Praise for *Wednesday's Child*

"Wilson gives her readers just what they want: more thrilling adventure and heartwrenching suspense.... Inspiring. Wilson is destined to become one of the suspense genre's brightest starts."
—*Romantic Times BOOKclub*, 4 1/2 stars

Rave reviews for *In Plain Sight*

Gayle Wilson is one of the best romantic suspense writers in the business, and *In Plain Sight* is proof of her ability to grab hold of the reader's imagination and not let go until the story is finished."
—*Chronicle Herald* (Halifax, Nova Scotia)

"*In Plain Sight* sizzles from start to finish. Compelling characters, great romance, nonstop suspense—I couldn't put it down."
—*New York Times* bestselling author Carla Neggers

"Wilson's novel mesmerizes from the first page to the last, with chilling twists and a compelling plot."
—*Romantic Times*

"Gayle Wilson pulls out all the stops to give her readers a thrilling, chilling read that will give you goose bumps in the night."
—*ReadertoReader.com*

GAYLE WILSON

DOUBLE BLIND

HQN™

ISBN 0-373-77073-1

DOUBLE BLIND

Copyright © 2005 by Mona Gay Thomas

Also by Gayle Wilson

To Patricia Potter...
For her service and dedication to RWA
And because her example always inspires me to
try to be a better person and a better writer.

DOUBLE BLIND

CHAPTER ONE

WILL SHANNON OPENED his eyes and then closed them against the painful influx of light. His pupils felt exposed. Dilated. Raw.

That immediate agony was compounded by a massive headache centered at the back of his skull. Gradually he became aware of other sensations. The coarseness of whatever his cheek rested against. A trickle of saliva at the corner of his mouth. Nausea.

He pressed his lips together, swallowing despite the dryness of his throat. Carefully, knowing he would have to do it sooner or later, he opened his eyes again, this time squinting in anticipation of the pain.

In front of him stretched a roiling gray fog. In the middle of it loomed the foot of an enormous bird, holding something in its claw. He blinked, trying to bring the image into focus.

He was eye level with the ball-and-claw leg of a coffee table. The fog slowly resolved itself into a couple of yards of the gray carpet, on which he was lying. And he had no idea how he'd gotten there.

Without moving—which would require an effort beyond his present strength—he listened. There was a strangely familiar ticking, faint enough that he knew whatever caused it wasn't in the room. There were no other sounds.

Despite a debilitating disorientation, he knew there was something he was supposed to be doing. He was incapable at the moment of remembering what, but his sense of urgency about it overwhelmed both the throbbing in his skull and his lethargy. Something important…

Vincent. The name floated to the surface of his consciousness. A fraction of a second later so did the handsome, fleshy face of the man it belonged to.

As soon as that happened, he knew he was in the upstairs office of Greg Vincent's mansion. The light that had seemed blinding seconds ago came from a greenshaded lamp on the millionaire's desk. The distant ticking was the grandfather clock at the top of the stairs.

It took longer for an explanation of his sense of urgency to form in his brain. When it did, the nausea became more powerful than the ache in his head.

Not again. Dear God, not again.

Somehow he managed to get his right hand under him, flattened against the carpet. The normally plush fibers felt stiff beneath his palm. Almost painful. As if his senses had been heightened, particularly the pain receptors.

Ignoring the unpleasantness of the sensation, he tried to lift his torso off the floor. Raising his head at the same time required a separate, but equally difficult, process.

When he had finally accomplished both, the resulting wave of vertigo forced him to close his eyes. Breathing in shallow huffs that echoed inside his head, he fought to keep from falling facedown again onto Vincent's expensive gray carpeting.

When the nausea eased, he began to work his outstretched leg back under his body. It felt as if he were directing the disembodied limb of a life-size puppet. For some reason his muscles were no longer under the command of his brain.

Swallowing the bile that crawled into his throat, he managed to get one knee under him, using both hands to push his body up. He rested, swaying on his hands and knees, from the effort.

Then he made the mistake of raising his head to survey his surroundings. The room swung round him in dizzying circles, just as it used to when he lay down on his bed after the occasional college binge.

He tried to think what he'd had to drink tonight. The last clear image he could dredge up was from dinner in the private dining room of a small Italian restaurant not far from the mansion. He had sat at a table adjacent to the one where Greg Vincent and his brother were eating, trying not to listen to their conversation.

He could picture the sweating glass on the table in front of him. Club soda with a twist of lime he hadn't asked for. As for what had happened next…

There was nothing. He remembered only the glass and the drone of conversation from the next table. Nothing about leaving the restaurant. Nothing about driving Vincent home—

That thought was comforting. Maybe he couldn't visualize any of that because Greg Vincent hadn't *come* home. Maybe he'd gone somewhere else after they'd left the restaurant. Some place he hadn't wanted a bodyguard tagging along.

The drug mogul had done that a couple of times since Will had come to work for him three months ago. Once when he had been meeting a woman at her home. Again when he'd gone to visit his mother, who was in some expensive residential facility in Maryland, her brain fogged by the dementia of Alzheimer's.

If Vincent wasn't here, Will told himself, the realization slow to form, then maybe everything was okay. Maybe he'd stumbled and hit his head on the coffee table. Maybe...

Reaching out, he got his forearm onto the cold, slick cushion of the leather couch. Using its leverage, he pulled himself up.

He waited for the hammering in his head to subside. When it didn't, he gritted his teeth and put both hands flat on the surface of the cushion. More by luck than design, he ended up sitting on the edge of the sofa.

When the dizziness had passed this time, he turned his head carefully, attempting to view the room without setting it off again. Nothing was out of place. There was no overturned furniture. No signs of a struggle or a break-in.

The only thing that struck him as odd was a nearly empty bottle of scotch on the coffee table. Beside it sat a crystal tumbler containing perhaps half an inch of amber liquid. The scotch was Vincent's brand, which must mean…

Struggling to his feet, Will started across the room, determinedly weaving in the direction of his employer's bedroom. If Vincent was here, that should be the first place to look for him. And if he wasn't—

He jerked his mind away from the possibility, staggering toward the hall. *Head injury?* If so, this was a hell of a concussion.

When he reached the doorway, Will stopped, leaning against the frame to try to clear his mind. It didn't work. The fog that surrounded him wouldn't lift, nor did he feel any more in control of his faculties than when he'd regained consciousness.

Driven by all the unanswered questions, he started down the dark hall, right hand on the wall for guidance and support. As long as he focused straight ahead, he was able to maneuver. Any abrupt movement of his head set off the vertigo again.

As he approached the door to Vincent's suite, he automatically reached for the SIG-Sauer he normally wore in a shoulder holster. He was still wearing the holster— after all these years he would have felt naked without it—but the weapon it should have contained was missing. Panic surged with that discovery, making the hair on the back of his neck begin to lift.

He reached for the knob of the door and then hesitated. Instead of opening it, he put his ear against the solid wood, straining to hear Vincent's soft snore.

That was something he'd done a dozen times in the weeks he'd worked for the millionaire, using that sound to gauge his client's well-being without having to disturb him by opening the door. Tonight no reassuring noises came from inside the bedroom.

Will swallowed, closing his eyes against a cold certainty that was seeping, unwanted, into his brain. Something was very wrong here. Something—

The clock at the top of the stairs chimed. Despite the familiarity of its sound, it seemed unnaturally loud in the stillness. He waited through its three slow strokes, counting them. Then finally, in the following silence, he allowed his fingers to close around the knob.

He turned it, at the same time pushing the door inward. The room was completely dark, the heavy drapes at the windows pulled against the expected intrusion of the dawn sun.

Greg Vincent normally had no trouble sleeping, in spite of the controversy that swirled around him. He usually stayed up late and slept in the following morning.

Why not? When you own the company, you can get away with that kind of behavior.

Will listened in the darkness, hoping to hear the slow, regular breathing of a sleeping man. It wasn't there, but as he waited, he realized there *was* something in the stillness he recognized. The heavy, copper-tinged smell of blood.

Knowing there was no longer any need for stealth, he reached out, running his hand down the wall beside the door until his fingers encountered the switch. He flicked it up, turning on the overhead light.

For a moment he was forced to literally shield his eyes with his hand. Gradually he lowered it, at the same time raising his head to peer, eyelids opened only a slit, into the king-size bed that dominated the room.

Vincent was lying on his side, a pillow clasped in his arms. He looked perfectly natural, at peace even, except for the blood that stained the other pillow his head rested on.

The discovery that his employer was dead wasn't a shock. It was what Will had been expecting since he'd identified the scent in the room as fresh blood, a smell that had been burned into his memory two years ago.

Despite the passage of time, he had never forgotten the sights and sounds and odors of that day. Just as he would never forget these.

He closed his eyes, willing himself to make the necessary journey across the room. Despite his absolute certainty, he needed to physically verify that his client was dead.

The nearest phone was on the nightstand. Even if there was no longer a need to call the paramedics, there would obviously be a need to call the police.

He started across the room, wavering without the support of the wall he'd used to navigate the hall. As he approached the bed, everything snapped into a more vivid focus.

The starkness of nearly black blood against the white pillowcase. A splatter of brain matter on the gleaming mahogany headboard. The section of blond hair below the bullet hole, stiff and darkened by what had exploded outward from the gaping wound in the back of Greg Vincent's skull.

Will took a breath and blew it out, attempting to control the recurring nausea. Then, aware enough now to know he shouldn't disturb anything, he leaned across the bed.

Despite his reluctance to touch the body, he forced himself to lay two fingers against the carotid artery in his employer's neck. Vincent's skin was cool, the pulse that should have beat beneath it nonexistent.

He had already straightened, beginning to turn toward the phone, when something in the expanse of white sheeting draped over the dead man's shoulder caught his eye. He stopped, again leaning toward the body.

The butt of a handgun lay perhaps half an inch below the top of the sheet. *Suicide?* Except the guy would have had to be a contortionist to shoot himself in the back of the head.

Again being careful not to touch anything, Will stretched as far as he could across the bed without losing his balance. From that angle he could identify the weapon that had been shoved under the sheet.

It was a SIG-Sauer. And unless he should add delusions to his disorientation and memory loss, the gun was his.

Before he could decide what that meant, much less what to do about it, there was a noise from the street below. Someone had stomped down on the brakes of a car that had been traveling fast enough that its rapid deceleration caused tires to squeal. The sound was followed by that of car doors—multiple—being slammed.

Will stepped away from the bed, stumbling in his haste to get to the window. He pushed the drapes aside an inch or so to look down on the street below.

Two police cars pulled up to the curb as he watched, joining the other that had driven up to the wrought-iron security gate. Which, he realized in bewilderment, was standing wide open.

Although there were no flashing lights, there was sufficient illumination from the streetlamp to leave no doubt as to what those vehicles were. If there *had* been any doubt, it was destroyed when the cops who'd been inside the first of those cruisers, their weapons now drawn, began making their way up the brick drive, which gleamed from the recent rain.

If they had entered the mansion five minutes earlier, they would have found him face down on the carpeting, and Vincent dead in his bed, apparently murdered with Will's gun. Their immediate and unquestioned assumption would have been that he'd killed his employer.

Had he?

The question was startling, and Will examined it as

carefully as he had the others that had occurred to him since he'd awakened. Was it possible that sometime during the time he had no memory of he'd pointed the muzzle of his weapon at the back of his employer's head and blown out his brains?

Will probed his memory, searching for some clue about what had happened after dinner. The last time he could remember looking at his watch, and that, too, had been at the restaurant, it had been 9:00 p.m. And now, according to the hall clock, it was after three.

Six hours of which he had no recollection at all.

But he also had no recollection of putting his gun to Vincent's head. No memory of the sound of its report. Or of the impact of bullet against bone. The only thing in his brain now was his absolute certainty that he wasn't capable of that.

He could kill. He had killed. But he hadn't done this.

The problem was he couldn't prove it. He couldn't even tell the cops where he'd been when this had happened. Or how he'd ended up in the condition he was in.

All he knew was that he was in the house with a dead man. One who had, in all probability, been murdered with his gun.

From downstairs came the sound of breaking glass. Apparently the cops weren't going to take time to ring the bell.

He let the curtain fall and stepped back to the bed. He reached across it and, without disturbing the sheet, used two fingers to pull the SIG-Sauer out.

As soon as its familiar weight settled into his palm, his panic eased. He hadn't killed Greg. Not with this gun. Some part of that action would still be inside his consciousness if he had. Some physical memory of squeezing the trigger if nothing else.

He could now hear other noises coming from the floor below. Maybe the cops were opening the window they'd broken. If so, they would be upstairs in a matter of minutes.

He didn't glance at the body again. Greg was dead. There was nothing he could do for his employer now. All he could do was try to save himself.

He recrossed the room, turning off the overhead light as he did. Then he eased open the door, thankful he hadn't turned on the light in the hall.

It was obvious the cops were inside. He could hear them moving around downstairs, but he had the advantage. After living here for three months, he knew the layout of the mansion as well as all its entrances and exits. Checking them each night had been a part of his routine.

Except tonight…

All he had to do was get out through one of those many doors, cross the back lawn and disappear into the vast wilderness of the capital's Rock Creek Park. Once he'd done that, maybe he could figure out what the hell had gone wrong.

He slipped into the hall, easing the bedroom door closed behind him. His left hand on the wall and his weapon in his right, he hurried in the direction of the office. There was a utility staircase there that led down to the restaurant-sized kitchen.

Although he was moving more easily, his coordination was still off, and each step he took jolted through his head like a bolt of lightning. He made it to the back stairs, starting down them in the darkness as the cops topped the main staircase. Behind him he could hear the telltale jingle of someone's utility belt.

He switched his weapon to his left hand, leaning heavily on the railing that ran down the right-hand side of the stairs. Despite holding on to it, he missed his footing about halfway down. As his foot slid out from under him, only his grip on the railing prevented him from crashing to the hardwood floor below.

Above him, a subdued pandemonium had broken out. Apparently the police had discovered Vincent's body, which meant they'd be calling for reinforcements. And he still had to cross the relatively open expanse of lawn behind the mansion in order to reach the dense woods that skirted this very upscale neighborhood.

Trying to make as little noise as possible, he ran across the dark kitchen. Moonlight poured in through its wide windows, bouncing off the stainless-steel surfaces.

He couldn't be sure how bright it really was, given the sensitivity of his eyes. Bright enough, he decided. And too damn revealing.

He had reached out to punch the security code into the keypad beside the patio door before he realized the cops would already have set off the alarms. Someone would eventually realize that the back door had been opened *after* they'd entered the house, but it couldn't matter now. All that mattered was getting the hell out of here.

He needed time to think. A chance to clear his head and recover the memories of whatever had happened earlier tonight. He could always turn himself in later if he decided that's what he needed to do.

By that time he had the patio door open. The resulting rush of cold air seemed to help. He scanned the area around the empty pool, its tile surround shining with an unnatural brightness in the moonlight.

Cross the patio. Avoid the gaping hole that was the pool. Skirt behind the cabana and then run for the safety of the woods and the park.

A siren on the street out front was the incentive he needed to push him from thought to action. He was halfway to his goal before he realized it had begun to rain again, something that would make it harder for them to see him.

He was only a few feet from the sanctuary of the pool house when the floodlights came up at the back of the house. "Hey."

That single syllable was all the warning he had before a bullet chipped plaster from the pediment above its doorway. Reflex action and years of training made him duck as a second thudded into the corner of the building.

He threw himself down beside the foundation plantings, trying to blend with the shadows. Weapon in hand, he crawled, elbows propelling his motion, through the mulch, which was soaked.

When he reached the back corner of the building, there was nothing between him and the park but fifty yards of closely mown grass and a low rock wall. No cover. Nothing to offer shelter.

The smart thing to do would be to return fire in an attempt to keep the cops locked into position. That wasn't something he was willing to attempt, considering the darkness and the problems with his vision. And if he wasn't going to shoot back—

He took a breath and pushed off with his left hand against the dirt. He ran, heading for the nearest stand of trees, which looked like something seen through the wrong end of a telescope.

He didn't have the balance necessary for any evasive maneuvers. He simply ran as hard as he could, breath sawing in and out of his aching lungs. Almost loud enough to drown out the sound of the gunshots coming from behind him.

He closed his mind to them, concentrating on reaching the wall and the shadowed darkness under the trees. He was almost there. Only a few more steps…

The bullet caught him high on the outside of his left arm. It felt more like a blow than anything else, so that at first he believed he'd run into something in the darkness. Only when the burn began, a good ten seconds after he'd been hit, did he realize what must have happened.

That was time enough to carry him into the edge of the woods he'd been trying for. Now all he had to do was to vault over the wall and stay on his feet until he reached the stream that centered this section of the vast park. If he could do that, even the dogs they would inevitably bring in wouldn't be able to track him.

The problem with his plan, he realized only as he began to push through the dense underbrush, was that he had no idea where he should go from there.

CHAPTER TWO

CAIT MALONE HAD BEEN ABLE to weave the first noise into the fabric of her dream. The subsequent one, either louder or clearer, pulled her from sleep, so that she opened her eyes, staring into a darkness unmitigated by the moonlight that normally filtered in through her bedroom curtains.

She lifted her head so that her right ear was no longer pressed against the pillow. Then she remained motionless for perhaps thirty seconds, listening to the rain falling in the predawn quietness of her suburban Maryland neighborhood. Whatever sounds had dragged her from sleep were not repeated.

She turned to look at the small digital clock that stood on her bedside table. Four forty-seven. Later—or earlier—than she'd imagined. Hardly the opportune time for a burglary.

Garbagemen, maybe? Except it wasn't Thursday. Some kind of delivery? Or someone having car trouble?

Whatever it had been didn't seem to pose a threat. She eased down against the pillow once more, her eyes still open as she thought about the day ahead. She was supposed to meet her mother for lunch at the mall, something she wasn't looking forward to.

She blew out a breath, her cheeks slightly puffed. Before the exhalation ended, there was another unexplained noise. Something metallic.

This time it was clear the sound had come from the direction of the attached garage, which held, in addition to her six-year-old Altima, an accumulation of junk she'd moved from dorm room to apartment and finally to this house. The collection had grown during those eleven years, encompassing everything from prom dresses to sports trophies to half-used cans of paint.

Although she navigated through the boxes every time she needed to reach the washer and dryer, someone else might not be able to manage the obstacle course it had become. Not in the dark. And at a quarter of five in the morning, it would be like pitch out there.

The next noise was even more distinct than the previous one had been. A falling carton? Or someone falling over one? In any case…

Cait threw off the covers, sitting up on the edge of her bed. She had already reached for the phone, when she pulled her hand back, taking another breath.

What she'd heard could be anything. A raccoon in the garbage cans. A stray dog. Or, as she'd thought before, one of the neighbors having car trouble. After all, it was nearly daylight. There was no reason to panic and call 911. Not yet.

She put her left hand on the top of the bedside table,

and then with her right, she eased open its single drawer. Her fingers closed around the cool metal of the semi-automatic she kept there.

She could imagine her mother's reaction to the thought of her going out to confront an invader, gun in hand. And her mom wasn't the only one who would doubt her ability to defend herself. That Cait believed she was still capable of doing that would come as a surprise to the people she'd worked with in the Secret Service as well.

She lifted the weapon, relishing the familiar heft as it settled into the palm of her hand. She knew from the immediate comfort the feel of it gave her that the hours she'd spent on the range during the last few weeks had accomplished exactly what she'd hoped.

Although her damaged arm had trembled with weakness the first time she'd picked up her gun after a hiatus of nearly two years, she had persevered until she could not only hold the SIG-Sauer steady on the target, but could regularly place two or three shots into the kill zone. Despite everything she'd been told about the nerve damage her injury had caused, she had proven, to her own satisfaction at least, that protecting herself, if not others, wasn't beyond her capabilities.

Damn straight.

With the surge of adrenaline that mental affirmation gave, she stood, stepping off the small braided rug and onto the coolness of the hardwood floor. Her bare feet made no sound as she tiptoed across to the open door of her bedroom.

Breathing suspended, she stopped to listen when she reached it. She thought briefly about turning on the hall light, but decided she didn't want to give whoever was outside warning that she was awake.

Despite the darkness, she walked down the narrow hall with a surety honed by familiarity and into the main room of the small Craftsman-style bungalow she'd moved into more than four years ago. Almost unaware of the familiar ache in her shoulder, she held the gun with its muzzle pointed downward to the side, her other hand extended in front of her.

Exactly when she expected them to, her outstretched fingers touched the frame of the kitchen doorway. Even if they hadn't, she would have known where she was with the next step. The slate tile produced a measurably colder sensation under her feet than the wood had.

Trailing her fingers along the countertop, she followed the line of cabinets toward the door leading to the garage. She stopped when her hand encountered the knob of the pantry louvers, which meant she was within three or four feet of her destination.

Once more she paused to listen, again holding her breath. What she heard this time was definitely human in origin. A man's voice muttered a profanity, accompanied by another thud.

She leveled her weapon at the door to the garage, slipping her left hand under the right to steady it. At the same time, she took a step back.

It was well and good to play Annie Oakley when she was shooting at paper targets. It was something quite different to face an assailant about whom she knew nothing. Not even if he was armed.

She had already turned, taking the first step toward the phone, when whoever was out there began to pound on the door. She responded automatically, swinging around, weapon extended.

"Cait?"

Her name. And spoken by a voice she would have known anywhere. Anytime. Under any circumstances.

She closed her eyes, slowly lowering the semiautomatic until it once more pointed downward. She could feel the sting of tears behind her closed lids, and she hated them. Hated herself for responding like this just to the sound of his voice.

She opened her eyes, blinking to clear the unwanted moisture. Of all the scenarios she had theorized to explain the sounds coming from her garage, she could never in a million years have contemplated this one. A confrontation that—despite all the battles she'd fought and won during the last two years—she was least equipped to handle.

"What are you doing here, Will?"

"Somebody set me up."

For a split second she thought he was talking about the recording the hotel security camera had made on that fateful night two years ago. The night before the assassination attempt during which she'd been shot.

She quickly realized that didn't make sense. No one, not even Will himself, had ever suggested that what had happened then had been anything other than what the official inquiry had determined: *Faulty judgment exhibited by the agent in charge.*

"What are you talking about?"

"Somebody murdered the guy I was working for. Only they did it with my gun. Then the cops showed up and…"

"And what?" she demanded when he didn't go on.

"I need your help, Cait. I need… I need somebody I can trust."

Below the belt, Shannon. Way below.

Quickly, before she could change her mind, she took the three or four steps that separated her from the outside door. In the darkness, she fumbled for the chain lock. When she located it, she gripped its knob and slid it out of the slot.

Then she released the hold her teeth had taken on her bottom lip. With her left hand she turned the dead bolt and with her right she gripped the knob. Finally she stepped back, bringing the door with her.

"What the hell—?"

Instead of answering, Will stepped inside, brushing by her so closely she flinched from the contact. The knob was pulled from her hand as he closed and then relocked the door.

She could see little beyond the white dress shirt he was wearing, but he was close enough that she could hear him breathing—small, irregular inhalations as if he'd been running. She took a step to the side, hitting the switch beside the back door. The overhead fluorescent sputtered on, flooding the kitchen with light.

Squinting against its brightness, she looked back at her former supervisor. His head was lowered, his right hand shielding his eyes.

"What's wrong?"

"I'm okay. I just need…"

In her shock she was almost unaware he hadn't finished the sentence. Her eyes had adjusted enough to take in the details of his appearance. The bloodstained sleeve of his shirt. The fact that every stitch of clothing he wore was wet and that he was visibly trembling like someone with a chill.

Even as she watched, his body began to sag. Almost in slow motion, he slid down the door to end up sitting on the floor in front of it, one long leg stretched out before him, the other still bent at the knee.

"What the hell happened to you?" she asked, automatically stooping beside him.

"I told you." Will didn't bother to open his eyes, his head against the door behind him. "The cops showed up. I wasn't in any condition to talk to them. I knew what they'd think, so…I got out. Just not quite fast enough."

She used to know intuitively what he meant, even when he talked in this kind of verbal shorthand. He had told her once that he loved her because he never had to explain.

He loved her…

She hadn't expected that memory to hurt as much as

it did. She thought she had dealt with these feelings a long time ago. After all, her relationship with Will Shannon was one of the first things she'd *had* to deal with after she'd been shot. And now...

"You took a bullet." Her intonation was flat because it wasn't a question. Not with all the blood.

"And not even for the man." There had been a breath of laughter at the end, quickly cut off.

"How bad?"

She reached out, intending to unbutton his cuff to push up the sleeve and evaluate the damage. She accomplished the first, but his sharp intake of breath as she tried to expose the wound made her realize she couldn't do that without hurting him. She would have to cut away his shirt instead.

"I need some scissors."

Before she could begin the motion to stand, the fingers of Will's right hand wrapped around her wrist. Surprised, she looked up and straight into his eyes. The same deep chocolate that had mesmerized her from the day she'd met him, they hadn't changed at all in the two years since she'd last seen him.

"It's a graze. Lots of blood, but obviously no arterial damage, or I wouldn't be here. And nothing's broken."

As if to demonstrate, he tried to straighten his left arm. This time his gasp was followed by a sighing release.

Still, the arm *was* functional and, as he'd assured her, apparently not broken. Some of her terror receded to be replaced by anger. The kind a mother feels after she retrieves her toddler from his dash into traffic.

"Why in the world would you run from the cops? Of all the idiotic—"

"I told you. I wasn't in any shape to explain what had happened. Hell," he said with that same short, unamused breath of laughter, "I didn't *know* what had happened. All I knew was that the guy I was supposed to be guarding had had his brains blown out with my gun."

I wasn't in any shape to explain what had happened....

"Are you saying…you'd been drinking?"

She'd heard the rumor from one of the agents who'd visited during her recovery. He'd said that Will was drinking too much because he wasn't dealing well with his dismissal.

And who the hell would have? Given the circumstances.

"No." Will's denial was immediate. And satisfyingly decisive. Until he spoiled it. "At least…I don't think so."

"What does that mean?"

A longer pause. This one she waited through.

"That I don't remember." He leaned back, putting his head against the door again and closing his eyes.

"You don't remember getting drunk?"

"I don't remember *anything*. Dinner." Clearly an amendment to his previous statement. "I was drinking club soda. I can't remember anything after that. I thought it would come back, but…" His head moved slightly from side to side.

"So you *could* have been. You could have been drinking and blacked out."

"I can't even remember the last time I had a drink. Maybe six months ago. Maybe more."

"Things happen—"

"You can verify if I'm telling the truth." He opened his eyes to look at her again.

"How?"

"Smell my breath."

She laughed, but there was nothing remotely funny about the thought of getting that close to him.

"I'm not your personal Breathalyzer. If you want to take a breath test, you're going to have to call the cops. And if you haven't managed to destroy every brain cell you ever possessed, you'll do it right now."

"Somebody set me up to take the fall for a murder, Cait. My weapon was in his bed, shoved under the sheet. And I was unconscious on the floor. When I woke up, I was… I don't know. Disoriented. Uncoordinated."

"As in drunk."

His sigh was audible. Instead of arguing, however, he put his head back against the door.

She waited, thinking he would go on with what he'd been saying. Try to convince her. Do something.

When he didn't, she began to think about what *she* needed to do. Call the cops was first on the list.

For some reason she didn't move. She continued to stoop beside Will Shannon, remembering things she hadn't allowed herself to think about in months.

Except sometimes late at night. Always at night.

"What do you want from me?" It wasn't what she'd intended to say. But at some point in the midst of those memories, she had realized that no matter what Will might have done, she was going to help him.

Her decision would make no sense to anyone else. No more than his coming here would.

They were two people whose lives had been torn apart by circumstance. Now it seemed they had been put back together by a situation that was as fraught with physical and emotional danger as the other.

"I don't know. I just…" He took another breath. "I couldn't think of anywhere else to go."

And no one else to trust…

He didn't say that this time, but he might as well have. That's why he'd come here. Why he'd come to her.

Whatever else had been between them, they had once been partners in a very dangerous occupation. Partners trusted one another. It was inherent in the relationship.

"You need a doctor."

"No."

"Look, you can't possibly tell how serious—"

"Just give me a couple of minutes, and I'll get out of your hair. If I'd been thinking clearly—"

"At least let me look at it."

"I told you. It's a graze."

Ignoring that disclaimer, Cait got to her feet and walked over to the drawer where she kept the scissors. When she turned around, he was watching her.

The intensity of that dark gaze made her conscious for the first time of the thinness of the nightshirt she was wearing. Not only did the damn thing end at mid thigh, she was wearing nothing underneath. She was far too aware of that as she again stooped down beside him.

Despite her mockery of the request he'd made a few minutes ago, she took a tentative breath, testing for the smell of morning-after alcohol. Instead, the pleasantly masculine scent of the aftershave Will had always worn assaulted her.

They said that smell was the sense most closely tied to memory. Whether that was true or not, desire roared through her lower body.

"What's wrong?"

She realized she was simply holding the scissors, paralyzed by memory. Spurred to action by a question she couldn't answer, she took his wrist and turned it—this time ignoring his gasp. She inserted one of the blades in the opening she'd revealed when she'd unbuttoned his cuff.

She split the sleeve up to the shoulder seam. The fabric above the elbow was stiff with blood and in places glued to his skin. Although the shirt was damp from the rain, the injury appeared to have stopped bleeding some time ago.

"How long has it been?" she asked.

"Since I was hit? I'm not sure. A couple of hours maybe."

"The bleeding seems to have stopped."

As gently as she could, she pulled open the edges of the fabric, exposing the wound. *Graze* was the perfect description. And a very ugly one. The path of the bullet cut across the dark skin on the outside of his arm, literally removing a chunk of flesh in its passage.

Gingerly she pressed around the area, trying to see if any fragments of the slug remained. She had felt Will's body stiffen as soon as she began her exploration, but this time he didn't make a sound.

"There are probably bits of thread and cloth embedded in the wound. If we don't get them out, they'll become infected."

She glanced up as she said the last. Will had turned his head to look down at the injury.

The overhead light emphasized the late-night stubble that darkened his cheeks. She knew exactly how that would feel moving against her skin, its masculine roughness as seductive as the softness of his lips had always been.

"Can you clean it?"

Dazed by the effects of that remembrance, for a second or two she couldn't even think how to answer him. And when she realized what he'd asked…

"Look, I'm not a doctor. And obviously you need one. A real one."

"Who is required by law to report any gunshot wound."

"Tell them you scraped it on something."

"Would you buy that?"

She wouldn't. Anyone who had ever worked in an emergency room would recognize this for what it was.

"You have alcohol?" Will asked.

He meant the medicinal kind, she realized. And she did. Peroxide, too. Along with half a dozen other salves and ointments of various ages in her medicine cabinet.

"In the bathroom."

For what seemed like an eternity, nothing happened. Maybe he expected her to go get the stuff and clean the wound. Or at least to offer to bring the alcohol to him.

Just as she decided that might be the smartest thing she could do, he began to struggle to his feet. She rose, taking a step back to put the necessary distance, both for her peace of mind and his impairment, between them. She found herself backed up against the counter, watching as he completed the obviously painful process.

As he rested against the door, gathering strength for whatever came next, she realized that she hadn't even asked how he'd gotten here. If he was running from the cops—

"You have a car outside?"

Will shook his head. "I took a cab. Don't worry. He brought me into the neighborhood, but not to the house."

"If they really *are* looking for you, they'll trace the fare."

"I know. All you have to say is that I came, but you wouldn't let me in. Anybody who knows anything about us…"

Would believe that she'd refused to help him.

She finished the sentence mentally when he let the words trail. He was right, of course. As a result of the inquiry into the assassination attempt in which she'd been shot, Will had been dismissed from the Service.

The public had taken his dismissal to mean that he'd been to blame for what had happened, especially for what had happened to her. Despite her attempts to explain that wasn't true, her mother was still convinced of that.

Maybe because you never said publicly that he wasn't.

"Lead the way," Will said.

"I'm sorry?"

Lost in that familiar guilt, for a second or two she had no idea what he was talking about.

"If you aren't willing to clean this—"

"I didn't say that. I said you needed a doctor."

Along with the antiseptics, she also had painkillers, she realized. Almost a full bottle from her last refill.

Those, too, had been something she'd decided she was going to learn to live without. Along with the sense of fragility that had dogged her since she'd awakened in the hospital, unable to move her right arm.

"Going to a doctor is out of the question. I'd be very grateful if *you'd* try to do something with this instead." He lifted the injured arm slightly.

Humility wasn't a characteristic she had ever associated with Will Shannon, but it went hand in hand with pain and disability. Something she'd learned the hard way.

Unable to deny him the help he'd asked her for, she

nodded. Even if he were somehow discovered here, no one would blame her. She would again be the victim.

"Then…?"

At his question, she resisted the urge to gesture toward the back of the house. It wasn't necessary. Will knew the way as well as she did.

"The alcohol's in the bathroom."

He walked past her, his gait unsteady, cradling his left arm against his body. She followed, aware of the damp dress shirt clinging to the hard muscles of his back and shoulders.

On some level she was also aware of the irony of all this as well. If Will Shannon hadn't literally been running for his life, he would never have come here. And if she were not the woman who'd been injured because he had supposedly failed in his duty, she could never have afforded to let him stay.

CHAPTER THREE

"I CAN'T GUARANTEE there's nothing else in there, but...I think that's probably as much as I should do."

And just about as much as you can stand...

Cait had honestly expected Will to pass out a couple of times while she'd worked on the wound. Given the blood loss, as well as whatever had happened to him before he'd been shot, she understood that he was functioning on sheer guts and willpower. Not that he hadn't always had an ample supply of both.

"It's fine," he said, glancing down on the rawness of the injury she'd just abused. "If you could wrap something around it before I put my shirt back on..."

"Of course."

She turned, looking into the open medicine cabinet above her lavatory as an excuse not to look at him. Although Will was still wearing his undershirt, helping him take off the damaged dress shirt had proved a far more intimate act than she'd been comfortable with.

Added to that sense of intimacy was the size of the bathroom, small enough that it had been a tight squeeze for both of them to be here at the same time. Finally she'd suggested Will sit on the closed seat of the john while she played doctor.

The position had still put them into a very close proximity, but it hadn't been as bad as if he'd been standing beside her. She had already been too aware of him physically. Looking into his face every time she raised her eyes would have reminded her, as it had in the kitchen, of exactly what that dark stubble on his cheeks would feel like brushing across her body.

As she rummaged around among the contents of the shelves, she knew he was watching her. It made her hands tremble slightly, just as they had done when she'd begun to wash out the wound.

As soon as he'd realized that, Will had looked away, concentrating on the opposite wall instead. Only by his occasional intake of breath was she able to gauge the effect of her clumsy ministrations.

Her fingers closed gratefully over a couple of gauze pads she discovered, still in their cellophane packaging. Maybe those, held in place with Band-Aids, would serve to protect the injury from the friction of his clothing.

She set the box of Band-Aids on the rim of the sink, and then tore the ends off the wrapping that enclosed the bandages. Careful not to touch the side that she put against his skin, she placed the pads over the wound.

"Could you hold them?"

Will turned his head to look at what she was doing, then obediently put two long, dark fingers over the gauze to hold it in place. She unwrapped four of the

Band-Aids, laying them out in a row. Using them, she taped the pad into place over the wound, careful to avoid contact with his fingers.

"That should do it," she said, as relieved this was over as he would be.

He turned his head again, looking down at her handiwork. "Thanks. I know that just saying that isn't enough—"

"Yes, it is," she interrupted quickly. She didn't need to hear Will Shannon's gratitude. It simply added to the guilt she already felt where he was concerned. "Believe me," she added, trying to mitigate the abruptness of her tone, "it's more than enough."

With that she looked up, meeting his eyes. Again a frisson of desire ran through her body, reminding her that this, too, was part of what she'd lost the day of the assassination attempt. A major part.

"I've been thinking…" he said hesitantly. "Would you mind if I cleaned up a little before I go? Maybe… take a shower."

One part of her, the still rational, thinking part, knew that the best thing she could do for both of them was to get Will out of here as soon as possible. Another part, the one that kept remembering all the other times he'd been here, didn't want him to leave. Letting him take a shower, hardly an unreasonable request given his condition, would accomplish that.

"It might help clear the cobwebs," he added when she didn't reply at once.

"That's fine." Her voice sounded thready in her own ears, but Will didn't seem to notice either that or her confusion.

"Thanks."

"I'll see what I can do about your shirt. I can at least put it in the dryer."

He nodded as if that made sense. He didn't mention the sleeve she'd cut, and neither did she. Instead, she took the garment off the towel rack where she'd thrown it after they'd managed to ease it off.

"I'll leave you to it then. The clean towels are in the closet—" she began before she remembered he knew where she kept the towels.

He knew that and just about everything else about her life that there was to know. At least her life as it had been then.

He nodded again, this time holding her eyes. Seeing what was in the dark depths of his, she opted for the better part of valor. Maybe the media had dubbed her a heroine for what had happened the day the militant had tried to shoot the Saudi prince they'd been assigned to guard, but she and Will Shannon knew the truth.

Like the coward she was, Cait clutched his still-damp shirt to the front of her nightshirt as she beat a retreat, leaving alone in her bathroom the man she'd let the press crucify two years ago for something that had been her fault.

WILL STOOD IN THE SHOWER, head bowed and eyes closed, as hot water cascaded over the back of his neck and shoulders. Although the headache he'd awakened with had gradually lessened, it hadn't completely disappeared. At least now he could walk without worrying about running into walls.

Except, of course, the one that loomed between him and the events of last night...

He opened his eyes, using the fingers of his right hand to rub water from them, before he allowed his arm to fall again. Maybe if he gave himself some time. Stopped trying to remember. Stopped thinking about it altogether.

Of course, the only other thing his brain seemed determine to think about was no less dangerous for his peace of mind. Although his gaze was focused on the white tile wall of the enclosure, what he saw were the features of the woman he'd thought about every day for the last two years. Nothing he'd imagined during those years had matched the reality that had confronted him this morning.

He wasn't sure what he'd expected Cait's reaction to be when he'd shown up here. He wasn't even sure the question had crossed his mind.

The one thing he *had* expected, based on everything he'd been told and on what he'd read in the papers, was that Caitlyn Malone would be physically and emotionally very different. That she would no longer be the woman who, against all the strictures of his position and hers, he'd fallen in love with.

Despite the guilt that had gnawed at his guts for two

long years, other than a discernible fragility, Cait seemed to be exactly the same as she'd always been. Calm. In control. Capable of making intelligent decisions in a crisis.

And eminently desirable...

He closed his eyes again, leaning forward until his head touched the tile. He rested his forehead against the coolness, moving it back and forth as if he could rub away the images that had assaulted him since he'd stepped through Cait's back door this morning.

Her hair was the same as she'd always worn it. The long, straight auburn strands had tangled around his shoulders as they'd made love. Her eyes were still the russet of oak leaves in the fall. Alabaster skin that should, with her coloring, be dusted with freckles and was not.

Even the house hadn't changed. The paint on the walls, most of which he'd applied, was the same color.

Only he was measurably different from when he'd been a frequent visitor here before. Back when he'd had a life stable enough to share with someone. Now...

Enjoy wallowing around in your victimhood?

Will hadn't realized until the painful moment of self-awareness that was how he viewed himself. He knew only that he'd lost both a job and a woman he loved. His colleagues and most of his friends. And his self-respect.

He had finally acknowledged that the latter was the only thing he had any chance of getting back, so that's what he'd been working on during the last eighteen months. Then last night...

I didn't kill Greg Vincent, he reiterated mentally as he pushed away from the wall. He knew that with as much certainty as he'd ever known anything in his life.

He also knew that if he hadn't gotten out of Vincent's mansion, he would not only have been arrested for his employer's murder, but ultimately convicted for it. And unless he could stay away from the cops long enough to figure out who had framed him, that would still happen.

He understood, however, that he couldn't stay here. He'd screwed up Cait Malone's life enough two years ago. He couldn't involve her in this. If he'd been able to figure out nothing else since he'd left Greg's house, he had at least been able to reach the correct conclusion about that.

Which again brought up the question of why he couldn't seem to think straight. Or remember.

It was as if those missing hours had been wiped out of his brain. Exactly like the effects of an alcoholic blackout. Just as Cait had suggested.

Except he hadn't been drinking last night. The image of that sweating glass on a white tablecloth was again in his head.

Maybe that was the place to start. At the restaurant. Backtrack there before the police could. Ask his questions before they got around to it.

Coming to a decision about what to do next made him feel marginally better. As if he had taken one step closer to normality.

He reached behind him and turned off the water. The silence after its steady pulse seemed strange. A little disorienting. He stood listening to it, droplets streaming off his body, until he realized that he had again fallen into that deadly inertia that had plagued him since he'd awakened facedown on the carpet.

He made himself push back the shower curtain and grab a towel off the bar. As soon as he brought it near his face, he knew that had been a mistake. The fragrance of the shampoo Cait used clung to it, pulling him again into that web of memory that was already too strong.

He stepped out of the enclosure and dropped the towel on the seat of the john. Then he opened the linen closet and took out a fresh one. As he turned, he caught a glimpse of movement in the clouded mirror.

With the speed and duration of a flashbulb, an image exploded inside his brain. A man whose black hair glinted with moisture. Sunken eyes. Gaunt cheeks darkened with a couple of days' growth of beard.

He stopped in the middle of the motion that would have taken him away from a line of sight with the mirror, but it was too late. Whatever he'd just remembered was gone.

He had no idea who that man was. Or where he'd seen him. All he knew was that he had. And that if he could only see him again…

He stepped over to the mirror and wiped off the steam that had collected on its surface with the still-folded towel. His reflection became clearer, but it was unmistakably *his* reflection and *not* whoever he'd seen before.

His own hair was black and wet. His eyes gave evidence of both blood loss and trauma. And he hadn't shaved since yesterday morning.

Those things had undoubtedly triggered the memory. But the flashback—if that's what it was—had definitely been the image of someone else.

Someone he'd encountered during those missing hours? And if so, someone who might hold the answers to the questions he so desperately needed answered?

Despite his concentration on his reflection, nothing else happened. The flashback was gone, and he had no idea how to bring it back.

Almost unconsciously he raised the towel and began to rub the water from his hair as he tried to recreate the face he'd seen for that fraction of a second. *This* time.

The last time he'd seen it had been in a very different setting. Different circumstances. And there was something about that he should know. Something important.

Frustrated, he tossed the towel onto the counter, his body still not completely dry. It didn't matter. He needed to lie down somewhere and close his eyes and try to will that face into his consciousness again.

Discovering this man's identity seemed far more important right now than anything the people at the restaurant could tell him. They might not even remember the Vincents. After all, Greg and his brother had done nothing to draw attention to themselves.

How the hell did he know that? he wondered. The same way he was so sure the image he'd seen in the mirror was important?

Maybe the guy who had shown up in his subconscious had loaded his groceries into his car the last time it had rained. Or accosted him on the street corner, begging for a handout.

Although the last possibility had been intended to point out the ridiculousness of trying to pinpoint where he'd met a man whose name he didn't know, something about the idea resonated. It *had* been on the street where he'd seen him.

That's why his hair was wet. He'd been out on the street, and it had been raining.

But no matter how hard he tried, that was all he could remember. And even with that promising start, this didn't seem to be going anywhere.

Probably because he was so wiped out. Maybe if he could get a couple of hours sleep—

And where do you think you're going to do that?

He walked across the bathroom, opening its door so he could see Cait's bed. Its king-size mattress dominated the room. Obviously she had been asleep when she'd heard him stumbling through her garage.

The covers had been thrown back neatly. As if she had just slipped out of them and planned to return momentarily.

Cait in that bed was not an image he wanted in his head. It was not as disturbing as the last one that had been there, but troubling enough.

He needed to let his brain relax before it imploded. Just lie down and close his eyes and let his mind rest from the frenzied attempts to figure out what was going on. Just lie down…

"YOU OKAY?"

There was no response to her knock or to the question that accompanied it. Despite Will's disclaimer that he was all right, nobody who knew anything about gunshots would take one lightly. With her experience, she certainly wouldn't.

The idea that he might be passed out on the floor of her shower had finally driven her from the kitchen. She had already finished two cups of coffee from the pot she'd put on to have something to do with her hands while she'd waited. And waited.

Now, with Will's silence, it appeared there might have been some justification for her concern. She opened the bedroom door a crack to be met by a darkened room. A hint of soap still floated in the air. Underlying the fragrance, she could still detect the sharp, almost pleasant tang of the rubbing alcohol she'd used earlier to clean the wound.

"Will?"

As she waited for an answer, she became aware of soft, regular breathing, punctuated occasionally by a light snore. Apparently her uninvited guest had fallen asleep in her bed.

Her options were to wake him up and get him out of

here as quickly as possible or to let him sleep for a couple of hours—something he obviously needed to do. She wasn't really worried about any legal repercussions of letting him stay. She could always say that she hadn't known what had happened, only that he was hurt. The downside of leaving him where he was…

Was that Will Shannon was back in her bed. And like it or not, back in her life.

Momentarily. A few hours at the most, she promised herself. She would do the same for any friend who had shown up at her door. Whatever else he'd been, Will Shannon had once been a friend.

She stepped inside the room and in front of the bureau that stood beside the door. Trying not to make any noise, she opened the top drawer. Taking out a bra and a pair of panties, she laid them over her shoulder, then bent to open the third drawer, locating her favorite pair of jeans. From the bottom one she removed a cream V-necked sweater.

Because of yesterday's rain, the shoes she'd worn to the gym were still by the front door. Although she hadn't had a chance to brush her teeth, there was baking soda and salt in the kitchen and chewing gum in the pantry.

Clothes in hand, she had turned toward the door when she remembered the phone on the bedside table. Folding the garments she'd picked out, she laid them on top of the chest and tiptoed across the room toward the bed.

She knelt and reached behind the nightstand. She pulled the plug from the jack and laid the wire over the back of the table. Then, putting her hand on the top of the nightstand for balance, she rose.

Despite her intent not to look at Will, knowing that to do so would be like probing a sore tooth with her tongue, she glanced down at the man lying in her bed. Her eyes had adjusted to the dimness of the room enough to allow her to see him quite clearly. Too clearly.

He was sleeping on his back, his lips slightly parted. The darkness of his hair contrasted with the white pillowcase, as did his unshaven cheeks. Their slight gauntness and the circles beneath his eyes made him appear… vulnerable. That was another word she would never before have associated with Will Shannon.

The sheet covered most of his chest, rising and falling with his breathing. He wore nothing from the waist up, exposing the makeshift dressing on his arm.

Unconsciously, her eyes traced along the length of his body. How many nights had she lain in this bed beside him, cuddled against his warmth?

More than she could afford to remember. Not and keep any kind of self-respect.

After all, he'd been very clear about why he'd come. And that had nothing to do with the memories that had plagued her since he'd been here.

Tearing her mind away from the temptation Will Shannon had always been, she tiptoed back across the room. Retrieving the clothes she'd placed on the bureau, she slipped out of the door, closing it behind her.

She leaned back against it, releasing a slow exhalation. Until this morning she'd believed that she had adjusted very well to how her life had changed. To the discipline rehabilitation required and to the requisite loneliness it imposed.

That had been before the man whose life she'd destroyed had shown up, asking for her help. Invoking memories she had thought she'd put behind her. Making her realize despite all the hours she'd managed to fill during the last two years, how empty every moment of them had really been.

CHAPTER FOUR

CAIT HAD LISTENED to a local station on her way home from the nearby discount store where she'd bought Will a new set of clothes. Although she'd watched the TV news before she'd left, only now was the story of Greg Vincent's murder getting significant media play. Because of Vincent's wealth and his family's social standing in the Beltway, she knew it would get a lot more as the day wore on.

The Metropolitan police had released Will's name, but so far only as a person of interest. Although it had been difficult to tell from the radio report, it sounded as if they were as yet unsure if Will, too, might have been a victim. There was no doubt, however, that they were now actively looking for him for questioning.

At some point while she was picking out a jacket to go with the sweater and jeans she'd purchased, she had realized the seriousness of what she'd been doing. Aiding and abetting a fugitive.

Of course, buying clothing for him couldn't be any worse than letting him stay at her house, she decided as she unlocked her back door. All the more reason to get him on his way as soon as possible.

If he persisted in his determination not to turn himself in, at least there would be nothing about his clothing that would draw attention. And with the insulated barn coat she'd bought, he would also be warm.

There was nothing else she could do to help, other than again urge him to call the cops. She just needed to wake him up, hand over the new clothes and send him on his way.

And then try to repair all the subtle tears his presence here had created in what had once been the smooth, uneventful fabric of her life.

As she walked by it, she automatically checked the answering machine on the kitchen counter. The light reassured her there were no new messages.

Her sense of relief was out of proportion to the possibility that someone she'd worked with might have called to tell her about Will. Of course, most of them would assume she'd be the last person interested in what was happening to him.

Before she went back to the bedroom, where Will had been sleeping soundly when she'd decided to run her quick errand, she stopped in the den. She set the bag holding the clothes on the coffee table and picked up the remote, punching the on button.

As she slipped out of her coat, she glanced at her watch. It was only a minute or so after noon, which meant she should be able to catch most of the midday news. She would find out the latest about the investiga-

tion and then, armed with that information, she would
go in and wake Will.

"...the murder of Vincent Pharmaceutical's CEO
Greg Vincent in his 27th Street mansion last night has
shocked the capital today. Vincent, eldest son of the well-
known Maryland philanthropist, James Harper Vincent,
who founded the drug company that bears the family
name, was found shot to death in his home before dawn
this morning. Acting on an anonymous tip, the Metropolitan police broke into the house to find Vincent's body
in his upstairs bedroom. Dolmer Pharmaceuticals and
Vincent's company have been involved in a bitter patent
battle over the product Hestapin, which had, until the
challenge by Dolmer, been a frontline weapon in the
fight against HIV. Will Shannon, Mr. Vincent's bodyguard and the former Secret Service agent discredited in
the assassination attempt on Saudi prince Ahmed al-
Faisal two years ago, is also missing. Police acknowledge
that Shannon is a person of interest in the homicide, but
say that it's far too early in the investigation to know what
role he might have played in the events of last night."

"How about scapegoat?"

Cait turned to find Will standing at the end of the hall.
His right hand was on the wall, as if for support, and his
eyes were focused on the blonde who'd been reading the
story from the teleprompter.

Cait pressed the mute button, creating a silence she
found she wasn't ready to fill. That was brought home to
her even more forcefully as she took in Will's appearance.

He had pulled on his water-stained slacks and his T-shirt. The two-day growth of beard that had made her think of him as vulnerable while he'd slept now made him appear almost sinister.

"They're already implying I did it." He almost sounded pleased to have been proven right.

"Right now, you're a 'person of interest.' You had no motive for killing Vincent, Will. Why would you think—"

"I was alone in the house with him. They call that opportunity. Trust me, the cops wouldn't have worried about motive. Not until later. And for all I know whoever set this up may have taken care of that question, too."

"The longer you're at large, the more convinced they'll become that you *did* have something to do with Vincent's death. You *know* that."

"Or I could turn myself in and let ballistics prove beyond a shadow of a doubt that I was involved."

"You're sure it was your gun that killed him?"

"I'm sure it had been fired. And that it was lying in the bed with the dead man. It seemed pretty convincing at the time. Believe me, it would take less evidence than that to make the cops believe I did it."

"They could test for residue on your hands. If there isn't any—"

"There are a hundred ways to get around that, and you know it. Maybe I was wearing gloves when I shot him. Or maybe the shower I took this morning was designed to take care of any lingering traces. It was *my* weapon beside his body, Cait. And as far as anyone knows, me included, I was the last person to see Greg Vincent alive."

It was hard to argue with the scenario as he laid it out. Even without the presence of residue, the cops, under pressure to make an arrest in a high-profile case, wouldn't hesitate to charge him based on those things alone.

"Vincent hired you because he must have felt he needed a bodyguard. So who were you protecting him from?"

"*Supposedly* protecting him." Will's comment was bitter. Cradling his left arm against his chest, he walked into the room and sat down on the edge of the couch. "Actually, according to Greg, it was his brother Ron who thought he needed a bodyguard. He didn't seem all that concerned himself."

"But…there *had* been some kind of threat? Something his family took seriously."

"Greg was waging a legal battle to protect a drug his company had developed while his father was still CEO. Some other manufacturer had come up with a variation, one they said differed markedly enough to qualify it as a new product, which would not be bound by Vincent's patent. Four months ago they got FDA approval of that drug. Vincent filed a patent suit to stop its production."

"And his family thought the other pharmaceutical company constituted a threat?" She hadn't realized the drug business was quite that cutthroat.

"The generic version offered the same treatment at a significantly lowered cost. A cost that a lot of the third-world countries and low-income people in this would be more able to afford. Since the government subsidizes a huge proportion of the care for those patients, I'm sure they were delighted by a less expensive treatment option."

"And Vincent objected to it. Sounds like a nice guy."

"He had a company to run. Shareholders to protect. Besides, according to Greg, profits fund research and development. Without them, new drugs aren't developed because there is no incentive to produce them."

"It sounds as if he convinced you."

"I liked him," Will admitted. "And my radar is pretty well attuned to phonies."

She couldn't argue with that. Will's instincts about people had usually been right on the money.

And you wouldn't be biased about that, of course.

"Greg's father built his company by hiring the best researchers he could find, paying them well, and turning them loose to do their job. Greg wanted to continue that success, but he knew it depended on protecting the profitability of the products his labs developed as long as he legally could. The drug he was fighting infringed on his patent. At least he believed it did."

"Clearly the other company didn't."

"And they tried to influence the FDA to that effect by arguing their case in the media."

"Apparently they were successful."

"Probably more than they'd intended. The thought that Vincent was blocking production of a cheaper alternative because it would cut into their profits angered a lot of people. Some of them reacted violently."

"How?"

"Pickets. Vandalism at the main lab. Nothing serious, but enough to cause the family concern. I was hired to make sure the protestors didn't try to do anything to Greg personally."

"So why aren't the cops zeroing in on the protestors as suspects?"

"Maybe they are, but… Frankly, they seemed pretty tame to me. Mostly the typical fringe element you'd expect in any protest of that kind."

"Except Greg Vincent is dead." She waited, expecting him to offer an alternative to the one he had just rejected.

"I know how it looks, but I swear I didn't kill him, Cait."

"I wasn't suggesting that. I'm trying to figure out who might have. And I'm also trying to figure out what happened last night. You're too good to be taken by surprise."

"Yeah, right."

The bitterness was again apparent, but she ignored it. "You said that when you woke up, you were disoriented."

He shook his head, the movement slight. Unthinking. "The closest I can come to how I felt was what you said earlier."

"That you were drunk."

"Except…" Again there was a small, side-to-side movement of his head. "There was a nearly empty bottle of scotch on the coffee table. I have no idea how it got there. No recollection of drinking from it."

And no recollection of anything else...

Of course, to be fair, she hadn't been able to detect the smell of alcohol on his breath. Maybe the liquor had been stage dressing. Like the gun that had been shoved under the sheet.

"So...what did they expect to prove by putting the scotch there? Surely the cops would have done some kind of test of how much you'd had. If it showed you hadn't been drinking..."

"I think it was part of the setup. Maybe they figured that if my impairment was so obvious when the cops tried to wake me, they wouldn't bother with a Breathalyzer."

"Maybe they hit you over the head when they came for Vincent. A concussion could cause the symptoms you described."

"I thought of that, mainly because my head hurt like hell, but there are no lumps. Not even a sore place. There would have to be to cause that kind of damage."

The lack of those telltale signs of injury should probably have made her feel better, but it didn't. If a concussion or alcohol wasn't the cause of his self-professed dysfunction, that left drugs. If she wanted to consider those, then there was the question of whether they'd been self-administered.

Except that, too, was completely foreign to the man she'd known. Despite everything that had happened as a result of the failed attempt on al-Faisal's life, she couldn't believe Will had changed that much. Or maybe she just didn't want to believe that because of the responsibility she bore for his dismissal.

"Will—"

"I didn't mean to get you involved," he interrupted before she could voice her regrets. "I just needed somewhere to sleep for a couple of hours until I could think straight."

"Can you?"

"Probably as much as—" He stopped, looking up at her. "I'll be fine. I just need to get out of here before I do any more damage. Thanks for... Thanks for everything," he finished softly.

The emotion in that quiet declaration as well as what was in his eyes disconcerted her. She didn't want Will's gratitude. God knew she didn't deserve it. The fact that he would even offer it made her uncomfortable.

"I bought you some clothes. That's where I went while you were asleep."

A small crease formed between his brows. "I don't understand."

"Look, I really do think the smartest thing you can do is turn yourself in. Let the cops sort out the evidence. The truth will eventually—" She stopped because he had begun shaking his head again. "*But,* if you're determined not to do that..." She picked up the sack from the discount store, holding it out to him. "...At least there won't be anything about your appearance that will draw unwanted attention."

Will hesitated a moment, still holding her eyes. Then

putting the palm of his uninjured arm down on the coffee table, he pushed himself to his feet, and took the sack.

"Thank you."

"I really wish there was something more I could do."

That wasn't what she had intended to say, but she didn't regret making the offer. No matter how much Will might have changed, she knew in her heart he wasn't capable of doing what had been done to Greg Vincent.

"You have any cash?" he asked.

Which would be untraceable. Unlike a credit card or an ATM withdrawal.

"If I do, it won't be too much," she warned. "But you're welcome to whatever I've got. My purse is in the kitchen."

"Thanks, Cait. I mean that. As soon as I've changed into these and gathered up my things, I'll meet you there."

His things? As far as she was aware, he hadn't been carrying anything when he'd arrived. Other than his weapon, she realized.

That was something Will would always have at hand, no matter how exhausted or disoriented he might be. She was willing to bet that right now it was either on her nightstand or under the pillow he'd been sleeping on.

"What about transportation?" Offering her car would only involve her more deeply, but thanks to what had happened two years ago—and to Will's silence—she had enough public goodwill to get away with a lot.

"I'll do what I did last night. Walk until I'm far

enough away and then grab a cab or hop a bus. I can take the Metro back into the city. I used most of what I had for the cab this morning, so I'd be grateful for whatever money you have on hand. I can mail it to you when things have settled down."

"I don't want you to mail me the damn money, Will. You're welcome to whatever I have. But I warned you it's not going to be much. I do have the diamond earrings my father gave me. You could take them and—"

"Just the cash, Cait," he said before he walked across to the hallway. Once there, he turned back to look at her. "It'll be fine, I promise."

It was a phrase he'd said to her a dozen times. She was the worrier. The one who obsessed about things. Will took everything in stride, no matter what the Service threw at him.

In a few minutes, she would hand over the money she had on hand, and he would walk out her back door and once more disappear from her life. Until he'd arrived this morning before dawn, she hadn't realized how cold and colorless and empty her existence had been.

Because there was no longer any danger or excitement? No adrenaline rush? No reason to be on her guard? Or because no man fell asleep in her bed, leaving the scent of his body on her sheets?

She realized she was still holding the remote. She started to punch the off button, but before she could, her eyes focused on the screen.

It was filled with images from the assassination attempt. Since the television was still on mute, there was a strange, almost hypnotic quality to the pictures she had never seen before.

Just before she was forced to turn away, unable to watch the chaos that had followed those gunshots, the clip was replaced by one of Will leaving the Secret Service building. His head was down, as he attempted to ignore the press of reporters surrounding him. After a few seconds, the blonde reappeared, her mouth moving as headlines from the newspapers that had carried the story of Will's dismissal appeared in a window beside her.

Cait hit the off button, destroying the picture. She knew she couldn't let Will leave without at least trying to explain why she'd never spoken out in his defense. Explain *and* apologize.

The first couple of weeks she had literally been fighting for her life. By the time she'd learned about the image captured by the hotel security tape and the resulting inquiry into where Will had been the night before the assassination attempt, everything was over. The story had faded from the airways, pushed aside by the next scandal.

Still weak, faced with both the loss of her job and what she'd been told would be a permanent disability, she'd let herself be convinced by people she trusted that it would be far better if she kept her mouth shut. Better for the Secret Service. Even better for Will, they'd said, who would have to endure more public exposure if she talked.

Besides, her confession that Will had been in *her* room that night wouldn't get him his job back. It would instead be another black mark against the Secret Service, which had taken a major public-relations hit when the security tape had surfaced.

It hadn't been until later that she'd realized how much they had needed the good PR provided by her supposed heroism that day. By then, that had become fact in the public's mind, and Will had disappeared. Just as he would again.

She realized she was still holding the remote. She laid it down on the coffee table, glancing toward the hall as she did.

She had no idea how long she'd stood there, reliving the past, but she knew Will would be dressed and ready to go in a matter of minutes. She had promised to have the money ready for him when he was.

The kitchen seemed chill when she entered it. With everything that had been going on this morning, she realized she'd forgotten to turn up the thermostat. It was possible she hadn't noticed the temperature when she'd come back from the store because it had been so much colder outside.

Her mind on what she wanted to say to Will, she didn't grasp the significance of the cold. Or of any of the other clues she should have picked up on long before she reached the counter where she'd put down her purse. Not the faint smell of cigarette smoke, like that carried in the clothing of a habitual smoker. Or the distinctive odor of damp wool. And by the time she had begun to put those together, it was too late.

A hand, its fingers reeking of tobacco, closed over her lips and chin. The man it belonged to ruthlessly jerked her head back and held it against his shoulder. At the same time he caught her right wrist, twisting her damaged arm behind her back until its forearm was pinned between her shoulder blades.

If his hand hadn't been over her mouth, her scream would have warned Will. As it was, the sound she made was low and guttural. Like an animal in pain.

That's exactly what she'd been reduced to. Even if the agony in her shoulder had allowed her to remember any of the self-defense moves she'd been taught, she was helpless to carry them out.

One quick twist and she'd been incapacitated. The only thought left in her head was a plea for him to release the pressure on the screaming muscles and traumatized nerves in her arm.

"Shh..." the man who held her cautioned, his lips pressed against her ear. "Don't do anything stupid, and you won't get hurt. You understand me?"

She nodded agreement, able to think only because he'd finally relieved the tension on her arm. With her surrender, he released her wrist. Almost mindless from the pain he'd inflicted, she was still incapable of trying to free herself from his hold.

In seconds, the hand that had grabbed her wrist came around to the front of her body. Something cold and hard was pressed against her larynx.

She had time to think *knife* before the sting warned

her that it had already bitten into her skin. Her fingers automatically wrapped around the hand that held it, attempting to pull the weapon away. Instead, it was pressed more forcefully against the delicate cartilage of her throat.

A trickle of blood slipped into the indention at the base of her neck. And she knew with absolute certainty that whoever this was, it wasn't the cops.

She had thought they'd consider her to be simply another victim. Now it seemed she would be. Not of Will, of course, but a victim of whoever had murdered Greg Vincent.

CHAPTER FIVE

WILL TOOK ONE LAST LOOK around the bedroom to verify he was leaving nothing behind. His eyes touched on the unmade bed, its sheets rumpled from the few hours of sleep he'd so desperately needed. Not only had those helped the headache, but the mental fog seemed to have cleared.

Enough for him to know what a mistake it had been to come here. A mistake on so many different levels.

The only thing he could do about that now was to get out before anyone remembered the tie between him and Cait Malone. A connection formed long before the seminal event that would make most people believe she'd be the last person he'd turn to for sanctuary.

She should have been, he admitted, his eyes considering the indention his head had left on her pillow. The fragrance of her hair had been caught in the fabric of its case. He'd only had to close his eyes and the memories of all the nights they had spent here together had been full-blown in his brain. If he weren't careful—

A sound from the direction of the kitchen brought his gaze back up. Although too faint to identify, the noise brought him out of that reverie of remembrance and re-crimination. He needed to get the money Cait had prom-ised and then get the hell out of here before he said or did something he'd regret.

Cait was obviously doing well. Far better than he would have believed possible based on the prognosis he'd heard after she'd been shot. Which should have been a relief.

It was, of course. The fact that she seemed so little changed had lessened the guilt he'd lived with for the last two years.

More surprising than how well she was doing, how-ever, had been the discovery of how much he still wanted her. *And why the hell wouldn't you? She's the sexiest woman your sorry ass has ever been privileged to make love to.*

He turned away from the bed, knowing this was get-ting him nowhere. Not out of Cait's house. Or, more im-portantly, out of her life.

If there was one thing she didn't need, it was him. Not with their shared past. Certainly not with his present.

He strode across the bedroom, refusing to allow him-self a backward glance. There had been enough nostal-gia for one day.

He stepped out into the hall, taking a steadying breath in preparation for the task of saying goodbye. And then, head cocked slightly, he took another one. Slower. Deeper.

Finally he lifted his nose, drawing air through it like

a hound running a scent. By the time he lowered his head, his hand had already closed around his weapon.

He drew it out of the shoulder holster, at the same time taking the backward step that would put him inside the bedroom. He eased the door closed, praying its hinges didn't creak.

Cait didn't smoke. She hadn't since he'd known her. Besides, that whiff of tobacco hadn't been here when he'd entered the house this morning. After the cold, clear crispness of the night air, he would have noticed.

The cops? Except they would have rung the bell. Or knocked. Despite the memories that had washed over him in the bedroom, he knew he would have heard either.

Even if they'd come because they had somehow figured out he was in the house, they would have made their presence known. Especially since, according to the news, he hadn't yet been charged with anything.

So…whoever was in the house wasn't the cops. Certainly not a SWAT team, who might not knock on the door in the conventional sense, but who could be counted on to force their way in with enough shouted warnings that no one would be left in any doubt about who they were.

So who the hell would come in unannounced, bringing the smell of cigarettes with them?

The answer that occurred to him was so unexpected Will literally had to examine it to see if it made sense. It didn't. Not really.

Whoever had murdered Greg Vincent had had every

opportunity to kill Will last night if that had been their intent. Why would they be hunting for him now?

No matter who was here, Will knew he had only a couple of options. He could go out through one of the bedroom windows and take his chances on getting away as he'd done last night.

The problem with that was that he had no way of knowing what was happening with Cait. The police wouldn't hurt her, of course, but for some reason, he couldn't get the other possibility—that this invasion might have some other, more sinister connection to Greg Vincent's murder—out of his head.

Rejecting escape as an option, he eased the bedroom door open again and listened for the sound of voices. There was none. At least not any he could hear from this vantage point.

He took the single, giant step that would carry him to the other side of the hall. Then, his back against the wall, he froze, breathing suspended as he listened.

No noise came from the direction of the kitchen. Not even the soft movements he might expect to hear if Cait was in the process of retrieving the money he'd asked to borrow.

Maybe she'd already done that and was simply waiting for him to show up. But that didn't explain that alien smell.

He took a couple of side steps, stopping just before he reached the end of the hallway. Another would carry him into the main room, which was visible from the kitchen.

By now the hair on the back of his neck had begun to lift, just as it had done last night before he stepped into Greg Vincent's bedroom. There was a waiting stillness about the small house that would have been instantly recognizable to anyone who'd ever seen action.

He brought his left hand up to steady the right, holding the semiautomatic out in front of him in the classic shooter's stance. Adrenaline pumping, he was no longer conscious of the path the bullet had plowed through his arm. He was conscious of nothing but the threat he'd brought into Cait's life.

He tried to visualize the layout of the rooms he'd passed through on his way to the bedroom, especially the kitchen. Of course, until he took that final step out of the hallway, he couldn't know where Cait was. Only where she'd been headed.

He did remember there was a back door that led in from the garage. Would it be better to climb out through one of the windows at the front of the house and reenter from a direction they wouldn't expect?

The seconds ticked away as he tried to figure out the best way to do this. The approach that would put Cait in the least danger.

Before he'd had time to decide what that would be, he heard the noise he'd been waiting for. The shuffle of feet across a hard surface. Like kitchen tile?

"Shannon? You there? I got something here you might want to take a look at."

He didn't recognize the voice, but it was obvious

whoever this was, they were trying to draw him out. Or to get a fix on his position.

It was the kind of ploy that took discipline not to respond to. Especially if it were used in a situation where you didn't have visual contact with everyone in the detail.

Will waited, refusing to rise to the bait. This was going to get much worse before it got better. And they had all the advantage because they had Cait.

"I don't want to hurt her, Shannon. I don't think you want her to be hurt. So why don't we make a deal? I let her go, and you come on out here and talk to me."

The man doing the bargaining was undoubtedly holding Cait. If Will was stupid enough to step forward from his position in the hall to confront him, the guy would use Cait's body as a shield.

"You want to talk to her? Just so you'll know she's all right? You say the word, Shannon, and I'll let her talk."

The voice sounded fractionally closer. With the rug that covered most of the floor in the living area, Will knew he wouldn't have been able to hear the guy advancing once he'd gotten into that room. Which meant he could now be standing just beyond the opening to the hall.

Will relaxed his hold on his weapon before he let his fingers slowly refasten around its grip, trying to relieve the tension that had been building as he waited. He would have one shot to take the talker out. If he were right that the guy was holding Cait, it would have to be a head shot. The most difficult to make.

Cait was tall for a woman, maybe five-eight. If this

bastard was smart, he'd be propelling her along in front of him. Will adjusted the angle of the semiautomatic slightly to approximate a height of just under six feet.

Of course, the guy who had Cait wasn't alone. No one would be fool enough to come into this kind of setup flying solo. Two-to-one odds were the best Will could hope for. And nothing he would count on.

"Come on, Shannon. None of us have all day. Certainly not Ms. Malone."

Will reacted to the mockery, just as he had been intended to. He wasn't green enough, however, to let that surge of anger interfere with what he would have to do. And whoever had sent these clowns after him should have known that.

If they had done their homework. And if they hadn't—

"What do you want?" he asked, working to keep the tone of the question free of emotion.

"To talk."

"About what?"

"Greg Vincent's murder."

"Sorry, I wasn't there."

There was a heartbeat of silence.

"That's not what I hear."

"Whoever told you different was wrong. Maybe *he* wasn't there, either."

"My sources are very reliable."

"Then why don't you ask *them* what you want to know?"

Will eased forward half a step, his muscles tensed for the final move that would take him into the room. He'd have only a fraction of a second to evaluate the situation. To locate Cait. To determine her condition.

The last thought sent a wave of nausea through his guts. *Why the hell aren't you giving me any help, Cait? Why aren't you talking to me?*

She would know exactly what was going through his mind. His desperate need for the information her silence wasn't providing.

All he'd learned from the verbal exchange was that, whoever this was, it definitely wasn't the cops. There had been no offer of identification. No request for him to surrender.

Which meant he was free to do exactly what they would do. Shoot first and deal with the fallout later.

Adrenaline roaring through his veins like a drug, he dove through the opening, rolling toward the safety of the sofa that was positioned in front of the small fireplace. The man holding Cait was standing just about where he'd expected him to be. Almost dead center of the room.

But the shots that had tracked his movement across the floor hadn't come from there. They'd originated in the shadows to the other man's right.

It was there Will directed his return fire. Three quick shots in succession.

All unanswered. And the thud that followed the third let him know he'd gotten luckier than he deserved.

His attention returned to the man in the middle of the room. And this time he took in the detail he'd missed before.

The bastard had a knife to Cait's throat. His other hand covered her mouth, holding her head against his body so that the length of her neck was exposed above the vee of the sweater she wore. A rivulet of blood streamed down its smooth white column, staining her fingers, which were wrapped around the hand holding the hilt.

Either Cait was taller than he'd estimated, or the man holding her was shorter. There was perhaps an inch difference in their heights. Not enough to allow him to try for the high-risk shot he'd considered.

That assessment took Will perhaps three seconds. Long enough that the man had begun to move, dragging Cait backward toward the kitchen.

The reason he hadn't already cut her throat was because he was smart enough to realize that if he did, he was a dead man. Only fear of hitting Cait prevented Will's finger from squeezing the trigger again.

That might be a fatal delay, but it was the kind of judgment call Will's entire professional life had prepared him to make. At some point the man was going to realize that continuing to hold Cait was a hindrance to his escape. All Will could do was hope that when that happened, there would be an opening that would allow him to kill the bastard.

Crouching behind the sofa, he watched the backward

progress of the pair, joined in a bizarre parody of an embrace. Watched and waited for his chance.

Cait could do nothing but obey the physical demand. It seemed that the stream of blood had widened, spreading over the slender hand that was still on her assailant's wrist.

Unwilling to let them out of his sight for an instant, Will stood as Cait's captor inexorably increased the distance between them. As he considered whether to go over the back of the sofa or around it, the phone on the counter in the kitchen shrilled.

In the tense silence that had built after the gunshots faded, the sound seemed unnaturally loud. Although Will was unable to judge the degree of shock it had created in her captor, that had apparently been communicated to Cait, perhaps through a momentary relaxation of his hold.

The fingers that had been wrapped around his forearm dug in like talons, pulling it—and the knife—away from her throat. At the same time, despite the restraining hand, she managed to jerk her head forward and then slam it backward into the center of her assailant's face.

His nose took the impact of the blow. With a howl of pain that coincided with the second ring of the phone, he reflexively brought his hands toward his face. When he did, Cait ducked under them.

Then, instead of getting out of the way and giving Will a clean shot, still in a crouch, she drove her left elbow as hard as she could up and into the man's crotch.

Only as he doubled over in agony did she finally dive to the side.

By then Will had vaulted over the back of the couch. At a run, he kicked at the keening man, catching him under the chin. He could hear a satisfying crunch of bone as the toe of his shoe connected.

As the phone rang for the third time, the man toppled backward like a felled tree, the knife falling from his hand. His head hit the floor with an audible crack, literally bouncing a couple of times against the rigid slate.

Despite his need to know who'd sent the guy after him, Will didn't much care right now whether or not the bastard lived or died. He stood over him, the 9 mm pointing downward, hoping the guy would give him an excuse to pull the trigger.

When it was clear he wasn't going to, Will glanced over where Cait huddled against the counter, arms crossed over her body. "You hurt?"

She swallowed before she answered, her words coming on top of the next shrill of the phone. "Not really. He twisted my arm, but—"

"Then answer that," Will ordered.

"What?"

"Answer the phone before whoever's calling hangs up."

"Why?"

"To see if it might be somebody checking on how this went down."

She closed her mouth, using her left hand on the countertop to pull herself up. As she reached out for the receiver, Will could see that her fingers were not only bloody, they were shaking as well.

"Hello?"

Given what she'd just gone through, he couldn't fault the slight tremor in her voice. Even before she shook her head, he had known by the relaxation of her body that whoever was on the other end, the call had nothing to do with what had just happened.

"I'm sorry, Mom. Something...came up."

As Cait listened to whatever her mother was saying in response, Will moved to check the guy he'd shot. As he bent to examine him, he heard her explanation.

"There was a leak in the kitchen sink. I found it when I got up."

Satisfied that the shooter wasn't going to cause anyone any trouble, Will returned to the second man, the one who'd held the knife to Cait's throat.

"I did," she said into the receiver. "My neighbor came over and shut off the water at the street, but I'm waiting for the plumber to show up. Sorry I didn't call. It just slipped my mind in the mess."

Since there was a stream of blood coming out of the guy's ears and nose, Will knew what he'd probably find, but he put his fingers against the guy's carotid artery. There was no discernable pulse.

"No, I don't *need* you to come over, Mom. Everything is under control. We just need to reschedule our lunch for another day. Can we do that?"

Will got to his feet, feeling the normal, post-action let-down as the adrenaline began to fade. He turned toward Cait, needing reassurance that she really was all right.

"I have to go now, Mom. The plumber's at the door. I'll call you tomorrow. Okay?" And then, "I love you, too. Sorry about today."

She placed the receiver on the stand, before looking down on the body in the middle of her kitchen floor. "Is he dead?"

"Does it matter? You sure you're not hurt?"

She put trembling fingers up to the streak of red that ran across her throat. When she removed them, she held them out in front of her, looking down at the blood. "It's just a scratch."

"You said he twisted your arm."

She shook her head, the motion decisive. "It's okay. What about him?"

"He's dead."

"I meant who is he?"

"I don't know. I've never seen him before."

"He knew your name."

"*And* yours."

For a heartbeat neither of them spoke, thinking about the implications.

"We have to get out of here," Will said.

"*We?*"

"Look, I didn't mean for this to happen, but now that it has…"

"What has? I don't understand."

He could tell by her eyes that she did. She just

didn't want to admit he was right. He couldn't blame her for that.

"Somebody put us together. Despite what you thought."

"That doesn't make any sense."

"Maybe not, but the reality is, these two came to *your* house looking for *me*."

"And if you hadn't been here, they would have left."

He could tell that she was getting her equilibrium back. Her voice was more definite. Her denial surer.

None of that mattered, of course. Nothing mattered but the fact that someone knew enough about him to figure out this was where he might have come. And enough about Cait to know she'd let him stay.

"If they had, they would have taken you with them." As he said the words, the enormity of that responsibility he now had hit him.

"But...why? Why would you think that?"

Because whatever they want from me, they know you're the one thing in this world I'd give up anything for. Even my life.

"They believe they can use you to get to me," he said.

For a moment she didn't respond. When she did, the question she asked wasn't the one he had expected. The one he'd dreaded.

"To *get* to you? To *kill* you, you mean?"

"I don't know. They could have done that last night. Why they didn't..." He shrugged.

"You think they want something from you?"

The man with the knife had said they wanted to talk. Maybe that, too, was part of the lure, but if they'd only wanted him dead, that would have been easy enough to accomplish.

The fact that they'd tried to use Cait instead of killing her seemed to indicate that, just as she suggested, they wanted something from him.

"That's the only thing that makes sense of this. The problem is—I don't have a clue in hell what that might be."

CHAPTER SIX

"I TOLD YOU. Because I don't have a choice."

"Once you're gone—"

"And I don't have time to argue," Will said, throwing a handful of underwear he'd scooped out of a bureau drawer into the suitcase he'd found in the top of the closet.

Cait was standing in the bedroom doorway, looking more vulnerable than he could bear to think about. Blood stained the neck of the sweater she was wearing. It had also dried in the creases of her knuckles and around the rims of her nails.

"I'm not going, Will. This isn't necessary. I'm not the one they're after."

He didn't bother to dispute that, opening the next drawer instead and adding a pair of sweatpants and a matching top to the pile in the bag. He chose a flannel nightgown from the next drawer and a heavy cardigan from the bottom one.

"You want to pack your toiletries or do you want me to get them?"

"I'll call the cops after you leave. I promise I will. They can be here in a matter of minutes."

The problem with that was they wouldn't stay. Not 24/7. And he would trust nothing less than that.

Without answering, he walked into the bathroom. He opened the old-fashioned medicine cabinet above the sink and was momentarily at a loss. There were a couple of medicine bottles as well as the usual over-the-counter staples. He put the bag down on the lavatory and started tossing things into it.

"Makeup?" He threw the question over his shoulder.

"Stop."

He could tell from her voice that she was standing in the doorway behind him. He ignored the command, just as he had ignored her arguments.

"Last chance," he warned. "I think I've gotten the important stuff out of here, but if there are any other personal items you need, you might want to grab them now."

"I'm calling the police."

That at least got his attention, stopping the hurried motions with which he'd been pulling things off the shelf. He turned, looking at her again.

"No, you're not. You're coming with me. The sooner you realize that, the better it will be for both of us."

"I appreciate your concern. Really I do," she said, obviously trying for a reasoned tone. "But nobody's going to hurt me. Not once you're gone."

"We've been over this. Until I know what's going on, you're going to be wherever I am."

"Even if I don't want to be?"

That hurt, but he couldn't blame her. He had let her

down twice, once the day of the assassination attempt and again today. At least this time he hadn't let her get shot.

"Even if you don't want to be."

She closed her mouth, her lips flattening before she opened them again. "If you think they want something from you, you stand a better chance of staying out of their way without having me along."

"If I knew what they want, believe me, I'd give it to them. I don't. I don't have anything that belonged to Vincent. I don't know why he was murdered, so I don't have anything to bargain with. And in case you hadn't noticed, whoever this is, they're playing for keeps."

"So are you," she said quietly.

"They didn't give me a choice."

"If you went to the cops—"

"And told them what? You know that murder you want to talk to me about? Well, there are a couple more corpses we should discuss while we're at it."

"I can tell them what happened. They'd believe me. Besides, we have proof." With one slender finger she touched the cut on her throat. "Maybe if they can identify those two, they can figure out who killed Vincent."

"No ID," he said, turning back to the suitcase. "I checked."

He opened the doors of the cabinet under the sink, pulling out a clear plastic satchel that looked as if it held cosmetics. He also picked up a box of tampons, putting it on top of the rest. There was nothing else that looked absolutely necessary, so he closed the doors and zipped the suitcase.

"They have to have fingerprints," Cait argue. "Maybe they won't be in AFIS, but it's worth a try."

"Not to me. You have a coat?"

She shook her head. Her arms were still crossed, her left hand supporting the opposite elbow. She had said the bastard had twisted her arm. And the right shoulder was where she'd taken the Muslim fanatic's bullet that day.

His fault. As was this.

"Your decision," he said, his voice harsh with his sudden anger. Not at Cait. At himself for coming here. For getting her involved. For putting her in danger. "But it's cold out there."

He was reluctant to force her, but he would if he had to. He had the sense that time was running out and that they weren't moving nearly fast enough to escape whatever happened when it did.

"I could go to my mom's."

"You want *them* to follow you there? You want them to kill her, too?"

"You don't even know what they want. Or who they are. How can you know they'll pursue this—?"

"What I *know* is that I can't take the chance."

"I'm not your responsibility, Will. I never have been."

Except she was. Especially after that day. Especially now.

"I didn't know I was going to get you involved. I wouldn't have come here if I'd had any idea that anyone other than the cops would be looking for me. You have to believe that."

"I know."

"But that doesn't change what's happened. It doesn't change the outcome."

"I'm willing to take my chances."

"I'm not."

Not with you.

"How long?"

"I don't know," he said truthfully. "A couple of days. Until I can figure some of this out."

"What makes you think you'll be able to do that?"

"Because eventually I'll remember what happened last night."

That was probably wishful thinking, but he didn't have all that many options at this point. He could turn himself in to the police. If he did, that meant no one would try to find out who had really killed Greg.

Cait was right. By running away last night, he'd blown any chance of making them consider other possibilities. And he still couldn't explain—not even to himself—why fleeing had been his immediate response.

"And if you don't remember?"

"I'll turn myself in. Until then, you're coming with me. I can't do this any other way, Cait. I can't risk leaving you here." He watched her face, hoping for capitulation.

He knew the exact moment when she made the decision. She blinked, denying the glaze of moisture that formed in those copper-penny eyes. And then, head high, she nodded.

"I'M GOING TO HAVE TO TELL my mother something."

At her age, it was a stupid admission to make, but it was the truth. Her mother hadn't bought the story about the leaky sink. And if she then disappeared for several days...

Will took his eyes off the road long enough to look at her. She was holding her arm again, she realized, trying to ease the bone-deep ache. She released it, straightening in her seat.

She hadn't protested when Will had asked for her keys. He was guiding the Altima through the heavy D.C. traffic with the same unthinking competence he brought to any physical activity.

"Why?" he asked. "You think she'll come over to the house?"

They had left the bodies where they lay. Will had said he'd place an anonymous call to the locals as soon as they were out of the area. She hadn't known whether to believe him or not, but if he didn't, there wasn't much she could do about it.

"If she doesn't hear from me in a reasonable time. I promised to call her about lunch tomorrow."

"Overprotective?"

"Not really. She's just—"

There was no way to explain the complex relationship that had developed between them after she'd been shot. Cait had been on her own for so long before that they had naturally grown apart. She'd made a point to spend holidays and birthdays at home, especially after her dad had died, but there had been little more interaction.

When she'd awakened in the hospital, though, her mother had been there with her. She was the one who'd kept everyone else at bay, including the press, fiercely guarding Cait's privacy. Her role as confidante and caretaker during those first few difficult months had strengthened the bond that had once existed between them.

"We'll figure out some way to let her know you're all right."

"She won't go to the police if I tell her not to."

"That's good. In a few days it won't matter."

It had been a couple of days when he'd been trying to convince her to come with him. Although she had finally agreed, she still wasn't certain of her motivation.

She had been thinking when she'd walked into her kitchen that she didn't want Will to leave. Given what had happened after that, all the feelings of helplessness and disability had come roaring back.

At one time she'd been as much of an adrenaline junkie as Will. Coming close to death had been a sure cure for that malady. And the pain the guy with the knife had inflicted had reminded her of those long, agonizing months, first in the hospital and then in rehab.

Her indecisiveness about going with Will was the result of not wanting to be in danger again balanced against the realization that he might be right. After all, it had taken the guy with the knife two seconds to prove she was no longer capable of defending herself.

"And where are we going to spend those days?" she asked.

"There are a couple of options."

"Like what?"

"My college roommate practices law here."

"Paul Fisk."

"I told you about him?"

"You mentioned him."

Although she knew he and Paul were still close, she'd never met him. When her professional relationship with Will had slipped into a personal one, they had deliberately kept a low profile.

What they had been doing would have been frowned upon by the Service. They had both worked too hard to want to be officially reprimanded. Despite acknowledging that risk, neither of them had ever suggested that what was between them wasn't worth it.

"You think he'll let you stay with him?"

"You mean let *us* stay."

For some reason all this still wasn't quite real to her. That she wouldn't be going home to her own bed. That she would be sleeping wherever Will did tonight.

"I hope he'll take me as a client," Will went on. "Even if he doesn't, he's a friend. And he's been a good one, especially during the last two years."

"Then he'll tell you to turn yourself in."

"Probably. But if I chose not to, he won't call the cops."

"Does he have a family?"

"I guess that's one more thing we have in common."

They had talked about marriage. It had been vague enough she hadn't considered that Will had made a proposal by any means. It was almost as if they had taken for granted that some day…

She took a breath, trying not to think about the past. In spite of the fact that they were together again, this was by no stretch of the imagination what anyone could consider a romantic interlude.

"Warm enough?"

She wasn't sure if that was an attempt to change the subject or a legitimate concern. Once she had conceded defeat, Will had helped her into her coat, touchingly careful of her arm.

"I'm fine."

"Paul will take care of you."

"I thought you were going to do that."

It wasn't the smartest thing she'd ever said, but she wasn't sure what his last statement meant. Was he planning on handing her over to his lawyer while he continued to run?

"I meant if anything happens to me."

"Like what?"

"Like anything. If the police catch up to me. If whoever sent those two to your house decides to send out another search party."

"Maybe they already have."

He turned to look at her again, his eyes questioning.

"Maybe they're watching the people they think you might contact."

"Like Paul?"

"They knew about me. How can you be sure it's safe to go to his place?"

"I'm not."

"Then... I don't understand."

"I'm going to ask him to meet us somewhere."

It seemed he'd already thought all this through. And after the disconnect in his decision making that she'd sensed earlier today, the fact that he had a plan was reassuring. The lingering effects of whatever had happened to him last night must be lessening.

"I still need to tell my mom something. She's probably worrying because I stood her up today. If she does decide to come over to check..."

She would find two dead men. Then all hell *would* break loose.

"Use your cell," Will suggested.

"They'll be able to pinpoint the tower."

"It won't matter. We're close enough to your place that it won't tell them anything they don't already know. Actually, the sooner you make that call, the better."

Which meant he would hear every word she said. She wasn't sure why that made her uncomfortable.

Will had asked if her mom was overprotective and she'd denied it. Cait knew, however, exactly what kind of third degree she was in for.

She reached into her coat pocket and pulled out her phone. Then she hesitated, trying to prepare for the lies she was about to tell. Finally she turned on the phone. After calling up the menu, she punched the first number on her list of contacts, which, sadly enough, was her mom's.

She waited through the rings, wondering if her mother had cut off her cell while she was shopping. If she had to, she could always leave a voice mail. Actually, that would be easier because she wouldn't have to answer questions.

As if on cue, her mother's voice came over the line. "Hello."

"It's me. I just wanted to touch base."

"Did you get your sink fixed?"

"They just finished."

"You want to come on over to the mall? I haven't eaten. I wasn't going to bother since you weren't able to make it."

"Actually, something's come up."

The same phrase she'd used before. If she were going to lie to someone who knew her so well, it would have been better to think everything through first.

"With the plumbing you mean?"

"No, that's fine. I'm… I just wanted to let you know that I'm going away for a few days."

"Away? Away where?" The tone of her mother's questions was bewilderment rather than shock. And that was probably justified.

Cait couldn't remember making an out-of-town trip

since she'd been shot. At first she hadn't thought she could afford to miss rehab. Even when the results she'd gotten had surpassed everyone's expectation, she had continued to work doggedly, determined that her recovery would be as complete as she could make it. Ultimately, she hoped, her arm would be as good as new.

Yeah, right.

"My friend Ann Cummings called. You remember. From Emory. She's in town— Actually, she's passing through on her way to New York. She asked if I wanted to drive up with her."

In the face of the silence that greeted that information, Cait fought the urge to keep talking. To add detail to detail until her mother was forced to believe her story by their sheer weight, despite the fact that she knew nothing screamed "lie" more than that.

"Mom?"

"For how long?"

"I'm not sure. A few days. She has some business to take care of, and then we're going to take in a couple of shows. See the Christmas decorations. Just…do the tourist things."

Another silence.

"I wanted to let you know so you wouldn't worry."

"How very thoughtful."

Sarcasm. Her mother's favorite weapon. But it was one Cait had lived with all her life. This she knew how to handle.

"I aim to please," she said pleasantly.

At this point, she really didn't care if her mother was annoyed. After all, she was too old to be expected to ask permission for whatever she did.

"Are you sure—?"

"I'm sure. Everything's fine, Mom. Trust me."

Everything's just peachy as long as whoever sent those two goons to my house doesn't find us. And as long as I'm right in believing Will had nothing to do with Greg Vincent's death.

"Do I have an option?" her mom asked, her tone sardonic.

"Not really."

"When are you leaving?"

"As soon as I can throw a few things into a suitcase. She's coming by here."

"Is there anything you want me to do at the house? Pick up your mail?"

Or a couple of corpses.

"Everything's taken care of. The only thing I need you to do is not worry. I love you. I'll call you when I get back."

She punched the off button, deliberately cutting off whatever her mother said in response. Then she slid the phone back into her pocket.

Although she expected Will to comment on the one-sided conversation, he didn't. The only sound in the car was the fan on the heater.

"What about *your* call?" she asked to break the silence she felt was uncomfortable. "You want to use my cell?"

"I'll find a pay phone. I don't want you implicated in this any more than you have to be. If the cops ask, your mother will tell them you're in New York. They shouldn't be able to pinpoint the time of death precisely enough to put you in the house with those two."

"So…they'll think I was gone before you showed up?"

"If we're lucky."

"And if we aren't?"

"They'll be looking for me not only in connection with a murder investigation."

It took her a second or two longer than it should have. "They'll think you kidnapped me."

"That's better than the alternative."

Which was that she'd been an accessory. An accessory to murder.

Whatever else Will Shannon had done since he'd come back into her life, he had certainly added another dimension to her relatively uneventful existence. One she wasn't sure that she was up to dealing with.

CHAPTER SEVEN

"WHAT ARE YOU DOING?"

Will had pulled up to the curb on a crowded street in Fountain Heights. Still thinking about the carnage they'd left behind in her house, she hadn't been conscious of her surroundings until he'd stopped.

"That's the place where we ate last night," he said, nodding to indicate the restaurant across the street.

"So...what are we doing here now?"

"I want to talk to the people who were here then before the cops do."

"You think they haven't already done that?"

"I don't see how they could have. Not this soon. Ron Vincent, Greg's brother, called and asked him to meet him here. The name won't be on Greg's appointment calendar if they've started looking through those."

"His brother will have told them where you had dinner, Will. People do that in a murder investigation."

"He might. *If* he thought it could be important."

"*You* do."

"Because it's the last thing I remember. Ron may not

know that. To him, this just may be a place he had dinner with his brother."

"His *last* dinner with his brother. That he wouldn't consider that to be important is a crock full of wishful thinking."

"Maybe, but it's a chance I have to take."

He opened his door, but before he could climb out, she put her hand on his arm. "What can you possibly hope to accomplish by going in there that's worth the risk you're taking?"

"I want to find out what happened last night. The last clear memory I have was here."

"None of the waitstaff who's on now would have been there last night," she warned.

"Then maybe they'll give me the name of someone who was."

Maybe. This whole pointless exercise seemed predicated on that word. "Will—"

He pulled his sleeve from her grip, getting out of the car and slamming the door. She expected him to leave her in the car while he went inside, but he came around the front of the car to open the passenger door.

As he waited for her to crawl out, his eyes surveyed their surroundings. With his background, Will would be able to recognize a stakeout.

"Anybody watching?" she asked as he closed her door.

He shook his head. "Even if they know we were here last night, they won't expect me to come back. The only thing I'm worried about is whether someone inside might call them before we get the information we need."

Although Will had been identified as a "person of interest," the film clip from the inquiry had been included in the television coverage she'd seen. It was not a good picture, but still…

Of course, having her with him lessened the chances of his being recognized. People would see them and think couple-out-for-lunch rather than fugitive-from-a-murder. She wondered if that's why he was taking her in.

"This isn't smart," she warned as he took her elbow to guide her across the busy street.

"Maybe not, but I have to start somewhere."

He couldn't go back to Vincent's house, a place that would be far more likely to provide information about what had happened last night. The police would be in the process of collecting that at this very moment.

When Will pushed open the door of the restaurant, a wave of warm air, filled with the rich fragrance of Italian food, greeted them. There was a pleasant babble of lunchtime conversation, punctuated by the occasional clink of glassware or china.

The place was so crowded, people waiting for a table were lined up from the door to the reservation desk. No one seemed to be paying the slightest attention to them, including the restaurant personnel. She and Will were simply part of the midday crowd. Will worked his way through the mob, carrying her with him toward the desk.

"Two for lunch?" The hostess was young and obviously harried. She'd probably asked that question a hundred times today.

"Actually, I just need some information." Will smiled at the girl, a slightly crooked grin Cait knew from experience could be disarming.

"Would you like to see a menu?"

"No, not *that* kind of information."

Will seemed relaxed. Amused by the question. As if he were sharing an inside joke with the hostess. He'd always been good at putting people at ease.

"Then…exactly what kind of information are you looking for?" The woman's tone had become almost flirtatious. As if she expected Will to ask for her phone number in spite of the fact that Cait was standing beside him.

"I was with a party in one of the private dining rooms last night. I think I may have left my briefcase there. I wondered if it had been found."

"Not that I know of, but I can ask. Hold on." She used the phone at the desk to pose the question, punching in a couple of numbers before she spoke. "A gentleman thinks he might have left his briefcase in one of the back dining rooms last night. Did anyone find it?"

Again, the babble of conversation swirled around them as the hostess listened. A party of diners, in the process of exiting, pushed past them on their way out. Cait took a half step to the side, which put her in even closer proximity to Will.

He put his arm around her shoulder. She couldn't tell

if that was part of the act or the kind of naturally protective gesture she'd once taken for granted.

"Thanks. I'll tell him." The hostess replaced the phone on its stand. "Sorry. No briefcase. Are you sure you left it here?"

"I've looked everywhere else," Will said. "I wonder if I could talk to the guy who waited on us last night."

"If you're implying that someone here might have found it and not turned it in—"

"I'm not implying that at all," Will said quickly.

"You want to talk to the manager?"

"Was he here last night?"

"There's a different staff for lunch and dinner."

"So nobody who's on duty now was here last night."

"That's right."

Cait could hear the growing impatience in the hostess's voice, maybe because Will still had his arm around Cait's shoulder. She knew Will would be reluctant to give up on this, especially since there were so few avenues open to him.

"When does the dinner shift come on?"

"It's staggered to handle the crowd. Some come in early. Some later. Just like the patrons." The sentences had been staccato. And unfriendly. "Did you want a table for lunch, sir? Because if you don't…"

"How about just the name of the waiter who handled the back rooms last night?"

"We're not allowed to give out that information. Privacy concerns. And to protect our employees. I'm sure you understand."

"We do," Cait said, deciding that this had gone on long enough. "Thanks for your time. You've been very helpful."

She hadn't been, but it would be better to leave on a friendly note than to let the hostess stew all afternoon about Will's persistence. That was the kind of thing that could tilt people over the line about notifying the authorities. Maybe in the rush she would just forget this had ever happened.

Putting her hand on Will's arm, Cait began to turn toward the door, attempting to pull him with her. After the slightest, probably unnoticeable resistance, he acquiesced.

"What was that about?" he asked as they started back through the throng between the desk and the street entrance.

"I thought you didn't want to draw attention."

"I *wanted* information."

"Which she obviously wasn't going to give you," she said, turning to look at him. "If you'd kept on, she would have called the manager. What good would that have done?"

Although she wasn't watching where she was going, she had assumed the crowd would continue to part before them. Instead, something hit her, elbow high, with a resulting clatter of glassware.

"You okay?" The busboy she'd run into was even younger than the hostess. Except he was male. And black.

"I'm fine." She brushed at the liquid that had sloshed out of his tray and onto her coat.

"You sure?" He handed her the towel that had been slung over his arm.

"I'm sure," she said, looking up to smile at him although the towel was damper than her sleeve. "Anything broken? I'll be glad to pay—"

"Naw. Plastic tray," he said, lifting it as if to demonstrate. "They just bang around in here. And it's not a big deal if it did. Don't tell 'em I said that, okay?" His grin was friendly.

"No, I won't," she agreed, handing the rag back to him. Before he could move on, she added, "We were looking for the guy who waited on us last night at dinner. We ate in one of the back rooms. My husband thought I put down the tip, and I thought he put it on the card. We came back because we're leaving tonight—going back to Ohio—and we didn't want to stiff the waiter."

"One of the private dining rooms?"

"That's right," Will said.

"You're out of luck. That's Emilio. He won't be in until six." Again the kid attempted to walk past them.

"Our flight leaves at four," Cait said. "Is there any way we could get in touch with him?"

"You can leave the money with the manager."

"I don't like to leave cash. You never know if it gets to the right person. If you could just give us his last name. Or a phone number."

Even as she said it, she knew the story didn't add up.

No matter how young this kid was, he would realize that there was something strange about the request.

"We just want to do the right thing," Will added. "If there's anything you could do to help us out…"

"You want me to give him the money for you?" The brown eyes were suspicious.

"No," Cait said softly, deciding that the only way to get what they wanted was to give up the tale they'd spun and make it worth the busboy's while to cooperate. "But we *are* willing to give *you* something in exchange for the information."

The kid studied her face before his eyes moved to examine Will's. "You cops?"

"Not even close," Will said.

"Emilio in trouble?"

"All we want is to talk to him about the people in the back room last night." Will took his hand out of his pocket. Although she couldn't see what was in it, the boy's eyes widened. "You want to help us out or not?"

"She's watching," the kid said, glancing at the desk before his gaze came back to Will again. ·

"The hostess?" Cait guessed.

"You all talk to her first? She know what you want? Man, you're gonna get me in so much trouble."

"Is there somewhere else we could talk?" Will asked. "Outside maybe? I guarantee it will be worth your while." He took the towel from the kid's hand and brushed at his jacket in case the hostess really was watching this prolonged conversation.

"Behind the restaurant. There's an alley. You go out the front. I'll meet you back there."

"Stop at the clock-in board before you do. Look at Emilio's card. I need an address. Or a phone number."

"Go on. Get out of here," the kid urged, moving past them and continuing toward the back of the restaurant.

"You think he'll come?" Cait asked as soon as they were outside.

"For the fifty I showed him? He'll come."

"*My* fifty."

Although she'd told Will she wouldn't have much cash, she'd forgotten that she'd made an ATM withdrawal last night in preparation for the trip to the mall. And she'd had almost the entire two hundred left.

"I owe you," he said. "Actually…for a lot more than the money. That was good thinking to ask the kid."

As they turned the corner, she said, "You mentioned you were drinking club soda last night."

"Yeah."

"Here?"

"It must have been. I remember the condensation on the glass. The white tablecloth under it. And Greg and his brother were talking in the background while I was looking at it."

"But you don't remember leaving?"

"I don't remember anything after that. Not until I woke up on the floor of his office."

"They put something in your drink."

"*They?*"

"Vincent. Whoever he was with. Emilio."

Will's instincts *had* been good, she admitted. As always. This place *was* important in what had happened last night. More important than she'd realized.

"Rohypnol," he suggested.

"Or something like it. GHB. Ketamine."

Any of the so-called "date rape" drugs would cause the symptoms Will had described. Lost time. Headache. Disorientation. Lack of coordination.

"They're usually given in alcohol," Cait went on, thinking out loud. "It increases both the effects and their duration. And they wouldn't show up on a normal tox screen. Not unless you were looking for them."

Obviously Will had come to before they'd anticipated he would. Whoever had drugged him had expected that the cops would find him passed out on the floor, his gun in the bed beside his dead employer, and arrest him.

"It might be useful to know who told the police something was wrong at the house," she said, following that train of thought.

"All I can tell you is that Greg didn't call them."

"Nor did you."

Another beat of silence. She could hear her own breathing, a combination of the pace Will was setting and the biting cold.

"I can't say that for sure," he said finally.

"If you were the person who was supposed to take the fall, then you'd hardly be calling the cops. But someone did or they wouldn't have shown up so quickly. It might be important to know who."

They made the turn into the alley behind the restaurant. As the sound of traffic faded behind them, she began to wonder if this had been a smart move.

The same succulent aromas that had wafted out of the front door when they'd arrived grew stronger. They were evidently heading toward a back of the kitchen. And the busboy, who'd had plenty of time to make it here, seemed to be a no-show.

"I didn't mean to get you into this," Will said, coming to a halt near a pair of wooden, shutter-type doors that were standing open, "but I'm glad you are."

Before she could assimilate the compliment, if that's what it had been, Will straightened. The busboy stepped through the opening and into the alley. He lit the cigarette he carried in his hand, then slipped the lighter under his apron and presumably into his pocket. He glanced back inside, and without preamble, got down to business.

"His name's Emilio Garza. This is his number." He held out a slip of paper, which Will took. "I think it's a cell."

"How about the address? Just in case I can't reach him on this." Will lifted the phone number he'd been handed.

"He lives in Adams Morgan. Card says 1744 Trinidad." The busboy's eyes cut nervously toward the kitchen as he took another drag on the cigarette.

"Thanks," Will said, holding out the fifty he'd offered.

The kid took it, slipping it under the apron. He grabbed another pull on the cigarette before he flipped it in an arc across the alley.

"Emilio open to bribes?" Will asked.

The kid had already turned, heading to the kitchen. He looked back, the brown eyes no longer friendly. "Anybody who makes less than minimum wage is open to bribes."

He raised his brows as if challenging them to argue with his contention. When they didn't, with a dignity beyond his years and station, he nodded and then disappeared inside.

Neither of them said anything for a long heartbeat.

"We may not be able to find him from that," Cait warned.

"I'll find him," Will said.

He reached out to take her elbow, turning her in the direction from which they'd entered the alley. Suddenly he stopped, his eyes on the building across it. Faded letters and an arrow had at some time been painted on the bricks, pointing the way to additional parking.

"What's wrong?" she asked.

"It was back here."

"What was here?"

"The guy I saw. He was here."

She replayed the words in her head, but they made no more sense the second time than they had the first.

"What guy?"

"This morning. I had... I had what may have been a

flashback. I'd glanced in the mirror. I could see my reflection, but it was distorted by the steam. Then all of a sudden, this guy's face was there."

It took a minute for her to absorbed the information. "And you think you saw him here?"

"That was behind him. I didn't recognize it this morning, but…"

"Will? *What* was behind him? I don't understand."

"That sign. It was behind him in the flashback. And his hair was wet because it had been raining."

"Last night?"

"It was raining when we came into the restaurant last night."

"You came in through this door?"

"The front. I remember. I parked the car out there."

"Then…"

"I don't know. All I know was that the guy I saw in that flashback this morning was in this alley last night."

CHAPTER EIGHT

"THIS MUST BE IT," Will said, bending to look through the windshield at the numbers on the front of the run-down apartment building.

He had repeatedly called the number the busboy had given them, but gotten no answer. And there was no Trinidad Street in the area, something it had taken them more than an hour of searching to discover. Either the busboy had been dyslexic or he'd deliberately misled them. And this part of the Adams Morgan wasn't a place where you'd have much success asking directions. Finally someone had suggested they might be looking for Trinity, which indeed had an apartment building at 1744.

"You want me to wait in the car while you check it out?" Cait asked.

He didn't. However inhospitable the reception inside might be, it would be safer than leaving her alone out here. No one had followed them from the restaurant, but he wouldn't consider this neighborhood safe for a woman alone under any circumstances.

"You're the one who figured out how to get to this guy."

"I'm willing to take the credit for that. Just as long

as you promise not to be disappointed if Emilio can't tell you anything. They wouldn't have wanted anyone else to know what they were doing."

The assumption that whatever he'd been given had been administered in the club soda was only that—an assumption. In actuality, he could have been drugged at any time, before or after they'd left the restaurant.

He scanned the area surrounding the building as he walked around to open Cait's door. He saw nothing to cause his well-tuned radar to go off.

He slammed the car door and hit the remote to lock it. A couple of Latino kids were sitting on the steps of Emilio's building, a boom box blasting away between them. As they approached, the boys eyed them with open interest.

Although the kids were leaning back against the concrete banisters on either side of the entryway, their legs stretched across the steps in a way that would prevent access, neither made a move as Will and Cait reached the stairs. Will stopped at the foot, making eye contact with the boy who appeared to be older.

"We're looking for Emilio Garza. He live here?"

"Don't know no Emilio," the teen said, drawing out the syllables of the name.

Will judged he might be thirteen or fourteen, but it was hard to tell, given his small stature. "Dark hair. Mid twenties. He's a waiter at Maglianno's."

"I'm supposed to be impressed?" As he asked the question, the boy straightened, his air of indolence changing to one that was apparently supposed to threaten.

"Not really. We're just looking for information."

"We got none of that," the younger one said, imitating the other's belligerence. "Not for tourists."

"Emilio's apartment number?" With his left hand, Will fingered a ten out of his pocket, making sure it was visible to the boys.

There was a moment of hesitation, as if they were thinking about it, and then the older one asked, "You looking to buy? I can set you up. Stuff's better then Emilio's shit."

The kid turned his head to spit across the top of the banister. An editorial comment on the quality of what Emilio was selling?

"Just his apartment number."

"I don't know the number," the older one said finally, eyeing the ten. "Second floor. Door to the right at the top of the stairs."

"He up there?" Will carefully separated another ten from his dwindling reserve.

"I ain't seen him come out, but it ain't time for him to go to work."

"Thanks. Gentlemen, if you'll excuse us." Will held out one of the tens to the younger boy, who was perhaps nine or ten. He grabbed it as he rose, clearing a path up the right-hand side of the steps. "And to you for the information."

The older teen held his eyes, making no move to take the money or vacate the steps. "You a cop?"

"No."

The wary eyes regarded him a few seconds longer. Then the kid stretched out a thin arm and removed the bill from Will's fingers. "Don't matter. Emilio's an asshole anyway."

He stuck the ten in the pocket of his cotton shirt. Then without any sign of haste, he picked up the boom box by its handle and sauntered by them and down the sidewalk.

When the sound of the music had faded by several decibels, Cait said, "Nice kid."

"I'm just glad Emilio pissed him off."

She laughed. The familiarity of the sound echoed inside Will's chest, reminding him again of how much he'd missed the easy camaraderie they'd once shared. Almost as much as he missed everything else.

When they'd reached the top of the steps, he opened the outer door of the building. Ushering her through, he followed her inside, conscious of the sounds and smells as they began to climb the stairs.

The mewling cries of a baby drifted down the stairwell from one of the upper stories. The nearer they got to the landing, the stronger grew the odors of stale cooking and of too many bodies occupying too little space. Underlying those was the faint, unpleasant stench of urine.

"Even with the cost of housing in this town," Cait said, "I would think that someone who worked at Maglianno's could do better than this."

"Maybe he's supporting his family back in Ecuador. Or wherever home is."

As he said the words, another fleeting image, like the one he'd had in the bathroom this morning, flashed through his mind. A dark hand set a glass down on the expanse of white cloth. He had looked up to say thanks, encountering eyes as black as those belonging to the kids on the steps.

As dark as the man in the other flashback? Were they one and the same? Except the waiter's hair had been short. Dark and curling, but closely cropped. And his features had clearly been Latino and the other man's had not.

That memory of the waiter was another that hadn't been in his head before. And Will wasn't sure what had triggered it.

He realized that Cait had already reached the landing. She turned to wait on him, her hand still in contact with the stair rail, as he finished the climb.

The door to the right of the stairs, the one to which the boy had directed them, said 2B. Just as there had been no names on the array of mailboxes in the foyer, there was none on the door.

He stepped past Cait and tapped on it a couple of times with his knuckles. As they waited for a response, he was aware that Cait had moved to stand behind him.

Someone had finally quieted the baby. In the stillness, he could hear Cait's breathing. Despite the smells that permeated the dilapidated building, he was again aware of the fragrance of her shampoo. Just as when he'd lain down in her bed.

In her bed... The phrase resonated with connotations far beyond the reality of those hours he'd spent there this morning.

"Try again."

He had already raised his hand in response to her urging when he noticed that the lock wasn't engaged. On casual inspection, the door had seemed to line up with the jamb, but it actually sat slightly behind it. He changed his target, banging on the wood panel only an inch or two above the knob. As if he'd used a key, the door popped open.

"It's not locked."

"That makes no sense," Cait said. "Not in this neighborhood. Especially if he's not here."

"I guess we're about to find out. Emilio?"

As he called the waiter's name, Will pushed the door with his foot. As it swung inward, he examined the room its movement revealed.

His first thought had been that housekeeping wasn't Emilio's forte. It quickly became clear that the place had been trashed.

Not as in vandalized, but as in searched. Thoroughly and, in Will's opinion, professionally.

The cushions on the stained couch had been cut open, their stuffing scattered over the floor. Furniture had been pulled away from the walls and then overturned.

Sunlight streamed in from the window of the kitchen, which was in the direct line of sight from the front door. Even the crockery had been swept out of the cabinets there. Shattered glass and shards of china lay over the cracked linoleum.

"What the hell?" Cait asked softly.

"It's been searched. And by somebody who was serious."

Drug deal gone wrong? Had Emilio's supplier come looking for his goods or his money?

"What about Emilio?"

There'd been no answer to his repeated phone calls. A drug dealer who didn't answer his cell didn't last long in the business. Which added to the very bad feeling Will had gotten when he'd first seen the chaos inside the apartment.

Maybe Emilio had been smart enough to exit as his previous guests had entered. Or maybe he hadn't been at home at all.

"I don't know."

He hoped the waiter hadn't been here when this had been done. He couldn't be sure what Emilio's visitors had been looking for, but the search they'd conducted had been both ruthless and determined. The same attitude of the guys who'd shown up at Cait's this morning.

"Will?"

He could hear the note of concern in Cait's voice. "Come on."

He took her arm, drawing her with him inside the apartment. He shut the door behind them and threw the dead bolt. Until he knew exactly what was going on, he didn't want anyone to see them in here.

"Don't move," he warned.

She didn't answer as he began to pick his way across the room. Even the baseboards had been pried away from the walls. Whatever they'd been looking for, they'd taken the place apart in an attempt to find it.

He stepped over one of the slashed cushions, making his way toward the kitchen. Hardly bigger than a good-sized closet, it contained a small stove and refrigerator, topped by a couple of cabinets, whose doors were standing open. He walked across the room toward the sink, debris crunching under his soles with every step.

There was no fire escape outside the long, narrow window as he'd anticipated. Despite the sunlight pouring through it, the only view was of the brick wall of an adjoining building.

He turned, his gaze seeking Cait. She was standing patiently by the door.

"I'm going to take a look in the bedroom."

She nodded. And then, almost as an afterthought, she added, "Be careful."

In response to her warning, he drew his weapon out of its holster. His gut told him that the apartment was empty or someone would have reacted by now to the noise he'd been making. As well-honed as his instincts were, there was enough unknown in this situation that he wasn't going to take any unnecessary chances—not with Cait here.

Like the door to the landing, the one leading into the bedroom was not completely closed. Putting his left hand under his gun hand, he pushed the door open with his foot, stepping to the other side of the doorway as it swung away from him.

A sagging double bed, now stripped to its mattress, dominated the narrow room. On the wall opposite the open closet and the door to the bath stood a chest of drawers. Each one had been pulled out, its contents either scattered onto the floor or spilling down the front.

He walked far enough inside to check out the space between the bed and the chest. There was nothing there except clothing from the drawers and the wadded-up bedding.

Taking a deep breath, he walked around to the other side of the room. On his way to the window, he took a cursory look into the closet, so sparsely furnished with clothing that it was immediately apparent no one was hiding inside.

The fire escape he'd expected to find beyond the kitchen window was outside this one. He didn't take the time to open it, only enough to discover that the metal-work platform was empty.

He turned, for some reason reluctant to finish the search. All that was left was the bathroom. Despite the disorder of the rest of the apartment, its door had been carefully closed.

Will put his ear against the thin wood. There was no sound from inside.

With his left hand, he rapped. "Emilio? It's okay. The people who did this are gone."

He waited, hoping for, but not expecting, an answer. When none came, he put his hand on the knob and turned it, feeling the lock disengage.

Then, just as he'd done with the front door, he pushed this one inward with his foot.

It stopped abruptly, bouncing a little as it ran into something that blocked its movement. Before he stepped inside, Will surveyed what he could see of the room.

A shower curtain drooped onto the black-and-white tile floor. It had been partially pulled away from the rod, although the loops that had secured it were still attached to the plastic. His eyes automatically followed the mildew-stained material back down to the floor.

This time he saw the hand that had ripped the curtain down. The same slim, dark hand that had placed the club soda on the table in front of him last night, its fingers still gripping the yellowed plastic.

Taking another breath, Will slipped into the room through the half-opened door, leading with his gun. Emilio Garza's body lay on the floor, glazed eyes staring at the ceiling.

The handsome face he had remembered earlier had been battered almost beyond recognition, the back of the waiter's head resting in a pool of congealed blood. Since both swelling and discoloration marked the injuries, it was obvious the beating had occurred prior to his death.

A drug deal gone wrong, as he'd speculated before. Or had Emilio been worked over in an attempt to make him give up the location of something else. Like whatever those men at Cait's had wanted to talk about this morning. Maybe poor Emilio Garza had had no more clue about what was going on than Will did.

Although there was no doubt in his mind that the waiter was dead, Will knelt, automatically putting his fingers over the carotid artery. As Greg's had been last night, the flesh was cool to the touch. Almost cold.

Getting to be a habit.

He'd been an agent for more than a decade. During the last twelve hours he'd seen more death than he had in all that time. And he knew from the way this was going it probably wasn't over yet.

He straightened, looking around the small room. It had been as thoroughly searched as the rest of the flat. The contents of the medicine cabinet had been dumped into the rust-stained lavatory. A few threadbare towels had been shaken out and then thrown into a pile on the floor.

"He's dead?"

Will glanced up to find Cait looking in through the partially opened door.

"Very," he said succinctly.

"How long ago?"

"Long enough for the body to be cold to the touch."

"Rigor?"

Reluctantly Will bent and tried to move the hand that clutched the shower curtain. The resistance he met answered that question.

"Yeah."

He swiveled on the balls of his feet to look up at her

again. Her copper-penny eyes were focused on the dead man.

"That means he's been dead at least eight hours."

The apartment was cold, but not enough to retard any of the biological functions. Cait's estimate would put the time of death at around 6:00 a.m.

"What were they looking for?" she asked.

"I don't know. Whatever it was, it looks like they tried to beat the information out of him first."

"That's what they were trying to do this morning."

She meant the men who had come to her house. They had intended to use Cait to force him to give them what they wanted. And maybe what they had wanted was whatever his killers had come to Emilio's to find. And when they hadn't found it—

The knock on the front door brought Will to his feet in one motion, his gun extended in that direction.

"Mr. Garza? Police. Open up, please. We'd like to talk to you."

CHAPTER NINE

WILL KNEW HE'D TURNED the lock when he'd closed that outer door, but it was possible the cops had brought the building superintendent up with them. If they didn't get an answer, he'd be instructed to use his key. Even if the police had to go downstairs again to get the guy, it would still be a matter of minutes before they'd be inside.

Already wanted for one murder, Will knew the authorities would attempt to tie him to this one, despite Emilio's time of death. When they added the two dead men back at Cait's to the body count...

He took the single step that separated them, putting his mouth against Cait's ear to whisper, "Shh..."

She nodded her understanding, her hair brushing against his cheek. Despite the circumstances, his groin tightened at her nearness.

Ignoring the feeling, he squeezed past her and crossed the room to close the bedroom door. At least the cops wouldn't see them as soon as they entered the apartment's living area. That might gain them a few seconds at a time when each was vital.

He shifted his gun to his left hand and grabbed Cait's

elbow, practically dragging her with him toward the window and the fire escape. When he got there, he released her arm, at the same time shoving his gun back into the holster.

No matter what happened, he couldn't use it against the cops. They had every reason to believe he was just what the evidence implied—a murderer on the run. Besides that, even if he had wanted to exchange shots with them, he couldn't risk it. Not if there was a chance Cait might be caught in the crossfire.

He flipped the lock on the window and tried to push up the sash. Obviously it hadn't been raised lately. Either the wood had swollen with the recent rains or it had been painted shut, which would be the kiss of death for any hope of their getting out of the apartment before the police got in.

"Mr. Garza? We need to talk to you. Open the door, please."

Although the voice seemed more distant than before, due to the closed door, the cop's demand reiterated, as if Will had needed a reminder, that time was running out. He bent his knees, trying to get the power of the larger muscles of his thighs and buttocks into the lift.

Just as he was beginning to despair, the window gave with a creak, inching upward. Encouraged by that progress, he strained again, driving the sash up with every ounce of strength he possessed. When he had it open far enough, he stuck his head out, looking down to check out the alley below. No one had been stationed there.

Nor could he see the patrol car from this angle, he realized, which meant that if one of the uniforms had been left out front with the vehicle, he wouldn't be able to see what was happening on this side of the building. Reassured that they weren't going to be fired upon from below, not yet at least, Will put one leg over the sill and climbed onto the metal landing.

"Come on," he urged, holding out his hand to Cait.

The cops were knocking again, although they'd apparently given up trying to talk their way in. If they'd had the foresight to bring the super with them, they would be inside the apartment in a matter of seconds.

Ignoring his hand, Cait put her leg over the sill and crawled out onto the fire escape beside him. He had already started to turn away when she leaned back inside the window.

"What are you doing?"

"Pulling down the shade."

There indeed was a stained and tattered paper shade on a roller above the window. Cait pulled it down and then straightened out of the opening.

"Close the window," she ordered, shifting to give him room to come back to it.

She was right, he realized, hurrying to obey. The cops would eventually look out it, as he had, for the mandated fire escape, but Cait's idea might buy them a few more minutes.

The narrow fire escape again put them into a close proximity, something that seemed to be happening with surprising frequency. Once he'd closed the window, he looked down into the alley again, but it was still clear. If there had been a lookout at the front of the building, apparently he hadn't figured out what was going on.

"You first," he ordered, nodding toward the ladder.

He wasn't sure how much strength Cait had in the damaged shoulder. All she would have to do if she went first was to step on the lower rung and ride the ladder to the ground.

He would follow in the more conventional manner. The strain of the climb down would pull at his own injury, but that wouldn't affect his ability to hold on to the ladder. It might Cait's.

She moved past him obediently to wrap her fingers around the left handrail. Her face was colorless, but she hadn't protested what he had asked her to do.

"The descent will be fairly quick," he warned, "but we're only one story up so the landing shouldn't be too hard. Just hang on."

"I'll be fine."

"When it touches down, run toward the back of the building. I'll catch up to you." He could tell by the sounds coming from beyond the bedroom door that the cops were inside. "Go," he urged.

She put her right hand on the opposite rail and then stepped onto the ladder. It began to lower, metal squealing as it slid through the open trap and down onto the alley below.

Only when it touched down did Will remember to

breathe. Without waiting for her to step off, he climbed onto the top of the ladder and began his descent. Above him he could hear raised voices in the apartment they'd just vacated.

He estimated it would take the cops a couple of minutes to search the rooms—just as he had done—to make sure they weren't walking into a trap. Another few to examine the body.

If he managed to get three or four minutes before one of them stuck his head out of the window, he'd be extremely lucky. Will prayed that would be enough.

He stepped onto the pavement and turned to see Cait about halfway down the alley, which slanted downhill. With a final glance toward the street where they'd left the car, Will followed at a dead run.

At any second he expected to be told to freeze. He would, of course. Because if he didn't—

"Hey. Over here, dude."

The younger of the kids from the front stairs was standing in a low doorway near the end of the alley. A couple of steps led down to the entrance where he stood, but the area behind him was shadowed so that Will was unable to tell where it led.

"They got somebody waiting 'round the back," the kid said.

With that information, Will gave up any thought of refusing his help. He grabbed Cait's arm, drawing her with him across the alley. The kid moved out of the doorway as they came down the steps.

As soon they'd made it inside, the door closed behind them, shutting off the sunlight that had beamed into the alley between the two apartment buildings. The darkness that surrounded them was almost complete. A trap? Will wondered. Because the kids thought he was carrying a lot of cash?

As the idea formed, there was a metallic clang and the kid materialized out of the darkness.

"The door's got a metal bar. They ain't coming in this way. Come on."

Despite his doubts about the boy's motives, Will decided that following him through the basement was the lesser of two evils. After all, he *knew* what lay behind them.

It was possible the kid felt some kind of kinship because they were running from the cops. Law enforcement wasn't highly regarded in this heavily ethnic community, sometimes with good reason.

With Cait behind him, he trailed the ghostly paleness of the kid's T-shirt until it stopped, maybe thirty feet from the door. The boy was waiting for them, the whites of his eyes shining in the dimness as he watched their approach.

"Downstairs," he directed, pointing to a flight of stairs that angled to the right of the hallway.

"What's down there?"

"Whadda you care? It ain't the cops."

The kid had a point. Still, it wasn't smart to go into any situation blind, a feeling he'd become overly familiar with in the last twelve hours.

"Furnace room," the kid said, apparently deciding they weren't going to budge until he gave them some clue as to their destination. "There's a passageway that leads over to the next building. 'Course if you don't want to get out of here…" The upward movement of the thin shoulders under the T-shirt was visible despite the shadows.

"Okay," Will agreed, knowing there really wasn't much choice.

He heard the kid's tennis shoes slapping against the concrete as he started ahead of them.

"You trust him?" Cait asked as the sound disappeared into the darkness below.

"Yeah. I don't know why, but…yeah, I do," Will said, taking hold of the railing. "He didn't have to get involved."

"Maybe he's hoping for more money," Cait said, following him. "They've probably written you off as an easy mark."

The comment made him wonder about the older kid. Maybe he'd taken his boom box and gone home. Or maybe he was playing lookout. *Or maybe he's selling you out to the cops*….

"If he pulls this off, it'll be worth whatever it costs."

They reached the landing. In the increasing darkness of their descent, Will couldn't be sure if this was the furnace room or if there was another set of steps below this point.

"Over here."

The sound of the whisper and the pale blob of the

boy's shirt marked his location. When Will reached the spot where he thought the kid had been standing, however, all he found was the entrance to another hallway. At the end of it hung an exposed lightbulb, illuminating a brick wall.

"Come *on,* man. The super knows about that outside door. He's gonna bring the cops down here before long."

The kid's face had appeared around the corner of the wall lit by the bulb. Not an end of their journey, Will realized, but another turn. Maybe the beginning of the passageway the boy had mentioned. Judging the size of the building from its outside appearance, they would surely have reached its outside limits by now.

"I don't like this," Cait whispered.

Will removed the SIG-Sauer from its holster. After all, if the kid *was* leading them into a trap, there was no guarantee he was working for the cops. The memory of what had been done to Emilio Garza was fresh and very raw.

"Me, either, but we can't go back. By now the cops will be all over that alley."

It seemed they were being lured farther and farther into the darkness. Still, Will felt he had no option but to take the chance the kid hadn't sold them out, despite the fact the ten he'd slipped him seemed too little recompense to make anyone go this far out of his way to save them.

The sound of a door slamming somewhere in the basement echoed and reechoed, bouncing against the brick walls so that it was impossible to know whether it had come from behind or ahead of them. Unwilling to bet it hadn't been the former, Will increased his pace, hurrying along the passage toward the bare bulb. When he reached it, he turned left, almost running into the boy, who had again seemed to materialize in front of him.

"You gotta break that light," the kid said.

Will hesitated, thinking about the stygian blackness that would surround them if he obeyed. Another sound from above made the decision for him.

He stepped forward until he was under the light. Reversing the semiautomatic, he swung at the dangling bulb, sending it crashing into the wall. He shielded his face from the glass that tinkled down around him, automatically closing his eyes.

When he opened them, the darkness seemed to have closed in, becoming oppressive. As if there were no longer enough air. From above them came the sound of footsteps.

He reversed his gun, and then reached out, trying to locate Cait. His searching hand encountered nothing.

Panic roared through him. He had known since this morning that they would make her a target. Separating them had obviously been what the kid had been instructed to do.

"Cait?"

Without answering, she touched him. Her fingers were cold, but they were steadier than his right now. He gripped them, his relief so powerful it made him weak.

"Come on." The kid's whisper came from the direction of the passage. "We gotta get out of here. Ain't much farther."

Still gripping Cait's hand, Will moved forward, conscious that the quality of the sounds coming from above had changed. Whoever had entered the basement was now descending the flight of stairs they'd taken. Soon they would be on this level, but without the guidance of the light he'd broken, they would be at a greater disadvantage than he and Cait had been.

Will could hear the kid running ahead of them. Either his night vision was better than Will's, or this was a journey he'd made innumerable times, so that he could do it blind.

Suddenly, light flooded the passage, resolving into an open door as their eyes adjusted to the glare. The boy they'd been following was standing to the right-hand side, holding it wide. The older kid from the stoop was visible outside. As they approached, he motioned frantically for them to hurry.

Will moved ahead of Cait, passing by the younger of the two. He stepped into the opening, surveying the street. There was traffic, but no cops.

He motioned Cait forward. The boy followed, allowing the door to close, taking care to keep it from making any noise as it did.

"You drive?" Will asked the older.

The kid's eyes widened, but his affirmative was quick and decisive. "'Course. Whadda ya think I am?"

"Underage," Will said, retrieving the keys to the Altima from his pocket. "You see the car we came in? Beige Nissan?"

"Yeah."

"Go around the front and get it and then meet me."

"Where?"

"Somewhere close. Not too open. You tell me. This is your turf." Will held out the keys.

The boy's gaze fell to consider them, dangling from Will's fingers, before it returned to his face. "Cops got the car staked out?"

"Why would they? They didn't watch us drive up."

"It'll cost you."

Will almost laughed at the predictability of that demand. "How much?"

He could see the wheels turning inside the boy's head. He only hoped that what he asked for wasn't more than what he had.

"Hundred. Take it or leave it."

The last was bravado, judging by how quickly he'd jumped at the ten. And if Will met that price, it would leave them almost broke. Still...

"When you deliver."

The dark eyes widened again. Before Will could change his mind, the kid's hand came up, palm open.

Will dropped the keys into it. "So where do we meet?"

"Two blocks that way." The small, dark head tilted to indicate the direction. "Middle of the block there's a burnt-out warehouse. Says Merrill and something on the front. You can still see the sign. Alley beside it runs to a parking lot in back."

"Five minutes."

The boy nodded, clutching the keys. When Will nodded in return, he turned and started toward the other end of the block. He gestured to the younger kid, who fell in behind him as he passed at a jog. Will waited until they had rounded the corner and headed to the front of the apartment building before he looked back at Cait.

"What's to stop him from taking the car to some chop shop?" she asked. "There are probably a dozen within a square mile of here."

"I'm betting that despite the attitude, he doesn't have the sources," Will said, taking her arm to head in the opposite direction the boys had taken. "Besides, the way his eyes lit up at the sight of the ten, he'd sell his mother for a hundred."

"Then I guess the only other question is whether he can really drive. How old do you think he is?"

"I don't know. Maybe…thirteen. Maybe less."

"Thirteen going on fifty. If he can get the car out of that parking space, we'll be lucky."

"If he can't, we'll save the money and take the Metro."

"Take it where?"

It was a question he didn't have an answer for. Not a good one, at least. "I'll think of something."

As they approached the end of the second block, Will glanced over his shoulder to find the street behind them still deserted. He'd been expecting shouts or running footsteps since they'd emerged from the basement.

"Is this it?" Cait asked as he hesitated.

In actuality, they were only a block and a half from where they'd parted from the kids. When he glanced down the street, he could see the burned-out shell, just as the older one had described. He'd obviously been counting blocks from the front of the apartment building.

Without answering Cait's question, Will changed direction, cutting diagonally across the street, which was narrowed by cars parked along both sides. He could see the entrance to the alley on the far side and the name Merrill in fading paint above the damaged facade of the warehouse.

"Just ahead."

Almost before the words were out of his mouth, he saw a police car turn up the street they'd just crossed, approaching from the other end of the block.

Looking for them? Or simply a routine patrol of the area?

"Cops," he said under his breath.

He wasn't sure whether it would be better to keep walking toward the entrance of the alley or to cut down the street and continue in the opposite direction.

"Looking for us?"

"Looking for something."

The crawl at which the squad car was traveling made that clear. And the two of them stood out like a sore thumb in this neighborhood.

"There's a drugstore on the far corner." Carefully keeping his eyes away from the cruiser, he crossed to Cait's left, putting his body between hers and the street.

As the car passed, Will turned, following its progress. The cops were definitely casing the street, but they didn't seem to be interested in them.

A black man came out of the drugstore where they were headed, his eyes also following the cop car as he walked to the corner. He never glanced their way.

Will opened the door, letting Cait go in first. The girl behind the counter didn't look up from the magazine she was reading, despite the bell that announced their entrance.

He thought about walking to the back of the store, but decided instead to wait inside until the cop car had had time to clear the block. If they were searching for someone in connection with Emilio's murder, they obviously didn't know who they were looking for.

Hopefully they'd be gone before the two kids brought the Altima through the intersection and down the street toward the alley. Maybe he and Cait hadn't attracted the cops' attention, but he wasn't sure a thirteen-year-old driving erratically wouldn't. Will leaned toward the glass door, but he couldn't see all the way to the end of the block.

"Stay here," he said to Cait, intending to open the door and step outside just far enough to see if the cops were gone.

What he discovered instead were two cars—Cait's

Altima and the cruiser—stopped at the end of the street. And it appeared that the drivers were talking to one another.

Best-case scenario was that the cops were questioning the kid's age or skills. Worst case was that the boy was fingering them.

Of course, unless the Altima had rounded the corner before they'd entered the drugstore, he would have no way of knowing where Will and Cait were right now. And that was exactly how Will wanted to keep it.

CHAPTER TEN

WILL QUICKLY STEPPED BACK inside, causing the bell on the door to ring again. This time the girl looked up, her gaze considering his face before it moved to Cait's.

"Can I help you?"

"Back entrance?"

For a second she looked puzzled. Then, with a mental shrug he could almost see, she pointed toward the back of the narrow store.

"Come on."

"What happened?" Cait asked as she followed him down the aisle.

"The kids and the cops are parked side by side at the end of the street. They seem to be talking."

"Ask the girl where the nearest Metro station is."

It made sense. And although it would take a few seconds, it would probably save them time in the long run. Leaving Cait, he returned to the front.

"Metro?"

The girl looked up again. "Something wrong?"

"My wife. Labor pains."

"Go out the back and turn to your right. Walk…three blocks I think it is and look to your left."

"Thanks." He threw the word over his shoulder as he retraced his steps.

"Labor pains?" Cait repeated as they approached the exit sign.

"Invokes instant sympathy from women."

"Yeah, well, it might be more believable if I were pregnant."

"She didn't look at you that closely."

"Because she was looking at you."

"What does that mean?"

After a small hesitation, she said, "Nothing. Just… Nothing."

Will tried the outside door and quickly realized it was locked. He turned the dead bolt, expecting a buzzer to go off as he pushed it open.

Nothing happened. Maybe the girl up front had cut off the alarm. Or maybe, because of the multitude of mirrors in the place, the door wasn't considered that much a part of internal security.

The street they'd emerged on wasn't crowded with cars like the ones around Emilio's apartment. To reach the Metro station the clerk had directed them to, they would have to cross the exit of the alley leading to the parking lot where they had arranged to meet the boys.

Will hesitated, trying to decide if they should risk even walking by it. They could always go straight, then cut over and double back a block to reach the station.

There was a chance, however, that he'd read the situation wrong. Maybe the boy hadn't been giving the cops information. Maybe he'd been trying to talk his way out of whatever they'd stopped him for. After all, the officers hadn't gotten out of their car.

"It's worth a try," Cait said.

"What?"

"I thought you were trying to decide whether to check out the alley."

"Not worth the risk."

"What's he going to get from telling the cops about us?"

"Maybe out of a ticket for driving without a license."

The police hadn't seemed to be carrying out a traffic stop, Will admitted. They had appeared to be chatting. Maybe they knew the kids. Not so far-fetched if they patrolled the area regularly. Not if the boys frequented the stoop where they'd first encountered them.

"I think he'd rather have the hundred," Cait said.

It was a chance either way. Except in order to get to the place where he had intended to ask Paul to meet them, they would need a car.

Worth a try. Cait's words echoed in his head, reinforcing his own conclusion.

Without explaining his reasoning, he took her arm again, walking down the block toward the exit to the alley. When he reached it, he stopped, looking up the narrow passage between the two buildings.

He could see a break behind the shell of the warehouse that he assumed was the parking lot the kid had mentioned. He couldn't see into it.

Was Cait right? Would the kid do anything to follow through on the deal they'd made? More importantly, was he smart enough to figure out how to keep the cops from being suspicious?

The decision he faced boiled down to his judgment about a thirteen-year-old he'd met only minutes before. And his gut was saying "take a chance on the kid."

He didn't draw his weapon as he started up the alley. He wouldn't risk Cait getting hurt. Or the kids for that matter.

Too many people had already died as a result of what had happened last night, and he wasn't any closer to an answer to what that was than he had been when he woke up facedown in Vincent's den. If the cops *were* waiting there—

The Altima was parked at the far end of the lot, as close to the burned-out building as the collapsed back wall allowed. No cops. No cruiser.

He and Cait ran across asphalt still strewn with debris from the fire. As they approached, the passenger side door opened and the kid he'd offered the hundred to emerged.

For an instant, Will's heart caught, expecting one of the officers to get out on the driver's side, weapon drawn. Instead, another teen, a few years older than the one they'd dealt with, unfolded a lanky body that was a more mature version of the thirteen-year-old's. He leaned nonchalantly against the car and watched their approach.

"You slow, man," the younger teen said.

"Yeah, well, I saw you talking to the cops. They looking for us?"

"Just hassling people."

"Who's this?" Will nodded toward the driver.

"My brother. It's cool."

"I thought you said *you* could drive," Will said, pulling the folded bills from his pocket.

"You better be glad I wasn't. Not when they stopped us."

Will extracted two fifties, holding them between his thumb and forefinger. He lifted them so the boys could see.

"One more thing…"

"What's with 'one more thing'? You got your car. We done what you asked. You owe us."

"The money's yours. All I need is a few more minutes of your time. And a little distance. Move away from the car."

The boy cursed, but he didn't step away. From the corner of his eye, Will caught some movement from the older brother. Maybe it had been nothing more than a shift of his weight, but Will wasn't taking any chances.

He reached inside his jacket. The younger teen visibly started when he saw the weapon.

"Whoa, man," he said, backing up. "We done what you told us. All we want is our money—"

"You'll get it. Like I said, I just need a few more minutes of your time."

"To do what?"

"To take a ride."

With his left hand, Will opened the back door of the car. Using the SIG-Sauer, he motioned the youngest of the three out of the back seat. Eyes wide as saucers, he complied.

"Get in," he said to Cait. "And the three of you in the front, please."

"You want me to drive?" the older boy asked.

"Until I tell you to stop," Will said. "*Then* you'll get your money. I'll even foot the bill for you to take the Metro back here."

"We ain't gonna rat you out," the middle brother said, figuring out what this was all about. "If we was gonna do that, we would have done it when the cops stopped us."

"Except then you would have lost out on this." Will held up the folded bills again. "A fifteen-minute ride and it's yours. What have you got to lose?"

"What's to say you ain't getting rid of some witnesses?"

"To what?"

"To whatever got the cops all excited. Something to do with Emilio, maybe?"

"Maybe. But all you saw was us go into that building and come out of it. That's all you could testify to in court. Besides, if I was planning to get rid of witnesses, what's to stop me from doing it right here? I just want to make sure we are far enough away that when you get back here, you aren't going to be any help to the cops. You coming or not?"

Two pairs of dark eyes met over the top of the car. The younger one shrugged. He was obviously the natural leader of the three, despite his age.

"We ain't got nothing to say to the cops."

"Good. Take a ride with us and then go spend your money."

"NOW WHAT?" Cait asked.

They had let the boys off near a Metro station. Will had even done what he'd promised and given them money to ride back to the apartment building where they'd found Emilio's body.

"We get far enough out of town for it to be safe and then locate a pay phone."

To call Paul Fisk, she remembered. Maybe his friend would be able to talk some sense into Will.

Whatever was going on, the bodies kept piling up. Which meant that the cops were shortly going to stop playing the "person of interest" game and put out an APB on Will. And as far as she could tell, he was no closer to any answers about Greg Vincent's murder than he'd been this morning.

"I don't suppose you intend to use it to call the cops."

Will cut his eyes from the road, one dark brow lifted. "I told you who I was going to call."

"If your friend is a good lawyer, that's what he'll tell you, too."

"He is. And it is."

"Then why don't you?"

"You saw what they did to Emilio."

She had, and the brutality of it had sickened her. That didn't mean—

"I *saw* what they did to Greg," Will went on. "And to you."

"To *me?*"

He glanced at her again, something in his eyes that she didn't have time to identify before he turned them back to the road. Despite the fact that she couldn't put a name to the emotion she'd seen there, her heart had begun to beat a little faster.

"You have any idea what it did to me to watch him hurt you?"

She wasn't sure how to answer that. If she said yes, she'd be admitting that she thought he still had feelings for her.

Although he hadn't said anything about what had been between them, a dozen things he'd done today indicated he remembered what they'd once meant to each other. Putting his arm around her shoulders in the restaurant. Taking time to pack a bag for her. Watching her when he thought she wasn't aware of it.

Killing a man for putting a knife to your throat.

The stark reality of that put all the romantic nonsense she'd just celebrated into its proper perspective. Will had killed to protect her. And he would have taken a bullet for her as well.

Despite what she'd done to him.

And that was something they still hadn't talked about. She had been too much a coward to broach the subject because no matter what she'd been told at the time by those higher up in the Secret Service, not telling the truth about what had happened had been wrong.

If she had done the right thing, it might have made things easier for Will. At least he would have known that she didn't blame him for what had happened that day.

She had told herself that he'd moved on. That he would understand why she hadn't spoken out. That he would even have approved of it. She'd told herself those lies and a dozen others, but now…

Now she knew the truth about some of what she'd comforted her guilty conscience with for two years. Will Shannon still cared about her. In spite of the fact that she'd let him down. And now he was asking her to acknowledge that she knew he did.

"I know what it did to me to see *you* hurt," she said instead.

For some reason it was easier to confess to that than to make the admission he'd asked her for. Maybe because what she'd done to him had lessened the natural arrogance with which Will had always approached life. An arrogance that wasn't conscious or prideful, but the result of being the best at anything he'd ever undertaken. All of which she had stolen away from him.

"It brought back all the things I felt that day," Will said, ignoring her confession.

The day she'd been shot. She had known he would feel responsible. He'd been the one in charge. The senior agent.

"That wasn't your fault, Will. Neither was this morning. I just…" She shook her head. "I screwed up."

"Screwed up? Because you let somebody sneak up on you?"

He thought she was talking about today. And that was far easier than talking about the other. She would have to do that eventually. She owed it to him, but right now…

"I should have put it together." She seized on the excuse he'd given her to again back away from telling him the truth. "The kitchen was cold because they'd opened the door to the garage. The room even smelled different. It's my house. I'm supposed to know how it smells. For some reason—"

She had been thinking about Will. About the fact that he was leaving. And facing the hard reality that she really didn't want him to.

"Don't beat yourself up," he advised. "Believe me, it doesn't help. Besides, you had no reason to think anyone would come into your home and overpower you. At the time, *I* had no reason to believe that either."

"At the time?"

"If, in my worst nightmare, I'd ever thought they would come after me, I would never have come there. I would *never* have put you in danger. No matter what. I wouldn't have been that stupid."

It sounded as if he was trying to convince himself.

Which was okay. She'd done enough of that kind of thing during the last two years.

"That still doesn't make sense."

"What? In particular," he added with that small, bitter laugh.

"If Emilio is the one who put the stuff in your drink…"

She hesitated, trying to make sure that what she was about to say was logical.

"Why kill him?" Will finished for her. "Because he could testify as to what had been done to me."

"I understand that."

She did. If Emilio had done what she'd suggested, then he was a witness they wouldn't want around. A witness who could go a long way toward clearing Will.

"Then…?" Again he glanced over at her.

"What I don't understand is why they searched his apartment. What were they looking for that they thought he could possibly have? And more importantly, why would they think he'd have anything? He was the waiter, for God's sake. He saw Greg Vincent for a couple of hours at the most."

"And it got him killed."

"Painfully," she added. "So why would they beat him to death?"

"Maybe he kept some of the drug to use on an unsuspecting date. Maybe that's why I woke up before I was supposed to."

"They figured that out and then did that kind of

search to find the rest of it? Why? If they did find it, it wouldn't change anything."

"Maybe they were afraid he'd come forward if he saw the news."

"That was always a possibility, so why involve him in the first place. It doesn't seem worth the risk."

"They had to give me the drug somehow."

"But if it were something like ketamine and a strong enough dose, you probably wouldn't remember how it was administered. They could even have done it at the house."

"Are you saying ketamine could wipe out my memory of events that happened *before* I took it?"

"I'd need to do some research, but...I think it can. Maybe that's why you had flashbacks of the alley. Those memories are still there. After they gave you the drug, there's nothing."

"That doesn't help clear up what happened to Emilio."

It didn't. Actually, it complicated it.

And instead of being able to ask the kind of questions he needed to in order to make sense of that, Will was again on the run. This time heading away from the place where the answers—if they were out there—could be found.

CHAPTER ELEVEN

"WHERE THE HELL ARE YOU?"

Although those angry words were the first out of Paul Fisk's mouth, Will knew they'd been generated by concern. Paul was too old a friend to believe what the media was reporting.

Will was using a roadside telephone kiosk, the kind without the protective box around it, which left him feeling more exposed than he liked. At least he knew that no one would be eavesdropping on this conversation.

He'd left Cait in the car while he made this call. Despite the fact that the winter darkness had fallen, he'd parked the Altima near enough the light from the convenience store so that he could see her.

"I'm headed to water-ski."

Will waited through the resulting silence. There was no way Paul Fisk could have forgotten what that meant. They'd spent a half-dozen summers together skiing the lake in Virginia where Paul's family had a summer place.

"You should be on the way back to D.C."

"Where Metropolitan's finest are waiting not only to

arrest me, but to convict me all at the same time. I've heard some of the coverage."

"Yeah, well, they *have* got four murders with your name on them. You can hardly blame them for being anxious to inform the good citizens of the Beltway that they know exactly who they're after for them."

"Four?"

It wasn't that he didn't know which murders Paul was talking about. It was a surprise, however, that the cops had put them together so quickly *and* tied them all to him.

Actually, the last part wasn't surprising, he admitted, knowing too well how law enforcement worked in high-profile cases. By tomorrow, they'd probably have him responsible for most of the violent crimes committed in the capital this week.

"One of Caitlyn Malone's neighbors reported what sounded like gunfire coming from her house this morning. It took her a while to call in. She didn't want to look like a fool if it turned out to be fireworks or a backfire. The dead guys the locals found when they responded to the call took care of that concern pretty quickly. You take their IDs?"

"They didn't have any. It shouldn't take the police long to find their prints in AFIS. They didn't look like the upstanding-citizen type."

"Yeah? Well, right now, neither do you."

Will let the comment slide. After all, it was nothing less than the truth. "So how did they tie me to Emilio?"

"Is that the waiter?"

"Yeah."

"Busboy from the restaurant gave them the tip. Black kid. Said he recognized Greg Vincent's picture in the *Post* and that you'd had dinner with him there the night before."

"He was working last night?"

"Apparently."

They had only asked the hostess about the waitstaff. She obviously hadn't thought to mention the kid who bused tables. Which was why he'd been so sure who'd been on duty in the back room last night.

"He said that today you showed up at the restaurant asking questions about the waiter who'd served you," Paul went on. "An hour later the cops find Emilio Garza dead. You figure it out."

"He was dead long before I started asking questions."

There was a beat of silence. "You sure about that?"

"He was in full rigor."

Another pause. Will knew that no matter how sarcastic Paul was being right now, his razor-sharp legal brain was already processing the information Will was providing for a possible defense. After all, that was Fisk's specialty, as it had been his father's. The importance of the timing of Emilio's death had been duly noted.

"So how about Greg Vincent?" Paul asked. "What's your spin on that one?"

This time the hesitation was on Will's part. Even though he knew he was talking to a friend, he also knew this was the weakest part of his story. Cait was a witness for the attack of the two he'd killed at her house, as well as his alibi for Emilio, if it came to that. Vincent's death, however…

"I don't know."

That, too, was the truth. He had no explanation for who had killed his boss and no way to prove he hadn't.

"What does that mean?" For the first time, Paul sounded as if he thought there might be something to the charges.

"It means…" Will took a breath before he put into words the facts he knew would condemn him in the eyes of a lot of people. "…I don't remember. Nothing beyond eating dinner. Whatever happened after that is a void, until I woke up facedown on the carpet in Greg's office."

"You don't *remember* what happened last night?"

"Somebody staged the murder to make it look like I did it. As part of that staging, they tried to make sure I wouldn't be in any condition to say I hadn't."

"How?"

"Cait thinks it may have been something like GHB or ketamine."

"Cait? Caitlyn Malone? Then she *is* with you?"

Something about the inflection of the question bothered him. As if Paul had been hoping she wasn't.

"Considering the garbage I left on her kitchen floor, I didn't think I should leave her there alone."

"She went with you willingly?"

In this case, *willingly* was open to interpretation, but he had the feeling that wasn't what Paul would want to hear.

"Of course. *After* I pointed out that whoever was looking for me had obviously figured out the connection between us."

"Which is?"

Even now, that was a question he found impossible to answer. Former partner. Friend. And whatever echoes remained of what their relationship had once been were no one else's business.

Except when you dragged her into this, you made it everyone's business.

"What are they saying about Cait?" he asked, ignoring the question he couldn't answer.

"That you abducted her."

"*Abducted* her? Why would I do that?"

"Obviously because you've gone off the deep end. You're unhinged. After all, you murdered your employer, didn't you?"

"No, but putting that aside for the moment, even if I'm 'unhinged,' why the hell would I kidnap Cait?"

"The theory is because you're jealous of the accolades she received as a result of the assassination attempt."

Jealous because she'd reaped the glory that day and he'd gotten the shaft. It was neat, he had to admit. And it fit right into the scenario whoever had framed him for Vincent's murder had devised. That the person he'd run to had been Caitlyn Malone must have been an unexpected bit of good luck for them.

And absolute stupidity on my part.

Just like running from the cops in the first place. That, however, he could legitimately blame on whatever he'd been given.

Taking Cait… He took a breath, knowing very well what he could blame that on.

"That's a crock, Paul," he said aloud. "I took her with me because one of those goons had put a knife to her throat. She's still got the mark if you're interested."

"I suggest you take pictures of it."

Will examined both the words and the tone, but couldn't come to a conclusion, other than that neither sounded promising. "Does that mean you aren't going to help me?"

"The biggest help I can give you right now, my friend, is to advise you to call the local precinct wherever you are and turn yourself in."

"I didn't kill him."

"Then we'll prove that."

Some of the tension that had formed in Will's chest during his friend's last few sentences eased with his use of the plural pronoun. Having Paul at his side would at least guarantee that someone was doing their best by him legally.

"In a court of *law*," his friend continued. "That's the way the system works, in case you've forgotten."

"The system *doesn't* work—in case *you've* forgotten. Not when you have cops overly anxious to make an arrest. And someone working behind the scenes to make sure they've been presented with a likely suspect."

"You see the movie *Conspiracy?*"

"I saw it. Except I'm not crazy. Or paranoid. What I am is framed."

"What you *are,* just in case you haven't figured it out, is screwed. There's an eight-state 'armed and dangerous' out on you. According to the cops, you're a madman who's already killed four people and, in an apparent fit of jealousy, kidnapped the heroic woman whose life you ruined through your negligence two years ago. According to the press, you're practically foaming at the mouth."

"And what is there about all that that makes you believe I'll get *anybody* to listen when I tell them I had nothing to do with Greg Vincent's death."

The silence on the other end of the line lasted longer this time. When Paul broke it, he had modulated his tone. "You got any idea who did?"

"That's what I've been trying to find out."

"Well, it seems as if you might be going about it the wrong way."

Will ignored the sarcasm. "Maybe, but not by choice. I'd love to be asking Ronald Vincent what happened at the restaurant last night, but I don't think I'd have much success in getting in to see him. I tried to ask Emilio, but somebody had gotten there first. The place was tossed, by the way."

"Tossed?"

"Like they were looking for something and didn't find it."

"Like what?"

"I don't know. The search could have been staged as a cover-up for what they were really doing, but…it looked too thorough for that. He was dealing, by the way."

"Drugs? Then maybe that's what got him killed."

"That's a little too neat. His death has got to be tied to Greg's murder."

"So why kill the waiter?"

It was the question Will had been asking himself since he'd found Emilio's body. And the only answer that made sense…

"Because maybe he's the one who put the drug into my drink."

"Your drink? You want to elaborate on what that was?"

Paul was one of perhaps a dozen people who knew he'd drunk pretty heavily in the months after his dismissal. A lot of that had been having too much time on his hands and too few prospects for filling it. The rest had been remorse over what had happened to Caitlyn. As soon as he'd started working again, the drinking had become a non-issue. Protection wasn't a job you could do hungover.

"Club soda. Only, he brought the second one to the table with a twist of lime I didn't order. Maybe that was to disguise an altered taste or smell or a film on top."

"They paid some waiter to drug your drink, and then they killed him. Is that what you're saying?"

"Yeah. Except… He was beaten to death, Paul. Slowly. And in my opinion—for what that's worth—

professionally. I think somebody wanted something they believed Emilio had."

"But you don't know what."

"I know how this sounds—"

"Probably not," Paul interrupted. "I'm your friend, Will. I've known you most of your life. I don't believe for one second that you blew your client's brains out. But I'll tell you this. The story you're telling is going to be a hard sell."

"To a jury?"

"To anybody. It makes no sense."

Conspiracy...

"They drug me, use my gun to kill Vincent, leave it in the bed with him—"

"They haven't released that information."

At least Paul had been paying attention.

"Because they don't know about it. I took it when I found the body."

"And you're sure it's the murder weapon?"

"It had been fired. It was beside the corpse. Doesn't take a genius to get from point A to point B. If I'd left it there, even the Metro boys would have been able to figure that out."

"The fact that they don't have the murder weapon doesn't seem to have slowed them down any. Of course, Vincent's brother is now helping to whip up the frenzy. They interviewed him on the six o'clock news."

"What's he saying?"

"That the last time he saw his brother, he was with

you. That you'd been acting strangely. That you'd been drinking heavily."

He hadn't been, but he couldn't prove it. Not with Emilio dead. There had been more than one bottle of wine consumed at the adjacent table that night. Only he hadn't partaken of either of them.

Ron might have believed that the club soda he'd been drinking was something alcoholic. He wasn't sitting close enough to hear when Will ordered it. And besides that...

"There was a nearly empty bottle of scotch on the coffee table when I woke up," he said.

"Convenient. What else?"

"I don't know. I didn't have time to check the rest of the house. Even if I had..."

"So what you're saying is you don't know what other kinds of evidence the cops have."

"I don't know what was planted. All I know is somebody killed Greg and it wasn't me."

"Fair enough. The guy had a bodyguard, so...who wanted him dead?"

"The nutcases protesting the patent fight."

"You think they did this?"

"They seemed like... Actually, they seemed like kooks to me. Greg thought so, too. It was Ron who insisted he needed protection. Actually it was Ron who contacted me."

He had also done the initial interview, one that Will hadn't had a good feeling about. Greg's brother had seemed to be sizing him up the whole time and not liking what he saw. Will had walked out thinking there was no way he would get the job. The next day he'd been called to meet with Greg, and they had hit it off immediately.

"So Ron Vincent insists that his brother have a bodyguard," Paul said. "And now he's insisting that same bodyguard must have killed him."

"What are you getting at?"

It wasn't that he didn't understand where his friend was going with this. He just needed Paul to put it into words before he did.

"I'm wondering if there's any reason for Ron Vincent to want his brother dead."

"I don't know. I don't know what financial stake he has in the company. Greg was the CEO. I think Ron had some title in the research and development division. Whether that was the product of competence or nepotism, I have no idea."

"What did you think of him?"

"Ron?" Unconsciously Will shook his head. "Not as likable as Greg. Or as friendly. He was aloof. Condescending."

He'd treated Will like an employee, which he was, of course. Greg had treated him like a friend. Actually, despite the differences in their backgrounds, in the three months he'd worked for him, Will had come to consider Greg a friend.

"We should check out what he'd have to gain from Greg's death," Paul suggested. "Maybe nothing, but… It's worth a shot."

"If he really thought I was drinking… Cait said drugs like GHB are usually mixed with alcohol because it increases their effects *and* the duration."

"Meaning if Vincent *was* the one who gave you something, he may have misjudged the time you'd be out because he thought you'd already ingested alcohol."

"I guess that's pretty far out there."

"We're just looking for possibilities right now. The nutcases. Ron Vincent. Anybody else?"

"Greg was eager to get in on the bioterrorism stuff. Those were government contracts and meant huge money."

"Bioterrorism with government funding?"

"Antiterrorism," Will corrected. "Antidotes. Vaccines. That kind of stuff. The company couldn't seem to get its foot in the door, despite its reputation. If Ron really did have something to do with research and development, maybe that became a bone of contention between them."

"You hear anything to that effect?"

"They talked about it some at dinner that night."

He wished now that he'd paid attention instead of trying to give them privacy. That was a habit he'd deliberately cultivated during his years of providing security to government officials and visiting heads of state. His job was to see evil, not to listen for it.

Hear no evil…

"They seem animated to you? Angry? Contentious?"

"Not really. I wasn't listening to the words, but the tone of their voices was strictly conversational."

"Okay. Is that all you've got?"

Except for the guy whose face I saw in the mirror this morning...

Will weighed whether or not to tell his friend about the flashback. Although he was absolutely convinced that man was somehow connected to all this, he had no way to prove that either. And citing a broken memory as corroboration might verify for Paul that the cops and Ron Vincent weren't that far off in what they were suggesting about him.

As he had so often during his days with the Secret Service, Will went with his gut. Whoever the guy was, he had been at the restaurant last night. It was important Paul know that.

"One more thing."

"Okay."

Still Will hesitated, trying to find a way to frame his impressions. Given the fact that they *were* only impressions and that Paul was one of the most literal-minded people he'd ever known, there probably wasn't one.

"I'm pretty sure we went out the back last night."

"The back of the restaurant?"

He could tell Paul was puzzled by the detour. It wasn't going to get any better as Will went on.

"At least I did. I can't ever remember going out that way before, but... When Cait and I went back there today, I already knew what things in the area looked like. The only time that could have happened was last night."

It had also been raining then, which correlated to the man's hair being wet. Saying that, however, seemed as if he were trying to build a case in his head. He was sure enough about the man's presence in the alley that he didn't need to do that.

"And you think there's some significance to the fact that you went out the back door?"

"I don't know. Probably, but that isn't why I told you about it."

"So…?"

"There was a guy there. Dark hair, medium height, unshaven. He looked… I don't know. Sick. Drugged."

"And?" Paul asked when Will ran down.

"I think he has something to do with this."

"With Vincent's death?"

"Yeah. Or with setting me up."

There had to be some reason that was the only thing that had surfaced out of the hours he'd lost. The face of the man who'd been in the alley last night.

"Homeless? Panhandler?"

"I don't know."

"What was he wearing?"

"I didn't see. Actually… Look, I don't remember seeing him. I had a flashback. But it was only his face. And then when Cait and I were in the alley, I recognized that was the setting in the background of the flashback."

The silence this time lasted several seconds. Long enough that Will closed his eyes and leaned his forehead against the cold plastic of the kiosk he was using. The sensation was at least different. This morning's headache was back with a vengeance.

"You saw this guy in a flashback, and because you think you recognize the alley behind the restaurant in the background of it, you believe he's got something to do with the murder?"

"I know how this sounds," Will said, allowing his frustration expression. "If *you* think I'm crazy, then how the hell do you think the cops are going to react?"

"You just better hope they don't decide to shoot first and talk about your flashbacks later."

"Not funny, old buddy," Will said, the words tight, their consonants bitten off.

"It wasn't meant to be. According to the police, you're a mad-dog killer, and they're pulling out all the stops to protect people from your rampage. They aren't going to stop for explanations."

Paul was right, he realized. According to the cops, he'd killed four innocent people and kidnapped a woman. They wouldn't ask any questions at all if they saw him.

He'd made Cait come with him in order to protect her. Now it seemed that he had put her into more danger than if he'd left her alone in that house with the two corpses.

"I've got to find somewhere safe for Cait."

"I think you have."

Paul meant the summerhouse, Will realized. And he was right. It would be safe.

"Temporarily. But if they were able to track me to her place in just a few hours, then they may be watching everyone I've ever been associated with." He wondered if Paul would realize that by "they," he didn't mean the cops. Which led him to a more important conclusion. "That would include you, by the way."

"So I'll be careful."

"What does that mean?" He was almost afraid to hope, given Paul's skepticism.

"I'll be down there in the morning. And I promise you no one's gonna follow me."

Despite how much those promises meant at the moment, Will knew that he had no right to expect this much. "You don't have to do this."

"I know. I've always been a sucker for fools and lunatics."

"Which am I?"

"No one's ever accused you of being a fool."

"Just a homicidal maniac."

"It's going to be cold as a witch's twat on the lake. There's firewood. To the right of the back door. I chopped it the last time I was there, trying to work off a fit of rage."

"Over what?"

"A guy I defended in Maryland finally exhausted his appeals. They stuck the needle in his arm."

"And you believed he was innocent."

"Hell, no. I just don't like to lose."

"I'll keep that in mind."

"Most people do."

The silence this time was awkward. As if there was something else that should be said before they broke the connection.

Will knew that as soon as he hung up, the weight of all this, now shared with a sympathetic listener, would come crashing down on him. Paul knew that, too. That last bit of bravado was supposed to sustain him.

"Thanks," he said softly.

"Everybody says that until they see the bill," Paul said. "Tomorrow."

Although the connection had been broken, Will kept the phone to his ear for a few seconds. Despite everything Paul Fisk had said, the promise of that single word would allow him to return to the car and finish the journey he'd begun this afternoon without despair overwhelming him.

At this point, that was far more than he had any right to expect. And far more than he could ever repay.

CHAPTER TWELVE

NOTHING HAD CHANGED about the summerhouse, not even where they hid the key. Will could feel Cait shivering while he tried to fit it into the lock in the darkness.

When he finally managed to do that, he pushed open the door. The memories that flooded his mind were almost as powerful as those he'd felt while he'd been inside her house.

He'd spent a couple of months here during each of the summers between the years he and Paul had roomed together in prep school and college. This had always felt like a second home. Sometimes more welcoming than his own.

Now, with the drapes across the windows shutting off the moonlight, it seemed slightly alien. Threatening. White holland covers draped the furniture in the rooms on either side of the entry hall, adding to the sense of eeriness.

The air inside felt even colder than that outdoors. All he had to do was bring in the wood Paul had told him about and put it in the fireplace in the small den. If they shut that room off from the rest, the fire should make it warm enough that they could get some sleep.

"This way."

He started down the shadowed hallway, his footsteps echoing on the hardwood floors. When they reached the narrow doorway of the den, he stood to the side and allowed her to precede him.

"Paul said there's wood outside. I don't want to start the generator, in case there's anyone up here. It's probably a long shot that they'd make the connection—"

"That's fine," Cait said, cutting off the spate of words. "But…a fire would be nice."

He pulled the dust cover off the couch that sat directly in front of the fireplace, rolling it into a large, unwieldy bundle that he tossed onto one of the chairs.

"You can wait here."

He expected her to offer to help, not that he needed any assistance. Still, given the cold and how tired they both were, it seemed the natural thing to do.

Instead, she put her left hand on the covered arm and eased down on the edge of the sofa. She didn't settle back into the deep comfort of the well-worn couch, but continued to sit with her spine straight, her left hand now holding the collar of her coat around her throat.

"You okay?"

"Of course." She looked up, meeting his eyes.

Although his vision had adjusted somewhat to the dimness of the room, he couldn't read her expression well enough to determine whether or not she was telling the truth. She'd said nothing the last hundred miles, sitting in the passenger seat with her arms crossed over her body, but he hadn't really thought much about her quietness until now. He'd had too much else to think about.

"I'll light the lamp on the mantel before I get the wood."

"Are you sure that's a good idea?"

She was probably thinking of his concern about some of the homes up here being occupied. Given the season, however, that was doubtful. And unlike the generator, the oil lamp made no noise. He doubted much of its low light would escape through the thick curtains.

"I think being able to see is worth the risk."

The matches were exactly where they'd always been, beside the base of the lamp. He took the chimney and mantle off, and turned the knob until the wick appeared. Then he struck the match on the bricks and held it against the soaked wick.

Once it caught, he replaced the chimney unit. Although not bright, light invaded the darkness, leaving shadows only in the corners of the room.

"We'll be safe up here," he reassured as he turned back to face Cait. "Very few people outside of Paul's immediate family know about this place."

"Very few people knew about us either."

"They aren't going to come here. Not tonight at least."

"What if they're watching your lawyer friend? What if they follow him tomorrow?"

"Nobody's going to follow him over those roads. Not without him being aware of it."

Although Will had kept an eye on the rearview mirror, after he'd made the turn off the state highway and headed toward the lake, there'd been no headlights behind him. It would be just as easy for Paul to spot a car following him along that narrow two-lane in the daylight.

"I think they must have been watching me," Cait said. "Maybe even when I went to the store. When they saw what I bought, they knew."

"That I was there?"

"Maybe if I hadn't done that—"

Her eyes seemed to search his. Looking for absolution? If so, he was glad to give it to her.

"Even if they were watching you, you couldn't have known that. Obviously, I didn't think it was a possibility."

She nodded. "It makes me worry about Paul coming up here tomorrow. They may have everyone you were ever close to staked out. Although how they could have known about you and me…"

"If they chose me for this three months ago, then they'd have had plenty of time to do their homework."

If Ron Vincent had done any kind of background check before he'd interviewed Will, he would have known all of the information about his dismissal. Perhaps at that point someone had realized the potential for framing him and dug deeper.

Washington was an old-boys-network town, and the Vincents had been around it long enough to have friends in high places. Maybe someone had talked to people who had worked with Will. It's possible that's where his connection to Cait had been uncovered.

"You think that was the plan from the beginning? To hire you and then set you up?" she asked.

"I don't know. All I know is, if they did, I was perfect for their purposes."

He had been. He'd been dismissed from the Secret Service and vilified by the press. He had assumed the Vincents had overlooked that because of his résumé or because he and Greg had hit it off immediately. Now it seemed he might have been hired for another reason entirely.

"That's…diabolical."

"So is murder."

Cait shivered at the word, reminding him of the need for a fire.

"Wood," he said. "I'll be right back."

She nodded, finally leaning back against the couch. She closed her eyes, her arms once more crossed over her chest. In the light from the lamp, he could see the discoloration of the thin skin under her eyes, almost as if it had been bruised.

He hated to leave her alone, but according to Paul, the firewood was just outside the door. A matter of five minutes or less, he thought as he hurried through the frigid rooms.

As soon as he got the fire going, he'd collect blankets and pillows from the bedrooms. Cait could have the couch and he'd sleep on the floor.

He opened the back door, pushing against the leaves that had accumulated along the bottom. As promised, neatly split logs were stacked just to the right, covered by a small lean-to and a tarp. Sticks of kindling stood in a wooden bucket beside it, also protected by the overhang.

He remembered that the lock on this door engaged when it closed. As kids he and Paul had been locked out numerous times coming back from swimming. They would have to traipse in wet bathing suits through the front of the house. A habit that had annoyed Paul's mom.

He bent down and grabbed a piece of kindling, inserting it between the door and the jamb. Only then did he go down the steps to collect what he'd need for the fire. He slung the handle of the bucket over his arm and picked up as much of the wood as he could carry. He'd make another trip once he'd gotten the blaze going.

As he straightened, his arms loaded with the split logs, he looked out to where the lake touched the midnight sky. The line of demarcation between them was almost impossible to discern. Few stars were revealed by the drifting clouds, and the wind off the water seemed to hold the promise of snow.

Which would be good, he decided, as he turned to go back inside. Worse things could happen to them than being snowed in. With so few residents here at this time of year, the county wouldn't be in a hurry to clear the roads, effectively cutting them off from the outside world.

Another crock full of wishful thinking, he acknowledged. Paul would arrive tomorrow, and there was no doubt what his advice would be. Given the danger he had already put Cait in, Will knew that following it was something he would have to seriously consider.

Cait's eyes were still closed when he came back into the den. Even though the bucket bumped against the door frame as he came through, she didn't open them.

"This ought to do for a beginning," he said unnecessarily.

Her eyelids lifted, but other than that, she didn't respond. He wondered if she'd fallen asleep during the few minutes he'd been gone.

He set everything down on the hearth and methodically began to stack the logs in a crossing pattern, alternating them with the starter sticks, a skill Paul's father had taught him the first summer he'd spent up here. The wood was cold to the touch, but despite the nearness of the lake, he couldn't detect much dampness.

When he finished, he stuffed sheets of newspaper from the box that sat on the hearth under a few of the pieces of kindling and lit them with another of the matches from the mantelpiece. Then he sat back on his heels, waiting for the fire to catch. Although the first flickering flames did little to dispel the chill, the sounds they made as they ate into the wood were comforting.

When the blaze was beginning to blacken the logs, he reached up to the mantel and pulled himself tiredly to his feet. He realized that Cait was again sitting on the edge of the sofa, the glow of the firelight reflected in her eyes.

"It'll take a few minutes to feel the effects."

She nodded, her left hand running up and down the opposite arm. He watched the movement a moment, almost mesmerized by it, before he realized its significance.

"Your arm still hurt?"

Based on everything he knew about the Caitlyn Malone he'd worked with for three years, he expected her to deny it. He'd never heard her admit fatigue or disappointment or fear.

"Just from the cold and damp," she said, her left hand now massaging the damaged shoulder.

"This will take care of those when it gets going."

He'd forgotten to close the doors, he realized. And he hadn't made the second trip to the woodpile. Although several of the logs he'd brought were still stacked beside the paper box, there weren't enough to last through the night.

"There are blankets in the bedrooms. Maybe if I warmed one in front of the fire—"

"I'll be fine." Although spoken with finality, Cait's words were flat. Without conviction.

He had acknowledged this morning that she would never have allowed herself be taken by a man wielding a knife had she not been injured. Then, during the course of the long day, he had almost forgotten about the severity of those injuries. She hadn't uttered one word of complaint, and he'd dragged her all over Washington and points south.

"If I'd had any idea how things—"

"Don't."

Although he waited, there was nothing else. "Don't tell you I'm sorry?"

"You couldn't have known that anyone would figure out you were at my house. You didn't know Emilio was already dead when we went looking for him. You didn't know the cops would arrive while we were there. You couldn't possibly have known any of those things, so you don't have to apologize for them."

"I should have known that coming to you was a mistake."

She lowered her head, as if she were looking at her hands, which were now clasped together in her lap. When she spoke again, her voice was very low, so that he had to strain to hear her words over the growing crackle of the fire.

"So why *did* you come?"

"It seemed like a good idea at the time. Obviously, I wasn't thinking too clearly right then."

"You could have gone anywhere. You could have gone to your friend Paul. You didn't. You came to me."

"Proximity, maybe." Even as he said it, he admitted she was right. There were other friends who were just as near, especially if he were going to risk taking a cab. "Or because I didn't believe you'd call the police. And maybe... Maybe you were right about what you said before. Maybe because you'd be the last person they'd expect me to seek help from."

"Is that what you were thinking?"

"Not consciously. I just... Your house seemed safe."

"Then stop apologizing for the fact that you came to it. You knew I wouldn't turn you away. Or turn you in.

It was the logical thing to do. What you couldn't know was what a liability I was going to turn out to be."

"*Liability?* You haven't been a liability. Far from it. Actually, I was thinking—"

The sense of familiarity, of working with someone who knew him well enough to anticipate what needed to be done, had been there all day.

"Thinking what?"

"How much I've missed working with you."

Her mouth opened, whether in surprise or because she wanted to respond. She closed it again, visibly tightening her lips as if to prevent that from happening. She shook her head, but her eyes held on his.

"You don't believe that?"

For a long heartbeat, she didn't move. And then she lowered her head, again looking down at her hands.

"You don't believe I missed you, Cait? We were partners. Part of a team." He hesitated, wondering if he should say the rest. She looked almost too fragile to withstand anything else. Even this. "And we were much more than either of those."

The last had been almost a whisper, but her head came up. Her eyes locked on his again, holding them.

"You don't think I've missed that?" he went on. "Why the hell do you think I called you all those times?"

She shook her head. "I don't understand."

"I called you. I came to the hospital. They wouldn't let me see you."

"At first…" She shook her head again, licking her lips. "And then, even after I was better, I didn't want to see anyone. I told them that."

"Your mother told me."

"That I didn't want to see you?"

"She was pretty adamant about it."

The last time she'd threatened to have him arrested if he came back. Her bitterness had been enough to let him know that, like everyone else, she blamed him for what had happened to Cait. And like everyone else, it was obvious she'd had no idea about their relationship.

It was the same dilemma he'd faced with the board of inquiry, except on a much more personal level. How do you tell the mother of a woman you'd been responsible for that you hadn't let her get shot because you'd been with someone else the night before? Even if she'd known that the security camera had caught him returning from Cait's room, would it have made any difference in her condemnation?

"Are you saying she was wrong?"

For a moment Cait said nothing, and then, "She wasn't wrong. I didn't want to see you. She just didn't tell me that you'd come."

"You didn't think I would?"

"I thought… It doesn't matter what I thought."

"It matters to me."

"How can it? What possible difference can it make after all this time?"

"Because we're here. And we're together. And because we might not have many opportunities for telling each other the truth."

If Paul had his way, Will knew that after tomorrow he might not ever see her again. No matter what happened tonight, he couldn't imagine Cait coming to visit him in jail. Or in prison. He wouldn't want her to.

Just as she hadn't wanted anyone to see her in the hospital?

"I didn't take the shot."

Cait's words were so low he thought at first that he must have misunderstood what she'd said. When he replayed them in his mind, searching for a possible meaning—

"At the *assassin?*"

"I saw him. I don't know. Maybe it didn't register. What he was doing. Why he was there. But for some reason…I saw him, and I hesitated."

That wasn't how it had appeared on the video. He had watched all of it, over and over again, because he had thought if he studied that film long enough, he would finally figure out what had gone wrong.

He'd even watched those bullets impact Cait's body. So many times that he had eventually become desensitized to the sense of shock and outrage. And he had never noticed any hesitation on her part.

"You moved to cover al-Faisal, and then you fired. You did what you were trained to do."

"I had a chance to take him out *before* he shot, and I didn't take it."

"That's bullshit, Cait."

"And if I had, none of this would have happened. None of it."

"Vincent?" he said derisively. "You're responsible for Greg's murder?"

"Not for that. But I am responsible for your being there that night. If I hadn't screwed up, you'd still be with the Service, still doing what you *should* be doing."

He laughed and realized from her face it was the wrong reaction. He had no idea where she'd come up with this crap, but it was obvious she really believed it. And if she believed it now...

"You've thought that all this time? For two years you've believed that you were responsible for what happened that day?"

"I saw him, and I didn't react. Not quickly enough."

"And you think that was because of the night before."

Her eyes widened. He could tell it hadn't occurred to her. Apparently that was not part of the hair shirt she'd donned two years ago.

"That had nothing to do with it. We got enough sleep, despite..."

"You want to tell that to the board of inquiry?"

It was sarcasm, pure and simple, intended to mock her attempt to take the blame. He was the one who had been judged to be responsible. A decision he had never argued with.

"I wanted to."

"What?"

"I wanted to tell them what had happened."

"Thank God you didn't."

It was enough of a black eye for the Service that the agent in charge of a diplomatic security detail had been guilty of a lapse in judgment in staying out all night. He could only imagine the field day the press would have had if they'd known he had spent the night with a fellow agent. One under his command.

"Actually, the inquiry was over before I realized what was being said. I wanted them to reopen it. I tried to tell Jeff that they didn't know everything—"

"Jeff Eagles?"

Eagles had been his superior. The man who had the ultimate responsibility for the protection details in the capital.

"He told me it wouldn't help you. That it might actually make it worse. And he reminded me of what it would do to the reputation of the Secret Service."

"He was right."

"Do you think that made me feel any better? Do you think it makes me feel better right now?"

"Cait, you did *nothing* wrong that day," Will said, speaking with all the conviction he was capable of. "I must have watched that video a hundred times. I know that in a situation like that things seem to be happening in slow motion, but…believe me, you didn't hesitate. You moved to protect al-Faisal. You even got off a shot at the assassin. You did *exactly* what you were supposed to do."

"I got you dismissed."

He had no idea what to say to that assertion. He'd had no idea this was what she'd been thinking all these long months.

"What happened in those few seconds *wasn't* what got me dismissed."

"What happened in my room the night before did."

"I wasn't coerced into being there."

She looked down at her hands again before she raised her eyes once more. "I'm the one who…" She hesitated, obviously searching for the right words.

"So you're to blame for everything because you let me know you were attracted. Is that the point of this? Because if it is, I need to get in another load of wood."

"You can't deny—"

"Hell, yes I can. I knew the risks. I can't say that I thought our relationship would ever be exposed. It was a freak of circumstance that it was, but…I went into it with my eyes open. It was a chance I was willing to take. And frankly—"

He stopped, wondering if what he'd been about to say could possibly be true. Even after weighing everything that had occurred in the balance, he knew that it was.

"Frankly, if I had it to do all over again, even knowing the outcome, I wouldn't have done anything differently. Not about you. Not about us."

Her eyes, shining in the firelight, clung to his. From what he saw in them, he knew she needed to believe that as much as he had needed to say it.

"You did *nothing* wrong, Cait. Not that day. Not before. Whatever happens from here on out…"

Surprisingly, his throat tightened with emotion, but he made himself go on. This was the least he could do for her. Less than she deserved, but all he had to offer.

"I need you to believe that. And I need to hear you acknowledge that it's true. Nothing that happened two years ago was your fault."

He waited, watching what was happening in her eyes. Finally, they filled with moisture. One solitary tear coursed down her cheek before she scrubbed it away with the back of her hand.

"Cait?"

It was a demand. Just as she had always known what he meant, almost before he said it, she would recognize that.

"I need to hear you say it," he prodded. "And then I won't ever ask anything else of you."

"That's not fair."

"Nothing ever is."

The silence stretched, a battle of wills. The cheerful sounds of the fire seemed an inappropriate background for what was going on.

"But it wasn't—"

"Let it go, Cait. What you've thought all this time isn't what happened. I swear to you."

"On what?"

It took him a second to realize what she meant. "On anything you want me to swear on."

"Then…on us, I guess. I can't think of anything that ever mattered more to me. Swear on what we had."

Past tense. And she was right. No matter whose fault it was, what they had shared had been destroyed that day as surely as their careers.

"I swear on every memory we share that you weren't to blame. Not for any of it."

He waited, but although her lips had parted, she didn't do what he'd asked her to. "Your turn, Cait. I need to hear you say it."

I need to know you believe it.

"I'm sorry, Will. I never lied to you. And somehow… Somehow I don't think that now is the time to start."

CHAPTER THIRTEEN

WILL'S LAWYER FRIEND was nothing like Cait had anticipated he'd be. She finally figured out that was because he was nothing like Will.

Short and balding, Paul Fisk looked as if he'd never been inside a gym. His hand, when he extended it in response to Will's introduction, was very pale and softer than hers.

"It's an honor to meet you," he said.

She usually let things like that go. After all this time, she understood that any protest she made about the way her role in the assassination attempt had been presented to the public fell on deaf ears. People believed she was being self-effacing.

She might have let Paul's comment pass as well, if he hadn't been a friend of Will's. And if Will hadn't been standing beside her.

"If I'd been quicker to react that day, you'd never have heard my name. And no one would have heard Will's."

It was a truth she'd accepted long ago, and nothing Will had said last night had made any difference. She had seen the assassin. She had had the opportunity to take him out before he fired, and she hadn't. Thankfully she was the one who had paid the price for her split second's hesitation.

She and Will...

With her comment, something changed in Paul Fisk's eyes. She wasn't sure what had been there before, but for some reason their pale green irises appeared warmer. More friendly.

"Maybe you should have been quicker to react yesterday, too," he said, squeezing her hand before he released it.

"What does that mean?" Will asked.

"That getting mixed up with you wasn't the smartest move Ms. Malone has ever made."

"Cait," she corrected. "And I have no regrets about what I did. I would have done the same for any friend who was in trouble."

"Actually, I wasn't talking about taking Will in. I was talking about going on the run with him."

"He didn't leave me any choice."

"Yeah? Interesting. And not what I was told." Raising his brows, Paul looked pointedly at Will. "But that's the story you should definitely stick to," he added, as he turned back to smile at her.

"I beg your pardon?"

"If anyone asks why you went with him, you should say he forced you."

"I didn't mean that—" she began, only to be cut off.

"At gunpoint if you can manage it with a straight face. If Will goes down for the murder of that waiter, it will be to your advantage *not* to confess to having gone willingly into that apartment with him."

"Emilio was dead when we got there," she said. "And he'd *been* dead for quite a while."

"And the two of you went straight from the restaurant to his apartment."

"We had some trouble finding the address, but essentially, yes, we did."

"You may be called on to testify to that."

"I'd be happy to."

She was becoming a little angry, both with Fisk's rapid-fire suggestions about what she should and shouldn't have done and with his attitude, which seemed to imply she was incapable of deciding for herself what to tell the cops. She knew exactly what that should be. The truth.

"Look, I don't know what you think—"

"Anything new this morning?"

Will's question not only interrupted her protest, it broke the tension that had begun to form between her and his friend. Maybe that had been his intent.

"You were right about the men you left behind in Ms. Malone's house."

"They were in the database?"

"And suspected of far more than they've ever been convicted of. The proverbial hired guns. The problem is, with both of them dead, there's no way to determine in this case who it was that hired them."

"Sorry. I guess I 'reacted' before I had figured that out."

There had been no hesitation in the action Will had taken yesterday morning. Like the old saying, he had shot first and left it to God to sort the innocent out from the guilty. In this case, God would apparently have had it easy.

"Touché, I suppose," Paul said. "Admitting errors, however, doesn't get us anywhere."

"What will?"

With her question, the green eyes focused on her again. "I think I'm going to like working with you."

"Just as long as you know as much about what you're doing as you think you do."

Fisk laughed. "Tell her."

"He knows what he's doing," Will acknowledged. "So what have you decided?"

"We call the cops and arrange it so you can turn yourself in. The sooner the better."

It was the same advice Cait had given Will as soon as he'd shown up on her doorstep. Hearing it from someone she believed both of them had been counting on for a different kind of help created a sickness in the pit of her stomach.

They'd accomplished almost nothing in the last twenty-four hours that would go far toward proving Will innocent. And the chance of anyone being able to do that once he was behind bars seemed less than nil.

"And then what?"

She could read nothing in the tone of Will's question,

but her glance at his face told her all she needed to know. Paul's solution seemed to have rocked him, too.

"We go to work to find out who set you up and why."

"How the hell am I supposed to do that if I'm in jail?"

"*You* work mentally. We'll take care of the actual slogging."

"We?"

"The firm. I assumed you wanted me to represent you."

"If I hadn't, I wouldn't have called."

"Then let us get to the bottom of what happened. We have investigators who are skilled and experienced at this kind of thing. They do it for a living."

"And I don't. But I do have a vested interest. They don't. Frankly, it seems there are too many possibilities and not enough information to determine the truth. Besides—"

"For example," Paul went on, ignoring Will's caveat, "I'm wondering why they didn't just kill you, too, and blame the whole thing on the protestors? Wouldn't that make more sense than drugging you and hoping you wouldn't remember what had happened?"

"There are drugs that are known to produce amnesia," Cait said. "If they gave him one of those, they could be fairly certain of the results."

"Except drugs react differently in different people. Obviously the one they gave you—" Paul looked at Will again "—was supposed to keep you out until *after* the police arrived. It didn't. That seems a ridiculous chance to take."

"So why take it?" Despite his obvious disappointment over what Paul had suggested about letting the experts handle the investigation, Will sounded interested in the theory.

"I don't know. Maybe because they didn't have time to think things through. Maybe this was a spur-of-the-moment deal."

"I've been thinking that it must have been planned a long time. That's why I was hired. They were specifically looking for someone who would be easy to set up."

"Which takes us back to Ron Vincent."

"I wouldn't discount him as a possibility," Will said.

"No, nor would I. And I've got someone working on what we talked about last night."

"What he would gain by his brother's death? Why don't we just go ask him?"

"I might be amused if I didn't believe you're half-serious. That's the kind of thing I want to prevent."

"By turning me over to the cops."

"Yeah. But there's method in my madness, I promise. I also want to keep you alive."

"Until we run out of appeals."

"I shouldn't have told you that," Paul said, smiling.

"Told him what?" Cait asked.

"About a client of mine who was just executed."

It was ridiculous, but until Paul said the word, the possibility had never entered her mind. She had known from the first that Will hadn't cold-bloodedly put a gun to anyone's head and pulled the trigger.

She had, therefore, never entertained the thought that he might actually be found guilty of Greg Vincent's murder.

For the first time she was forced to confront what was actually at stake in the decision Paul had asked Will to make. Once he put himself into the hands of the police, the justice system took over his life. Life and death. There would be no backing out if it turned out that Paul couldn't prove he was innocent.

Until we run out of appeals, Will had said. He clearly understood that once he surrendered, there was nothing he could do for himself. He would be forced to depend on others to save his life—on Paul, on whatever investigators he hired, on the honesty of the witnesses who would testify. On her...

"That isn't going to happen to Will," she said.

"We'll do everything in our power to make sure it doesn't."

"But you can't guarantee it, can you?"

Fisk looked at her, his head tilted slightly to the side. "Nothing comes with a guarantee, Ms. Malone. Not in a court of law. I *can* promise you that I'll defend Will to the best of my ability, which is pretty damn good, if you'll pardon the self-adulation."

"What if someone lies?"

"I'm sorry?"

"Greg Vincent's brother. He's already decided Will's guilty. He'll be called to testify because he was there that night. At the restaurant. Since Will can't remember what happened, Vincent can say anything he wants to about what went on, and there will be no one around to deny it."

"Which may be why they killed the waiter."

Paul still didn't seem to get it. Now that she'd seen what might lie ahead for Will if one little thing went wrong… If one lie went unchallenged…

"What if the medical examiner who performs the autopsy on Emilio gets the time of death wrong?" she asked. "Or what if *he* lies. I mean if the FBI lab can be guilty of falsifying evidence, what makes you think the cops can't? They'll bring up everything that was said about Will two years ago—"

"You both need to understand that that's going to be brought up in any case. It's already happening. The fact that this murder has put the two of you together again is too good a story for the media to leave alone."

"We've been…a little out of touch," Cait said. "What are they saying?"

Paul's lips pursed slightly as he considered her face. "All the details of the inquiry two years ago, sensationalized, of course, because this time Will isn't simply an agent who did something stupid. He's a murderer on a rampage. And they're suggesting that's part of the reason."

"I don't understand. The inquiry?"

"That. His dismissal. His…dishonor, if you will."

"Will's killing people because he's angry the Secret Service let him go?" Her voice expressed how idiotic the accusation was. "Is that what they're saying?"

"Part of it."

"What else?"

"It doesn't matter," Will said. "There's nothing we can do about how they're going to twist things. It's their job. They'll say anything to boost ratings."

"So what else are they saying?" Cait demanded.

There was something they were keeping from her. Maybe Jeff Eagles or someone who had been privy to the information about their relationship had finally come forward.

No one had done that publicly before because even the Secret Service had recognized that promoting her as a hero would help detract attention away from the security failure the assassination attempt represented, as well as from the subsequent inquiry. Doing that had been even more important when the seemingly damning hotel video had been found.

"That Will kidnapped you because he was jealous," Paul said.

"Jealous? Jealous of whom?"

She wasn't involved in a relationship. She'd been too busy the last two years with rehab to think seriously about one.

If she were honest, there was another very good reason for her lack of interest in any member of the opposite sex. One who happened to be standing beside her.

"Of you?"

"Of…me? Jealous *of* me?"

"Of the attention you received. The recognition. The adulation, to overuse a word."

The idea was so bizarre, so foreign to what she knew about the way Will thought, that for a moment she was literally speechless. Then fury at the unfairness of it washed over her in a wave.

This was something she had wanted to straighten out then. She had wanted to come forward with the truth about where Will had been that night. Jeff Eagles had talked her out of doing that. Now her silence was being used against Will.

"That's one thing we can clear up right away."

"There'll be time enough for that," Paul said. "If you decide you really want to. First we need to get both of you somewhere safe."

"And for Will you think that's jail?"

"Far safer than being on the run with his picture on every television screen in the country."

"So get him *out* of the country."

"There are logistical problems with that, but even admitting the possibility… Is that what you want?" Paul's question had been addressed to Will.

He was right. This wasn't her decision. No matter how much she might want Will not to surrender, whether he did or not was ultimately up to him.

"I want to clear my name. I guess coming from me that sounds ridiculous, but… I didn't kill Greg Vincent. I didn't kill the waiter. As for the other two—"

His eyes fastened on her throat, before they lifted to meet hers. He took a breath, but it wasn't in order to finish the sentence he'd begun.

"You said you wanted to get Cait somewhere safe. Where would that be?"

"In protection. Mine, and not the cops'. For the time being here is as good a place as any. The house is even in my stepfather's name now."

"Not alone," Will said, ignoring the end of that. "I'm not leaving her here alone, no matter how safe you think it is."

"I didn't mean alone. There's a guy we've used before. He retired from the FBI a couple of years ago. He's done some investigative work for us as well as protection of witnesses."

"You trust him?"

"With you in jail, the threat level against Ms. Malone flatlines. The cops aren't going to be shooting at her because she won't be with you."

"I'm not worried about the cops. I'm worried about whoever might come after her because she's a potential witness."

"Which is why we'll protect her. Trust me, Will, whatever we do, she'll be a lot safer than she's been with you."

"She's still alive and relatively unharmed. I don't like the thought that I won't be around to make sure she stays that way."

"If you're dead, you won't be around to protect her either. I have it on good authority that the cops have been given the okay to shoot to kill."

"How can they do that?" Cait demanded.

"Because they have every reason to believe exactly

what the press is suggesting. That he's psychotic. Ron Vincent says that he blames himself for not picking up on the signs that were clearly there. And after all, Will did abduct you. Who knows what he may do next? It's a powerful argument. And there are some powerful people touting it."

"But to think they can just shoot someone down in cold blood without any kind of proof—"

"I ran from them," Will said quietly. "That's always a sign of guilt. That's the first thing you told me."

"I didn't know then what I know now."

"That doesn't make the argument any less valid."

"You do realize—"

"That people are convicted and even executed every day for crimes they didn't commit? It's not something I'm likely to forget. Even if Paul would let me."

"Then how can you agree to turn yourself in?"

"Because if I don't, what kind of life will I have?"

"*Life.* Don't you understand?"

For an eternity no one said anything. And then, pulling his eyes from hers, Will turned back to the lawyer.

"Set it up. But first, get someone up here to look after Cait."

"You're sure?" Paul asked, although he had been the one who had insisted on the rightness of this course of action.

"I'm not sure of anything except that I didn't kill Greg. I want a chance to prove that. If it has to be in court…"

"If you want any semblance of a normal life…" Paul said, shrugging.

Life. No matter which choice Will made, that's what it would eventually boil down to. Life or death. And that was a decision no one else could make for him. Neither she *nor* Paul. They didn't have that right.

The only rights they had were to care about what happened to him. And to do their best to make sure that what he chose had a chance of success.

"Then this is the right move."

She hadn't realized until he finished it that Paul's comment had been left dangling. And she supposed it didn't matter.

Whether this was a right move or not, it was the one Will had decided to make.

CHAPTER FOURTEEN

IT WAS AGAIN IMPOSSIBLE to distinguish where the lake ended and the sky began. The cause of their blurring wasn't a star-touched darkness this time, but a dawn mist, which lay low over the water.

The colors of the landscape that stretched before him were muted. Grays and browns and a shadowed slate. There was no sound but the soft, wind-driven lap of the water against the pilings of the pier and weathered boathouse.

Will had risen long before daylight, unable to endure another minute inside the house. As soon as he'd stepped out of the back door, again propping it open with a piece of wood, he had lifted his head, breathing in the familiar scents of the lake.

The happiest days of his adolescence had been spent here. It seemed appropriate that this might be the last place where he would be able to taste—and to savor—freedom.

He had walked out to the end of the pier, his footsteps echoing on its old boards in the stillness. A few ducks floated on the surface of the cold, gray water. They had watched his approach, but hadn't taken flight.

It seemed an appropriate metaphor. They were willing to chance an encounter with a hunter in exchange for a safe haven. A place where they could rest from their long and tiring journey.

He had stood there a long time, watching night give way to a false dawn and then to the first pale rays of the rising sun, shrouded by the mist and the low clouds. Eventually both would burn off, but right now, the tranquil, monochromatic world suited his need for solitude and peace.

"May I join you?"

Cait's voice. With a question for which there was no good answer.

He had known that he would have to say goodbye. He had tried to prepare himself for the inevitability of that, but this was too soon. And it was too hard. Besides, Cait belonged to the sunlit world of the day, not to this still-shadowed bleakness.

He turned to find her standing at the opposite end of the pier, wearing jeans and the sweatshirt he'd packed for her yesterday. She hadn't bothered with her coat, and the cold wind had already stained her cheeks.

"It's a free country."

His reply sounded curt. He hadn't meant it to, but there was no need to dress what was about to occur in sentiment. It wasn't fair, and it wasn't necessary.

They had grown accustomed to leading separate lives. They had done that for two years. What had happened between them during the last two days was an aberration. An interlude.

He watched as she walked toward him across the rough planks. As she did, she wrapped her arms over her chest, hugging her body for warmth.

"It's beautiful," she said, her eyes moving across the display of lake and shore and sky he'd been absorbing.

"I always loved it here. Even as a kid—"

He stopped the words, denying the memories. The long, heated days he and Paul had spent on this water. Swimming. Skiing. Canoeing. Cooking out on the old cement barbecue grill Paul's grandfather had built beside the shore. Sharing lies and dreams, mostly about girls and baseball and the embryonic plans they'd had for the remainder of their lives.

"I can see why you would," Cait said, her eyes still focused on the scene before them.

A polite and conventional response. Maybe that was for the best. They had only had time to scratch the surface of the emotional quagmire that had resulted from the events of two years ago. And now…

"You couldn't sleep?"

Like her comment, his question was safe. Acceptable. Unlike the ones he wanted to ask.

Did you think about the times we made love?

Did you wonder if we ever would again?

Did you go to sleep at night and awaken to find your body drenched with sweat, aching to be held against the heat of mine?

"Not really. I kept thinking—" She turned her head to look at him.

"About what?"

"About everything, I guess. Then. And now."

"That doesn't do either of us any good."

"I know, but… It's hard not to."

He held her eyes a moment, seeing a longing in them he couldn't answer, much less satisfy.

"*This* doesn't help."

"I know. When I saw you standing out here, I told myself it wouldn't. That I should just go back inside. But…I couldn't leave you out here alone."

He nodded as if that made sense.

"Do you want me to leave?"

No matter how convinced he was that being here together wasn't good for either of them, he didn't want her to go. He wanted her beside him. For whatever time they had left.

"It's all right."

"Paul's still asleep," she said, her left hand making that now familiar journey up and down her right arm and shoulder. "I could hear him snoring."

He began unbuttoning the jacket she'd bought him. She followed the movements of his fingers a moment before she looked up again.

"If that's for me…"

By that time he was shrugging out of the coat. He turned, holding it out for her to slip her arms into.

"It's okay, really. I didn't think about bringing mine. I didn't realize how cold it would—"

"Put it on."

The words were again too harsh, too much like a command. She hesitated until he moved his hands, lifting the coat as if to bring her attention to it.

She turned her back to him, slipping her left arm into the sleeve and then inserting the right, the movement slightly awkward. Another reminder, not that he needed any, of what her association with him had cost her.

He couldn't see her face as he held the coat. And maybe that's why it happened.

His hands released their hold on the garment, letting it settle over her shoulders. Then, as if acting of their own accord, they slid down to fasten over her upper arms.

He not only felt the depth of the breath she took, he heard it. Before he could react, she turned to face him.

With that movement, they were less than six inches apart. Her head had tilted slightly, so that she was looking up into his eyes.

He watched her lips open. And despite everything he knew about what he *should* do, his own lowered to meet them.

Her mouth was chill against his, but it clung exactly as it had the first time he'd kissed her. He'd forgotten how soft her lips were. How exquisitely sweet opening under his.

The duet their tongues engaged in echoed the sexual thrust and response their bodies had once enjoyed.

And might never again.

It was a reality he had not fully faced. Not even during the hour of introspection he'd just indulged in.

He slipped his hands inside the coat he'd put around her, finding her hips. Sliding his palms under her buttocks, he pulled her against his body.

His erection had been full-blown from the instant his lips met hers. Pressed against him as she was, there could be no doubt she was aware of it.

Suddenly, despite the control of his hands, she took a half step backward, breaking the contact between them. As she did, her head tilted and her eyes opened.

Slightly glazed, they looked just as they always had after they'd made love. As if she had not yet completely returned from the secret place to which that journey had conveyed her.

The sheen of moisture on her bottom lip gave evidence of their kiss. As he waited for whatever she wanted to say to him—protest or rebuke—her mouth closed. She swallowed, the movement visible down the long, slender column of her throat, before she opened it again.

"You don't have to do this."

"This?"

"Go with Paul. There are ways to get out of the country. We both know that."

"Except I didn't do anything wrong, Cait."

"That didn't keep you from being punished before."

"I *deserved* to be punished then. Maybe even more severely than I was."

"For what? For making love?"

"Maybe. It was the wrong time. The wrong place. And with the wrong woman."

Until her eyes widened, he hadn't realized how she would interpret that.

"I was your supervisor," he clarified. "If I hadn't allowed a relationship to develop between us, then maybe... Maybe none of what happened that day would have occurred. Maybe I would have seen the target, too. Or maybe you *would* have taken him out before he could get off a round."

"You said you'd watched the films. You said I didn't hesitate."

"I still believe that. *You're* the one who said you saw him and didn't react. If that *is* what happened, all I'm saying—"

"You're saying that it was *your* fault? I've heard of ego, Shannon, but that...? That's absurd."

"I know exactly how much sleep you'd gotten the night before. The same amount I did. And it wasn't anywhere near eight hours. Maybe the board of inquiry was right. Maybe that had an effect."

"You don't believe that. You *can't*."

"It doesn't matter what I believe. *They* believed it. And evaluating situations like the attempt against al-Faisal is their job. That and making sure senior agents aren't sleeping with people assigned to their detail."

She laughed and shook her head, her eyes expressing her disbelief and dismay at what he'd just said. "Well, you rather obviously aren't worried about that now."

A matching anger was in her tone, along with a hint of sarcasm. At least they were no longer dancing around the subject of how much he still wanted her.

"Maybe because I'm no longer your superior. Or because, please God, you aren't going to be in a situation today where anyone's life will be in danger."

"You do realize…" She hesitated, unsure how to give voice to the sudden fear he saw in her eyes.

"Everything you're thinking right now, I've already thought of. Believe me."

"And you're still going?"

"Paul's right. As much as I hate to admit it. I can't run from the cops and Greg's killers and at the same time try to prove I wasn't involved in his death. We pretty much confirmed the impossibility of that yesterday."

"I thought we did pretty well. Considering everything."

"Maybe. Or maybe we just got lucky that we didn't both end up dead. In any case, being on the run—always looking over your shoulder—isn't much of a life."

"Neither is being incarcerated."

"I can't argue with that. I do have two things in my favor, however."

"Two things?"

"I didn't kill Greg Vincent. And Paul really is as good as he thinks he is."

"Then I'm glad he's your friend."

He nodded. "Otherwise…there are only a couple of things I regret."

"Regret?"

"Actually, only one, now that I think about it."

"And what is that?"

With his hands he urged her forward again. There was a second of resistance before she melted against him. This time she put her arms around his waist and her cheek on his chest.

Under his jacket, his hands slid up her back, soothing the tension he could feel. It wasn't the kind of touching he'd been imagining when she'd appeared on the end of the pier, but perhaps it was better for both of them if it was the extent of the physical contact between them.

They had not only been lovers, but friends. Partners.

Maybe that was the right emotion to end this interlude on. The one that had begun it. The concern that was inherent in that relationship. Then, if Paul was somehow able to work another miracle—

"If you *did* decide to run…" Cait hesitated.

The cold-hardened tips of her nipples, separated from his chest only by her sweats and the sweater he wore, moved against his chest, sending a searing flood of heat throughout his body.

Some part of him didn't want to hear whatever came next, yet he was unable to formulate any statement that might prevent her from completing the what-if she'd begun. And he knew why he couldn't.

If she was about to make the suggestion he thought she might, then no matter what, he wanted to hear it. It would be something to carry with him through the long ordeal he faced.

"I don't really know how to say this," she began again.

"The same way we've always said things to one another. Straight out. It's a little late in the game to start pulling your punches."

"Then, if you decide that what Paul is urging you to do is not what you want to do…" She raised her head, looking up at him with a smile. "I haven't done anything in the last two years except try to get back to normal. I don't have a full-time job. And professionally… Although I've come a long way physically, I suspect that any kind of law enforcement job is out of the question—"

"Are you interviewing with me for some kind of position, Cait? Because if you aren't, then I'm not sure where the hell this is going."

Her laugh was embarrassed. "It's obvious that coming on to a guy isn't my strong suit. Although I guess I did pretty well the first time."

"The first time?"

"With you."

"You're coming on to me by telling me what you've been doing the last two years?"

"I'm trying to tell you that I'm not doing a damn thing that's so compelling I wouldn't be willing to do… something else. If you wanted me to."

"Like what?"

It was almost cruel to play this out, pretending he didn't know what she meant. It was a temptation he couldn't seem to resist.

He'd spent two years thinking she hated him. Just the

possibility that she might really make the offer he was anticipating—

"Like going with you. Or meeting you wherever you go."

"You'd really do that?"

"In a heartbeat. I've just been waiting for an indication that it's something you'd consider."

"Something *I'd* consider? You think I'd turn you down?"

"Despite my previous brazen behavior, in a word, yes."

"Then you aren't nearly as smart as I thought."

She searched his face a moment, hope growing in her eyes. It was so obvious, he felt guilty for leading her on. Despite his almost desperate need to hear what she'd just said, she deserved better.

"You'll take me?"

She had asked the question before he'd had a chance to articulate the reason that wouldn't work. Reservations that had nothing to do with whether or not he wanted her with him.

"If I were going anywhere," he said softly.

Her eyes changed with the realization of what that meant. "You're going to listen to Paul."

"It isn't that I haven't thought about the other. And, to be honest, about asking you to come with me. Sometimes we have to do what we know is right rather than what we *want* to be right. I'm not going to live the rest of my life branded a murderer, Cait. I'm going to fight to clear my name."

Something I didn't do before…

The unspoken words lay between them. Neither of them wanted to revisit the guilt associated with that day two years ago.

He'd been dishonored, but no one had accused him then of being a murderer. And this time, there was no one to shield from the devastation that would result from telling the truth.

"Clearing your name is still this important despite…?"

"Despite the fact that it's already associated in the public's mind with dereliction of duty? It may not make much sense, but…yeah. Yeah, it is. If Paul is able to bring this off, then I get my life back. At least the life I've been leading for the last two years."

He recognized the bitterness in his tone and regretted it. Self-pity was something he'd fought. He had made his choices, and he'd taken the chances they'd involved. He had deserved to have to pay for those when he'd been caught.

"And if he can't pull it off?"

"Then I'll have to learn to deal with it." Just as he had the other.

"You turn yourself in today, Will, and you're taking the chance that you may never see any of this again."

She meant the lake. And that wasn't what he feared losing.

Of course, you couldn't lose what you no longer possessed. He'd lost Cait a long time ago. Despite what she'd just said about coming with him, he had nothing to lose this time.

"Don't you think I've thought about that? I've thought about nothing else since Paul told me what he believes I should do."

That was a lie. Or maybe it wasn't.

Much of what he'd been thinking about throughout the sleepless night had had to do with placing his fate in a system whose flaws he knew too well. And a lot to do with the opportunity to reconnect with Cait it would cost him if the system failed in this case.

"Then maybe… Since this may be the last chance we have to make things right between us—" She stopped, looking up into his eyes. "Are you going to make me say it?"

"I think maybe you should. If I've learned one thing from the last two years, it's that nothing should be taken for granted."

"Not even tomorrow."

"Not even *today*. The ex-FBI agent Paul mentioned is on his way. He should be here by mid-morning. Paul and I leave for Washington as soon as he arrives."

Her eyes widened, but she made no further protest of his decision. Instead she did what he'd asked her to.

"Then…make love to me, Will. It doesn't matter why you do it. Reasons aren't important right now. Just please, Will, make love to me."

CHAPTER FIFTEEN

"ARE YOU SURE?"

Cait smiled, thinking that she had never been surer of anything in her entire life. But of course, Will wouldn't believe that kind of hyperbole. Not after everything that had come between them. Not after virtually being out of contact with each other for two years.

He didn't seem to realize that as far as she was concerned only two things had prevented her from running back to him and begging his forgiveness a long time ago. One was her physical condition, which, if she were honest, was no longer a consideration in any decision to resume their relationship. The other was her remorse over the things that had happened to him as a result of the last time they'd made love.

She still felt guilty, but the fact that he didn't blame her—that he had apparently never blamed her—had gone a long way in allowing her to put that destructive emotion behind her. It now seemed a foolish reason to deny what they both so obviously wanted.

"Almost the only thing I'm sure of is that I very much want you to make love to me."

He studied her eyes and then, without another word, he put his hand around her elbow and directed her back along the pier. For a few seconds, she believed he intended to take her back to the house. Then he stepped to the side and toward the entrance to the boathouse.

He went in first, ducking his head to clear the low doorway. Once inside, he turned and waited for her, extending his hand. She took it and followed him into the shadowed interior.

She was forced to wait until her eyes adjusted to the dimness. As they did, she discovered no boat hung from the rusting chains that dangled from the crossbeams. An ancient canoe lay bottom up on the opposite side, separated from them by the water that occupied the center portion. Fishing equipment was stacked in the far back corner. A variety of life jackets and oars were hung haphazardly on the walls, as if whoever had used them last had simply put them up on the nearest hook, without rhyme or reason.

Unsure what Will intended, her eyes came back to his. They held none of the uncertainty she was feeling.

"I realize it's not the ideal setting," he said, "but I didn't think you'd want to go back to the house."

Where Paul slept. And where the investigator was supposed to show up in a few hours.

"No," she said softly.

"Since I'm a little old to consider making love on cold, wet ground romantic…"

"Not to me."

He nodded, still examining her face. Her tentative smile was intended to be reassuring. Apparently, it worked.

He released her hand. Then he walked over to the wall and began pulling life preservers down. One by one he tossed them on the floor in the back corner, the one not crowded with tackle boxes and fishing poles. He arranged them so that they lay side by side, forming a makeshift pallet.

When he'd finished, he looked up to find her watching him. "Better than the bare wood."

She hesitated, wondering what she was supposed to do. Although she'd been the one who had initiated the first moves toward a personal relationship, once that had begun, Will had always been in charge.

Not only was it his temperament to take control, but she preferred it that way. She preferred *him* that way.

"If you'd rather go back to the house…" he began, obviously misinterpreting her hesitation.

"Paul's there."

"I can send him on some kind of errand."

"One he wouldn't see through?"

She had tried to inject a note of humor into the question, but she wasn't amused by his suggestion. The longer they waited, the more awkward this became.

It was one thing to do something unconventional in the heat of the moment. It was quite another to make contingency plans for it.

"Does it matter?" he asked, obviously puzzled by the question.

"I thought maybe it did to you."

For a long heartbeat he said nothing, and then, "I've got nothing to lose, Cait. Not this time."

Not this time.

"Not like before, you mean?"

"No one gives a damn if you and I make love. Not anymore. Not Paul. Not the Service."

"My mom probably wouldn't be too thrilled." This time her amusement was genuine.

But Will was right. They were consenting adults. They were no longer partners. No longer working for the government.

He laughed, breaking the tension. "Well, thankfully she's not here right now."

She wasn't. There was no one here but the two of them. And if they chose to make love, it would be without the danger of being found out, so she couldn't imagine why she was nervous.

At one time, despite the risk, moving into Will's arms had been as natural to her as breathing. The warmth and strength of them closing around her body had represented safety. Almost a sense of homecoming. Was she afraid that after all this time—

"There's no one here but you and me, Cait. Just like it used to be."

Tears stung behind her lids. Getting to be a habit, she thought. One she didn't like. She couldn't remember crying when she'd been shot, yet during the last two days, every time she turned around, she was tearing up.

"Don't mind me," she said. "I'm an idiot."

She reached into the pocket of her coat for the tissue she always carried and realized she was wearing Will's jacket. It had still been warm from the heat of his body when he'd slipped it over her shoulders.

The thought created its own sexual imagery. When she looked up, Will had closed the distance between them.

He stopped less than six inches away, putting his crooked index finger under her chin. He tilted it upward, wiping away the moisture that trembled on her lower lashes.

"Why the hell are you crying?"

"Because I didn't believe this would ever happen again."

"This?"

"Being together. Making love."

"You didn't?"

She shook her head, standing motionless, childishly obedient while he ran the pad of his thumb beneath her other eye.

"I *always* knew," Will said. "I didn't know it would be in these circumstances, but…I knew that someday I'd make love to you again."

"How could you know that?" she asked, smiling up at him through her tears.

"Because I knew God couldn't be cruel enough to take you away from me, too."

That should have sounded self-pitying, but it didn't. Maybe that was because she wanted so badly to believe what he'd said about knowing they would make love again, but to her the rest of it had simply sounded…honest. As if that were exactly what he'd felt.

Her heart too full to trust herself to respond verbally, she lifted her chin so that it no longer rested against his finger. Then she slipped between him and the wall of the boathouse, walking toward the area where he'd arranged the life preservers.

She slipped off the coat he'd loaned her, laying it down on top of the makeshift bed. Without looking at him, she bent to untie her running shoes, using the toe of the opposite foot against each heel to push them off her feet.

Her fingers trembled slightly over the task of unzipping her jeans. Despite that, it was quickly accomplished. Balancing first on one leg and then the other, she pulled off her socks, stuffing them into her shoes.

Only then did she turn around. Will's eyes came up slowly, moving over her exposed legs, which had already begun to get goose bumps from the cold. Conscious of that, as well as of the fact that the tan she'd gotten last summer had faded, she wasn't sure what to expect when his gaze finally reached her face.

She didn't have long to wonder. And what she saw in his eyes relieved any concerns she might have had that he would no longer find her attractive.

Despite the months that had passed since they'd made love, she hadn't forgotten how he looked at moments like this. That passion was in his dark eyes, reflecting the same memories that bombarded her.

He slipped off his shoes, using the method she'd employed. In spite of the cold, he hadn't bothered to put on socks for his dawn visit to the lake. He unbuckled his belt, allowing his slacks to fall around his ankles.

He stepped out of them and began moving toward her. He reached over his shoulder and grabbed the back of his sweater, just below the collar, to bring both it and his undershirt over his head. He threw them to the side and in almost the same motion took her in his arms, his mouth finding hers with a hunger that echoed her own.

She could feel the hair-roughened skin of his thighs against the smoothness of hers. The blatant masculinity of his erection was exciting, making her wish she hadn't stopped her own disrobing before she'd taken off her sweatshirt.

As if he had read her mind, Will tugged it over her head, revealing that she, too, had dressed in a hurry. In her haste to join him on the pier, she hadn't bothered with the bra she'd taken off in order to sleep more comfortably.

It was obvious her nudity excited him. He pulled her against his body as soon as her top joined the clothing he'd discarded on the weathered planks. The sensation of the hair on his chest moving against her breasts was a thousand times more evocative than the other had been.

Peaked with the cold, the sensitized tips of her nipples were crushed against his muscled torso. His hands flattened against her back, as his mouth continued to ravage.

Knees weak with desire, she was almost light-headed with the sensations created by Will's hands and tongue. He knew her too well. A knowledge gleaned from endless nights through which they'd made love, learning every conceivable way to give one another pleasure.

His mouth deserted hers as he bent to trail kisses along her throat. Her head fell back, allowing him access to the sensitive skin below her ear. Eventually, his lips began to trace lower, unhurried in their exploration.

They hesitated over the uneven texture of the scars, reminding her that this was the first time he'd seen the still-reddened evidence of the assassin's bullets. The last time they'd made love—

Had been the night before the morning that had changed both their lives forever.

She opened her eyes in time to watch his head come up. She couldn't be sure what was in his face, but she knew it was nothing she should fear. No revulsion. No pity.

"I'm so sorry," he whispered.

He bent to touch his lips to the marks she'd grown so accustomed to that she no longer even noticed them. She had been far more concerned about the nerve damage that had limited movement and affected strength.

The scars, in contrast, were cosmetic. Something they had told her could be reduced with plastic surgery if she wanted. She hadn't bothered. With what she now saw in Will's eyes, she knew that she wouldn't need to.

Those marks were part of who she was. The event

that had caused them was a part of both their lives. It always would be.

"You don't have anything to be sorry for," she said. "I've told you that."

"I'm sorry for this. For what you went through. If you had been anyone else on the team…"

"If I had been anyone else?" she prodded when he hesitated.

He laughed, a breath of sound. "I was going to say I'd feel the same way if this had happened to anyone else on the team. And that's a lie. I'd be sorry, but…it wouldn't make me feel the same. You were so perfect. So damn beautiful."

"And I'm not 'so damn beautiful' now? It's not too late for me to back out of this, you know."

This time his laughter was genuine and unrestrained. "Point taken."

"The scars don't matter, Will. Not to me. And if they don't matter to you, then…it's not worth talking about. Something we seem to be spending an inordinate amount of time doing."

Time we don't have.

The last was unspoken, but it didn't need to be said. They were both too aware of that reality.

Before she realized what he intended, Will bent, putting his left arm under her knees, while keeping his right behind her back. He picked her up as if she were a child, taking the final step toward the pallet he'd made from the life preservers.

Once there, he knelt, placing her on the center of the coat she'd spread over them. The lining was cool beneath her skin, making her shiver.

"Cold?" He attempted to pull the edges of his jacket around her nude body.

"*And* hungry. And you're the only one who can do anything about either."

The corners of his lips slanted upward just before he lowered his head, his mouth finding hers. At the same time his hand cupped under her breast, his thumb moving back and forth over its nipple.

Long before she was prepared for the kiss to end, he raised his head, his open mouth once more trailing moisture over her skin. His lips were hot in contrast to the damp chill of every inch of her skin his body wasn't in contact with.

Then his teeth closed over her nipple, gently teasing. Just before that sensation slipped over the delicate line that separated pleasure from pain, he released the pressure, running his tongue around the taut nub he'd created.

His palm, flattened, began to move over her stomach, inching downward as he continued to worship her breast with his tongue and teeth. Anticipation of his touch sang through her body. It had been so long. A long, lonely exile from how he had always been able to make her feel.

Her body arched with the first unerring stroke of his finger. She hadn't realized how close to the edge she had been. All she knew was that she ached with need. A need that only Will could satisfy.

The caress of his finger made her mindless, conscious of nothing but the once-familiar heat that was beginning to build in her lower body. It shimmered like summer lightning along nerve endings awakened from their long deprivation.

His mouth continued to caress her breasts, moving from one to the other. The moisture he left behind on each nipple when he deserted it was touched by the cold, another sensation added to the exponentially increasing sum of the others.

Her lips parted involuntarily, her breath sighing out. As it did, his finger dipped inside her body to find moisture, already there in anticipation of his entry. Once more he began to stroke her, tantalizing the nerve endings nature had so generously supplied to give her pleasure.

Almost before she had time to realize what was happening, the tremors started. Subtle at first, with each practiced movement of his finger, they grew in intensity, vibrating throughout her lower body.

He was obviously aware that the inexorable cataclysm had begun. Without hesitation, without allowing the sensations he'd created time to fade, he eased over her.

The familiar warmth of his body lowering over hers added to her driving need for release. With the same sureness he had brought to every aspect of their relationship, Will pushed into her, his entrance eased by her desire and his preparation.

Before she had time to relish the knowledge that, despite all odds, she and Will were again making love, he began to deepen his penetration. Perhaps it was the months she'd spent without this. Or the fact that he, too, seemed consumed with need.

For whatever reason, there was a heartbeat of panic as he began to thrust deeper and deeper, seeming to fill her more fully than he ever had before. Before she could convey, even unconsciously, the touch of uncertainty she'd felt, his mouth closed over hers again.

She relaxed into its caress. The movement of his tongue echoed the drive of his hips, raising and then lowering over hers. The scintilla of unease faded, as her body again responded to his touch.

This time the waves built more quickly than they had before. They rippled outward from the epicenter, each more powerful than the last until finally there was no separation, no release, between them.

Her breath came in short, even gasps, as her mind was consumed by what he could make her feel. If that qualified as thought, then it was the last she had before she gave into the surge of pure feeling. It swept everything before it from its path, filling her with an ecstasy that made the air thin around her and the world darken.

They clung together as the sea of sensation washed over them. When it had passed, they lay in its shallows, too spent to talk or move.

After a long time, Will raised his head, looking down into her eyes. Although they were still joined in the most intimate of connections, the world had again intruded.

She knew that in a matter of hours he would leave.

She might never again be with him like this. Never kiss him. Never hold him.

Yet she couldn't find the words to say any of the things that were in her heart. All she could do was to look up at him, holding on to what was in his eyes. Determined to memorize it so that when he was gone...

"You don't have to do this," she whispered.

He made no pretense of not understanding. "Even if I ran, I couldn't take you with me."

"Why not?"

He pushed onto his elbows a little, allowing enough space between their bodies for the cold to creep in. With his thumb he pushed a strand of hair away from her face.

"One person might make it. *Might*. If he had the gift of blending into his setting. Or never calling attention to himself."

She could tell that he had been thinking about the skills it would take to hide in a different culture for the rest of his life. If anyone could do that, Will could. He had the calm intelligence that kind of deception required.

"But for two people to carry that off?" He shook his head, the movement slight. And then he smiled at her. "Besides, you could never get away with being nondescript."

"I could do anything I had to. If you'd give me the chance."

The smile widened, his eyes filling with a tenderness she'd almost forgotten. Seeing it, she remembered that when they'd been involved before, he had thought her

GAYLE WILSON   225

naive. Young and inexperienced. Compared to him, she had been.

In this situation she didn't feel that gap. Maybe it was the fact that he was no longer her superior. Or maybe it was all she had learned about herself during the last two difficult years. Whatever had made the difference, she found that she resented his almost paternalistic attitude.

"Whether you believe that or not," she said, "it's true."

"I believe it. It just doesn't change anything. I want my life back. At least what's left of it. And if I somehow manage that—"

She waited for a promise, some crumb of hope, but he didn't finish the sentence.

"We better get back," he said instead. "Paul will think something's happened."

"You said he was smart. He'll figure it out."

"I wasn't sure you wouldn't mind if he did."

"The only thing I mind is having to say goodbye."

"Then don't."

"That won't change anything."

"It will change what I have to remember."

He was right. The time they had left could be measured in minutes, and she was wasting too many of them on arguments that she knew were fruitless.

Will had made up his mind. She knew from experience that nothing she could say could change it.

She raised her torso slightly off the coat. At the same time, she put her hand at the nape of his neck, her fingers spread, threading upward through the thick, midnight blackness of his hair.

Yielding to the pressure she exerted, his head began to lower. Her mouth opened, anticipating his kiss.

Instead of closing over hers, his lips lightly caressed each eyelid, their moisture mingling with tears she wasn't aware she'd shed. Then he touched her temples, cheeks and chin before his mouth covered hers.

They had exhausted the passion. This was benediction. And farewell.

She closed her eyes, denying the tears that burned behind their lids. If this was all they would have, she was determined not to mar the memory of it. She had told him she could do whatever he gave her the chance to do.

If what he asked her for was a goodbye without any further expression of fear or regret, then somehow she would manage it. *Somehow...*

CHAPTER SIXTEEN

"GODDAMN ASSHOLES."

Paul's profanity was so heartfelt Will had no doubt his friend was as shocked by the scene confronting them as he was.

The street outside the police substation where Paul had arranged for Will's surrender to take place was crowded with production trucks serving at least fifteen television crews. Barricades, manned by uniformed officers, had been set up to keep the reporters at bay on either side of the steps leading up to its entrance. A crowd had gathered, perhaps attracted by the media presence or by their reports from the scene, which had spilled over the sidewalk and out into the street.

"What the hell happened?" Memories of the humiliation he'd felt the day of the inquiry washed over Will in a sickening wave.

"Bastards couldn't wait to let the public in on the coup they'd scored."

"If you're talking about me, then they didn't do a damn thing that would qualify in *any* way as a coup. You made an arrangement to bring your client in. That's why the process is called surrender."

"All the cops care about is the fact that they're going to have you in custody. And that's all the good citizens of this city care about, too."

Why not? As long as the rabid killer the police had been publicly hysterical about during the last two days was behind bars, nobody gave a damn how it had been accomplished. They would celebrate that the crime spree was over.

With Will out of the picture, maybe it was. After all, whoever had murdered Vincent had intended for him to take the fall. That was exactly what was about to happen.

"This was supposed to be just me and you walking up those steps," he said bitterly.

"It will be."

"With an audience of a few million people."

"It doesn't matter. Everybody was going to know you'd surrendered as soon as Metro's spokesperson could get a mike and a reporter. They've simply eliminated a couple of steps in the process."

"I don't like it."

He didn't. This was like running a damn gauntlet, his every expression exposed to dozens of cameras.

And to everyone else.

"Relax," Paul said. "I thought about calling them myself."

Incredulous, Will pulled his gaze from the throng

lining the sidewalk to glance across the car at his friend. "What for?"

"Public scrutiny. Which equals protection. The more eyes watching this, the less likely anyone will try something."

Paul had a point. Will still didn't like it, maybe because he'd spent too many years scanning crowds, expecting something to go wrong.

"Look, whatever they've done, it's a little late to call this off now," Paul said.

"It's not too late until I walk up those steps and they put the cuffs on me."

"There won't be any call for that. You came in voluntarily."

"Don't put money on them not making a production of cuffing me. It's going to be part of the show."

It would be. Maybe it wasn't what Paul had planned, but he wasn't the only person who had a say in how this would go down. And the final say...

"This isn't how it was supposed to be," Will said. "Even if they leaked the information to the media, how did the rest of those people get in on this?"

"The stations have probably been hyping it since they were allowed to set up. People came to see—" Paul broke the sentence, his eyes going back to the mob. "Hell, Will, you know what they came here to see."

He did. After all, none of this was new to him. The inquiry after the assassination attempt hadn't attracted this kind of attention, but he'd had enough mikes and cameras thrust into his face then to last a lifetime.

He was a little surprised that none of the crowd had noticed them. Of course, Paul's black Lexus was fairly anonymous in this upscale neighborhood. And he had pulled it up along the curb almost a block away from the substation, chosen not only because it had jurisdiction over Greg Vincent's murder, but because it was located in this particular section of town.

"You aren't thinking about changing your mind, are you?"

Will wanted to. And his reluctance to go through with this would probably have been the same if there had been no one out there to watch what was about to take place. What he might be giving up forever had been made abundantly clear to him this morning.

And this is the only way you stand any chance of getting what you want....

"I haven't changed my mind."

"Good." Paul sounded relieved. "It's the right thing to do. And I'm telling you that both as your lawyer and as your friend."

Will nodded, having run out of things to say. Now that he'd reaffirmed his decision, he just wanted to get this over with.

"Let's go."

"Remember what I told you. Let me do the talking. And try not to react in any way to whatever questions the media throws at you."

"I've had a lot of training in that."

"It won't last long. The cops should keep them far enough away from you that we can make it up the steps and inside in a matter of minutes."

"I know."

"Then…you ready?"

"Yeah."

Paul hesitated before opening his door, making Will wonder if he, too, were having second thoughts. Just as that possibility brushed through Will's consciousness, Paul put his hand around the handle.

"Here we go."

Paul stepped out of the car, automatically adjusting his tie as he looked around. Will waited for his nod of approval before he opened his own door.

Together they started up the sidewalk that ran parallel to and across the street from the station. Like ripples on the surface of a pond, awareness of their approach spread through the crowd.

The indistinguishable babble that had been emanating from the throng began to die. By the time they reached the area occupied by the sound trucks, there was almost a complete silence from those lined up on either side of the steps.

The cops began to force the fringe element, the people who obviously lacked press credentials, away from the trucks, clearing a path that would allow them to cross the street. By that time, the noise had begun again. Will ignored the questions shouted at him, as did Paul.

Buffeted by the noise and by a renewed realization of the enormity of the step he was taking, Will had unconsciously been keeping his head down, attempting not to make eye contact with any of the reporters. He was almost halfway across the street before he realized what he was doing. And, more importantly, how that action would be interpreted.

He raised his head, making sure that no trace of the emotions he felt were reflected in his face. Instead, he lifted his chin defiantly.

He knew what they were here for. To get a look at a killer. To give their viewers a look at a mass murderer.

What he intended to offer them instead was the sight of a man confident of his innocence. And confident also of his ultimate acquittal.

"...can help you."

The first of that sentence had been lost in the clamor around him. Something about what he did hear drew his eyes in the direction from which the words had come. He scanned the crowd, all of whom now seemed to be yelling at him.

His gaze met and then held on a pair of dark eyes that were instantly—and eerily—familiar. The eyes of the man who had appeared in Cait's clouded mirror two days ago. The man Will believed had been in the alley behind the restaurant the night Greg Vincent had been murdered.

The same long, unkempt hair surrounded thin cheeks, still covered by several days' growth of beard.

There was no doubt in Will's mind that he was staring into the face that had triggered his flashback.

Shocked, he hesitated, failing to take the next step. Paul had already advanced a few feet ahead of him when he realized that Will was no longer beside him.

He turned back, shouting above the din. "What's wrong?"

"It's him."

"What? Who?" Paul's gaze searched the area where Will had been looking before it came back to his face.

"The guy I told you about. The one in the alley."

Comprehension lighting his face, Paul turned, again scanning the group to their left. "Where?"

Will had the presence of mind not to point or give any visual cue the cameras might pick up. If this man *did* know something about Vincent's murder, then like the waiter, he would also be on the list to be eliminated. Given the dwindling pool of people who could prove his innocence, Will couldn't afford to let that happen.

"Dark, stringy hair. He's wearing a gray jacket with a dark shirt. Unshaven."

While he watched Paul search for the man who matched that description, Will kept his eyes resolutely focused on the lawyer. He understood the damage he'd already done by stopping and gawking.

That knowledge was reiterated when he allowed the fragment he'd picked up out of what the man had shouted replay in his head. If the guy really *could* help him—

"Got him," Paul said.

For a second Will was afraid the lawyer intended to step across and present the man with his card. To prevent that from happening, Will took a few steps forward until he was alongside Paul. Then he put his hand under his friend's elbow, literally pushing him along.

Whether it was making that familiar gesture, one he had used on countless occasions to urge some dignitary or candidate through the closely packed bodies that surrounded them, or whether it was some instinct for survival, Will's eyes lifted, automatically scanning the roofline of the building they were approaching. Hardly conscious of what he was doing, he examined the ones of those adjacent to it as well.

A Secret Service detail was always made aware in advance of where police snipers would be located. That was part of the team preparation, which guaranteed everyone would be on the same page.

When he saw the distinctive shape of a rifle barrel on the roof of the building next door, for a split second he assumed that's what it was. A sniper whose job was the same as his. To protect their charge at all costs.

Except this time—

Even as the thought formed, Will was moving. He pushed Paul to the side, hard enough that the smaller man stumbled into one of the barricades beside the steps.

The first bullet struck the street where the two of them had been standing. By the time Will heard the sound of that shot, the second one had struck the concrete beside him.

The third, its trajectory possibly a reaction to his attempt to get Paul to his feet, thudded into the barricade, sending splinters of wood flying. That was all the incentive it took to panic the crowd into action—something the sound of the first two shots hadn't managed. Not for anyone but Will.

"What the hell?" Paul muttered, his eyes wide and confused as he looked up from where he sprawled on the ground.

"Assassination."

As he spoke the word, Will jumped over the fallen barricade, and then held out his hand. On either side of them, people ran screaming into the street, eddying around the downed man and the barricade.

"Run," Paul said, looking up into his eyes. "Get out of here. He's not after me."

Advice or permission? Will still wasn't sure when he took the first step. By the third, he was running full speed, one of dozens of people trying to put as much distance as he could between himself and the rooftop sniper.

He heard the fourth shot, and a cry of pain. He fought the urge to look back. Paul was right. They weren't after him. Will knew exactly who they were after.

As he ran, weaving through the maze of sound trucks, lost in the crowd that continued to flee, he began to work his right arm out of the sleeve of the jacket Cait had bought him. Paul hadn't allowed him to wear his weapon, so that the coat had only been protection from the cold.

Without decreasing his speed, he managed to slip the jacket off his other arm. He rolled it as he ran, holding it in front of him until he passed one of the metal grille waste receptacles.

He threw the coat into it, never breaking stride. The image that had been beamed to the television audience—and the one the sniper had seen—was of a man in a loden-green field coat. Perhaps the blue dress shirt and tie that Paul's investigator had brought to the lake with him wasn't much of a disguise, but it would change his appearance to the cursory observer.

The fact that there were dozens of other men fleeing the scene was the biggest thing in his favor. All he had to do was lose himself among them—

Someone bumped him from the rear, sending him staggering forward. He righted himself by reaching out to touch one of the trees lining the street.

His forward progress momentarily stopped, he took the opportunity to grab a quick look at his surroundings as people streamed by him. And he realized in those few seconds that he knew exactly where he was.

Greg Vincent's house was approximately three blocks away. And the Metro station he had always taken back to his apartment was around the next corner. He could take the subway to the train station and from there…

Although his feet had begun to move again, his brain seemed frozen. Locked in indecision.

Where the hell did he go from here?

The only answer that came immediately to mind

was back to where he'd come from. Back to where he'd left Cait.

Although the emotional pull to do exactly that was incredibly strong, he forced himself to consider the logic of it. No longer was the summerhouse known only to him and Paul. The P.I. was there, and others in Paul's firm might now be aware of the location.

Besides, his friend's face and undoubtedly his name had been a part of every broadcast that would emanate from the substation. If the people who'd killed Greg were as resourceful and determined as Will believed, then they were probably combing the records right now to discover any addresses associated with Paul or the members of his firm.

Will rounded the corner and saw the familiar entrance to the Metro ahead of him. Most of those who had been running beside him continued along the street he now deserted. He slowed his pace, attempting to fit in to his new surroundings.

He allowed himself one backward glance, but no one was following him. No one seemed to be paying attention to him, which was exactly what he wanted.

He stood aside, allowing a woman with a little boy in tow to precede him down the stairs to the station. He stayed close behind them in hopes that anyone who noticed him would associate him with the grouping. Family man and not a fugitive.

He pulled his Metro card from his wallet as he walked, pushing it against the red light to gain admittance to the platform. He wasn't sure whether or not the authorities would be able to track his use of the card. Even so, the risk seemed preferable to having to slow down to purchase a ticket.

Once through the turnstile, he walked toward the tracks. He paused briefly to verify the route he should take to the train station, peering over the shoulders of a couple who were obviously, by the array of cameras they carried, tourists.

Armed with the information he needed, he moved to the area where the train would arrive. The crowd waiting there seemed light, but then it was earlier than the normal commuter hours.

He took another look at the ramp leading to the platform. A few passengers drifted downward, but none of them appeared to be looking at their fellow passengers.

A couple were talking on cell phones. His training made him suspicious of that kind of activity, wondering if they were making a report or receiving instructions.

As he continued to study them, however, he realized that their eyes were downcast, and they were seemingly oblivious to their surroundings. If they were looking for him—

It was then that he saw them. Two men clattering down the steps, as their eyes searched the crowd. The look of the hunter was unmistakable. It was an aura they carried with them, one of danger and threat.

He quickly pulled his gaze away. As tempting as it was to watch, he deliberately turned his head back toward the track. He could hear the train now, the noise its approach made echoing through the enclosed tunnel, despite the sound-absorbing material of the overhead baffles.

He looked just like every other commuter standing here, Will reminded himself, except for the fact that, in spite of the cold, he was in shirtsleeves. Whether or not the men would notice that would depend on how good they were.

This was, after all, the Metro station nearest the precinct house. It was logical that someone would be sent here to check it out.

They were searching for a man in a green field coat, however. If his luck held—the same luck that had made him glance up at the rooflines—then they would decide this was a wild-goose chase. If not...

If not, then his only hope would be if the train arrived before they reached the platform. Its low rumble had grown to a roar that filled the underground station.

People began to edge forward, shifting toward the tracks. Will moved with them, trying to keep himself in the middle of the small crowd. Too few to hide him, but enough, perhaps, to keep the searchers from looking too closely.

He discovered that the woman with the little boy was again beside him. Unable to stand not knowing what was going on behind him, Will stooped, quickly untying and then retying the child's sneaker.

Peeking through the crowd, he saw that the men in

the overcoats were still standing at the foot of the stairs. They hadn't yet come through the turnstile, but their eyes were scanning the commuters.

Will looked away, in case his gaze might somehow attract their attention and right into the big, blue eyes of the toddler whose shoe he'd just tied. The boy held out his foot, pointing to it.

"What is it?" his mother said. "What's wrong?"

"His shoe was untied," Will explained as he got to his feet. He put his hand on the boy's head, ruffling the fine, blond hair. "It could be dangerous."

"Thanks."

Despite what she'd said, she looked slightly uncomfortable. After a second or two of holding his eyes, she pulled the child against her leg.

"I've got one about that age at home."

Her face relaxed, her mouth opening slightly. "Ah…"

"We can't ever keep his shoes tied. Even with double knots."

"I know."

Although she smiled as she agreed, Will decided he'd pushed this long enough. Maybe it had served its purpose. If the searchers had noticed him at all, he hoped it had been while he was in conversation with the woman.

"Here we go," the woman said.

She reached down to take the boy's hand, shifting the handles of the shopping bags she carried to a position farther up the wrist of the other arm. Hoping it was too late for her to scream for security, in case anyone was watching, Will put his hand on the small of her back, using it to gently propel her forward.

The muscles stiffened under his fingers as she turned to look at him over her shoulder. The child, however, continued to walk toward the opening door, so that she was forced to move with him.

Will followed, allowing a few people to enter between them. He was afraid if he pushed the attempt to appear to be part of the family grouping any more, she would start screaming. Just as he was about to step into the car, shouts came from behind him.

"He's getting on the train."

He made it through the doors, moving away from them as he did. Several people entered behind him, effectively screening him from the men who were now running toward the platform.

There was nothing he could do to make the doors close faster. And nothing he could do to slow down their arrival.

The passengers around him were beginning to notice the commotion. Some pointed, stooping to get a better view out of the wide windows. Some seemed to be looking around the car as if to try to spot the person those two were after.

Guns now drawn, the men in overcoats continued to pelt down the passage from the turnstile to the platform, shoving people out of their way. One raised his weapon, seeming to sight his weapon at the train.

Gasps and screams filled the car as finally—mercifully—the doors began to close. Whether or not the men after him were stupid or vicious enough to fire into a group of innocent people was a question Will couldn't answer, but he wasn't willing to take the chance.

"Get down," he yelled over the pandemonium. "Get down."

Most of them obeyed as the edges of the doors glided together. The men with the guns were almost to the platform, but the train began to move. Those who had been stooping without anything to hold on to were thrown onto the floor, adding to the cacophony.

Will eased up enough to take a final look back as the train pulled out of the station. The men who'd been sent to find him were standing on the platform, guns out, but lowered. They were still panting from the run they'd just made, but this time it seemed the tide had turned.

This time they had been the ones who'd been too late....

CHAPTER SEVENTEEN

"So you think he may be headed here?"

The private investigator Paul had asked to stay with Cait while he took Will to D.C. hadn't bothered to leave the room when the call came through on his cell. She had assumed that meant the conversation wasn't something she shouldn't hear.

Cut off as they were from any news, she was anxious to find out how the surrender had gone this afternoon. Somehow, judging from the P.I.'s response, that wasn't the information he was receiving. Maybe this was someone from the firm verifying that Paul was coming back to the lake house.

"Don't worry about a thing," Douglas Reemer said into his cell. "I understand perfectly."

Short and to the point, Cait thought. From her observations of the investigator, that was the way he operated. He hadn't attempted to make small talk in the time they'd spent together, which was fine with her.

Her mind had been miles away most of the afternoon. Spending it with a strong, silent type had actually been just what she'd needed.

Reemer closed his phone, slipping it back into the case he wore on his belt. The big Beretta he carried was worn in a shoulder holster, so the cell didn't interfere with that.

She waited, expecting him to offer her some condensed version of what the call had been about. Instead, seeming unaware that she might be interested, he picked up the magazine he'd been reading by the light of the lamp at the end of the couch.

That was another change from last night. With Reemer's help and encouragement, Paul had started the generator before he and Will had left this morning. They not only had light, but heat and hot water as well.

She'd actually been on her way to take a shower when the call had come through. Which was why she was now hovering awkwardly in the doorway to the hall.

"Paul's coming back here?"

She found she was unwilling to be kept out of the loop. She was too involved in what was happening on several different levels.

Despite the fact that she hadn't worked for the Secret Service in almost two years, she was unaccustomed to being treated like someone who didn't deserve to be informed about ongoing developments. That was something she could truthfully credit Will with—treating his team as equals, at least as far as keeping them informed. If Paul and Doug Reemer had any intention of keeping her in the dark about what was going on, they needed to rethink their plan.

"He's coming as soon as he can." The P.I. had lowered the magazine, looking at her over the back of the couch.

"Did he say how it went?"

"I'm sorry?"

"The surrender. Did he say how it went?"

The uneasiness she'd felt all afternoon seemed to explode in her gut as Reemer hesitated. She had known something was wrong. Call it woman's intuition. Call it any damn thing you wanted, but she'd known something wasn't right. And now this idiot—

"I'll let Paul explain when he gets here."

"You damn well won't let him explain. Something happened today, didn't it? Something went wrong."

Reemer's lips flattened, but apparently he decided that she wasn't going to be put off with waiting for Paul. "The cops had leaked the arrangements to the media."

It took a second for that to sink in. Another to wonder why that information would make Reemer sound as if he were expecting her to go nuts. That was something they all should probably have been expecting. Paul had told them how much pressure the Metropolitan police were under to make an arrest.

Or maybe Paul *had* been expecting this and hadn't told Will or her. Maybe that's why his firm's investigator was acting so strangely.

"So it turned into a media circus. I hope the bastards enjoyed it."

She wasn't sure which set of bastards she meant. There

were plenty of those to go around. The cops, the press and whoever was responsible for Greg Vincent's death.

"If you're talking about the police, I doubt it."

"Why not? If they're the ones who leaked the story…"

"Because somebody took a couple of shots at our boy."

At our boy…

"At Will? Is that what you're saying? Someone shot at Will?"

As she fired the questions at Reemer, she walked across the room and then around the couch to confront him. His eyes followed her every step of the way. At least he didn't try to pretend he didn't know what had happened.

"From the roof. The cops are denying it was a police sniper, but the news footage clearly shows *someone* up there. Either their security stunk—which is entirely possible—or one of their own got a twitchy trigger finger with the mob scene going on down below or misinterpreted something he saw."

"Was he hit?"

"The client?"

"Will. Was he shot, damn it?"

Reemer looked taken aback by her profanity. "Paul said he didn't see how he wasn't—how neither of them was—but… To answer your question, they're both okay."

Cait remembered to take a breath. The other automatic functions of her body, like her heartbeat, which had seemed to hesitate as she'd waited, began again.

"And so they're coming back here."

That hadn't been a question. She thought that's what the half of the phone conversation she'd heard must have meant. Only when Reemer shook his head did she realize she didn't yet know it all.

"You said Paul was on his way."

"He is, but… I'm sorry. The truth is, he doesn't know where the client is right now."

"Stop calling him that. His name is Will. Will Shannon. He isn't 'the client.'"

He didn't correct her, but he also hadn't told her what she needed to know. She took another breath, this one an attempt to control her anger.

"He doesn't know where Will is? Is that what you're saying? Someone shot at them and neither of them was hit, but Will— What?" she demanded. "What the hell happened?"

"He ran. Paul said as soon as the shots were fired, there was pandemonium. Shannon took the opportunity to escape."

So Will wasn't in police custody. Despite the threat against his life now that he was on the run again, she was glad. Glad he'd changed his mind. Glad that he wasn't trusting himself to those lying bastards.

"That's who you were talking about. Not Paul. Will. They think Will may be headed back here."

"Paul thinks it's a possibility."

"And what exactly was it that you 'understand'? What are you supposed to do if Will *does* come here?"

"Keep him—and you—here until Paul arrives."

"Me?"

"Paul thinks he may try to leave and take you with him."

Because she was his witness. One who could clear him of three of the four murders he'd been accused of. And maybe, just maybe, because after this morning—

She pushed that memory to the back of her mind. Even if what had happened between them was part of the reason Will would come back for her, it wasn't something that she could discuss with anyone else. And it wasn't necessary. They were obviously satisfied with another, less personal agenda as the explanation for Will's actions.

"How long before Paul gets here?"

"He said there were some things relating to the case that he needed to take care of before he left D.C. He wasn't sure how long they would take."

"So maybe tonight."

"It's possible. But more probably tomorrow."

"And he hasn't talked to Will since he ran?"

"I don't think so. Apparently he hasn't called."

"And you're sure he wasn't injured."

"Look, all I'm telling you is what Paul told me. If you want to call him back—" He pulled his phone from the leather case and held it out to her. "Hit Redial."

Maybe he expected her to refuse. Or to be satisfied with the half-loaf of information he'd offered. Obviously, he didn't know her.

She took the cell, studying its configuration a moment before she managed to redial the number Paul had called from. It rang and rang, but nothing happened. Not even a voice-mail message.

After waiting long enough to feel foolish, she folded the phone and held it out to Reemer. "He isn't answering."

"He said he'd be tied up for a while."

"You'd think he could answer his phone."

The P.I. pretended to devote his full attention to re-inserting the cell in its case. When he looked up, he raised his brows, his shoulders lifting in a slight shrug.

"You're welcome to try later."

"Thanks. I will. And if Paul calls again, would you tell him I'd like to speak to him."

"I doubt that will be anytime soon. Considering what he said."

"That's fine. I'll be in the shower. Just yell down the hall."

"You got it," Reemer said, his eyes falling to the magazine he held as if he couldn't wait to get back to it.

What he probably couldn't wait for, Cait decided as she retraced the path she'd taken around the couch, was to stop having to deal with her. But if she hadn't pushed the issue, she had the feeling that he wouldn't have told her any of what Paul had said.

If Will was headed this way, that was something she needed to know. And despite Paul's instructions about keeping him here, she doubted Reemer was capable of doing that.

Paul had had his chance to put Will in the hands of the authorities, and they had blown it. She didn't believe they'd get another.

Stupid bastards, she thought again as she closed and locked the bathroom door behind her. She expelled a long breath, trying to relieve the day's tensions, which had multiplied in the last few minutes.

She stepped over to the mirror above the lavatory. The effects of the last few days were etched in her face. Too little sleep. Too little real food. And way too much stress. None of which were likely to change any time soon.

And until Will got here...

She shook her head, watching the movement of the woman in the mirror. Will coming here wasn't something she should bank on. Paul could very well be wrong.

After all, she herself had advised Will to disappear. To just leave the country. Maybe, after today's fiasco, that's what he'd decided to do.

The long, hot shower she'd been anticipating fifteen minutes ago no longer held the same allure. It had been a couple of days since she'd had the opportunity for more than a quick wash in cold water, however. There was no reason not to take advantage of the heated water. Especially since she couldn't know what tomorrow would bring.

She gathered her hair in one hand, twisting it into a loose knot at the top of her head. She might regret not shampooing it, but it would take so long to dry without a blower that she decided not to chance it. She wanted to be dressed and ready just in case.

She stripped off the jeans and sweatshirt, letting them fall to the floor. Seeing them there evoked memories of this morning. And if the sniper in Washington had succeeded, those would be all she would have had left.

She stood in the center of the room, giving herself permission to remember. Allowing the images and the sensations of their lovemaking to flood her consciousness.

The slight masculine roughness of Will's hands sliding down her spine. His mouth teasing her nipples. His body straining above hers, driving into the center of her soul, leaving no room there for doubt that what they were doing was right.

Thinking about those moments was enough to create a sweet, hot flood of desire in her lower body. Her hands cupped over her breasts. Between them, underneath the tips of her fingers, she could feel the beating of her heart. Her head fell back as she closed her eyes, reliving those seconds of fulfillment.

Then slowly, reluctantly, she gathered the scattered remnants of her willpower. She lowered her head, opening her eyes to the present. Will wasn't here, and she had no way of knowing if he would return. All she could do was to be prepared if he did.

On legs that trembled, she walked over to the shower stall and turned on the water, putting her hand under it to test for warmth. Almost immediately it was hot enough to be slightly uncomfortable. She turned on a little cold, again testing the temperature before she stepped inside the enclosure.

She allowed the stream of water to flow down the front of her body before she turned so that it would strike between her shoulder blades. Although she had intended to bathe quickly so that there would be enough heated water for Reemer to shower if he wanted, its cascade down her spine changed her mind. She could feel the tension melting away.

After several minutes, she unwrapped the small bar of guest soap she found on the shelf and began to lather. She didn't linger over the process and was soon turning again under the flow of water, this time to rinse off the soap.

A sound she couldn't identify, but one that was loud enough to be heard over the shower, brought her head up. It had come from somewhere in the front of the house.

A door closing, signifying someone's arrival? If so…

Despite the fact that she hadn't completely removed all the lather, she reached out, shutting off the hot water. She wasn't quick enough in turning the knob on the cold to keep from receiving the shock of an icy deluge.

As soon as both spigots were off, she listened, shivering in the suddenly chill air of the enclosure. There were no sounds from the rest of the house. Certainly none that echoed whatever it was she'd heard before.

She debated turning the water back on, but there was something about the continued silence that bothered her. If someone had come in, whether Paul or Will, surely they'd be talking to the private investigator. If they were in the den where Reemer had been sitting, she should be able to hear their voices.

If Paul and the P.I. had gone outside to talk, that would mean that the lawyer didn't want her to know what he was saying. With that thought, her heart rate accelerated.

She threw back the shower curtain and stepped out onto the mat. She opened the utility cabinet and pulled out one of the bath towels stacked there, all the time listening for noises outside the bathroom.

She dried off quickly, discarding the notion of putting on the nightshirt she'd brought into the room. Without bothering with her undergarments, which would be difficult to pull on her damp body, she slipped on the jeans she'd dropped on the floor and then pulled the sweatshirt over her head. She didn't want to take the time to put on her shoes, so she stepped across the bathroom barefoot.

Maybe she'd been mistaken in thinking someone had come in. Maybe what she'd heard had been Reemer going out for wood. She couldn't remember how much had been stacked beside the fireplace, but she knew that he planned to keep the fire going all night despite the heat provided by the generator. Deciding that, whatever she'd heard, she was probably making a mountain out of a molehill, she opened the door.

When she'd left the den to go into the bathroom, the lamp the P.I. had been reading by had provided sufficient light to illuminate the hallway. Now only the light coming from behind her shone down its length. The room beyond was dark.

Where the hell was Reemer? It was too early for him to turn in. And if he'd gone out for wood, why would he have turned out the light in the den?

Thankfully, she had controlled her initial instinct, which had been to call out the investigator's name. Instead, she slipped through the doorway of the bathroom and, keeping her back against the wall, sidestepped her way into the bedroom where she'd moved her suitcase this afternoon. She had put Will's weapon on the bedside table there. Maybe she was overreacting, but she'd feel better if it were in her hand instead.

Because of the angle, the light from the bathroom didn't reach into the interior. She could see well enough to skirt the bed with its light-colored coverlet. Operating almost entirely by feel, she located the nightstand, drawing a breath of relief when her searching fingers touched the cold metal of the gun.

As she lifted it, there was a flash of déjà vu. She had felt exactly this same sense of relief on picking up her own SIG-Sauer the morning Will had shown up at her house.

Will.

There was no need for the panic that had driven her to the gun. She had known since Paul's call that Will could be on his way. Maybe Reemer had heard him arriving and had gone out to investigate. That would explain why he'd turned off the light in the den. He wouldn't have wanted to be silhouetted against it if he opened the back door.

Whatever was going on, she decided, turning and

holding the weapon out in front of her, she felt better equipped to figure it out with Will's gun in her hand. She crossed the bedroom toward the hall, pausing in the doorway to listen. The house was so still she could hear the faint crackle of the fire.

She blew out the breath she'd been holding in an attempt to calm her nerves. Then she put her left hand under the right, steadying the gun as she stepped across the threshold.

The floor was cold under her feet, reminding her once more of the journey she'd taken through the predawn darkness of her own house. Only three days ago, she realized. It seemed like a lifetime.

She advanced down the hallway until she could see a portion of the den. The flickering firelight cast shadows that made it difficult to recognize furnishings that should be familiar by now.

It was as if she were staring into a room she'd never seen before. And there was no sign of the P.I. in the part of it she could see.

She glanced back down the hallway, straight into the bathroom. Despite the time it had taken to retrieve the gun, a hint of steam still floated in the glow from the fluorescent bulb.

Having verified that her back was clear, she took another step toward the den, extending the weapon she held in front of her. Still no sign of Reemer.

Another step and she could see the fire. Despite her original idea that the noise she'd heard might be related to a replenishing of the wood supply, the flames were low, indicating that nothing had been added since she'd left the room fifteen minutes ago.

She stepped through the doorway and into the den. As she did, her gaze swept the room, tracked by the weapon she held. The room was empty and silent, except for the sounds emanating from the dying fire.

She straightened, coming out of the shooter's stance. Having verified that the P.I. wasn't in the den, she was faced with a choice. To her left lay the living and dining rooms and the front entrance. To her right were the kitchen and the back door. Given her theory about why Reemer may have cut off the light, that was the more logical area to search.

Decision made, she edged toward the right, again keeping the wall behind her until she reached the entrance to the kitchen. Cut off from even the firelight, the room was dark and cold and threatening.

She made the same careful scan of it she'd made on entering the den. And with the same result. Wherever Reemer was, it wasn't here.

She headed to the back door, her heart pounding in her throat. She could have locked herself in the back bedroom or the bath and stayed there with the big SIG-Sauer pointed at the door. It was what most people would have done. *Sane* people.

Somehow she couldn't do that. Not with the knowledge that someone's life might hang in the balance.

She had reached the back door. If Reemer had come

this way, then whatever had happened to him must have happened when he'd stepped outside.

Or maybe nothing had happened. Maybe she'd worked herself up for no reason. Maybe neither Paul nor Will had warned him about the back door. Maybe he'd let it close behind him, locking himself on the outside.

She reached out with her left hand, her fingers closing around the knob. It was cold to the touch. And what lay beyond it…

She turned it, easing the door open as the latch released. Pale moonlight illuminated the steps that led down to the ground.

At the bottom of them, Douglas Reemer lay. There was a dusting of snow on his dark jacket and pants. His face was turned away, as if he were looking out on the lake and the trees.

Her eyes lifted to trace across that landscape. Nothing moved in the stillness. Nothing disturbed the silent sweep of flakes drifting downward.

Maybe he'd fallen, she told herself. Or suffered a heart attack. Maybe this had nothing to do with the murders that had brought her and Will to this desolate place.

Despite his stillness, she couldn't know if Reemer was unconscious rather than dead. Why assume the worst?

Because of everything else that has happened during the last three days.

Ignoring the answer her logic had provided, she stooped, picking up a log off the stack. She put it against the jamb to keep the door from closing and then, her gaze and gun simultaneously sweeping the area around her, she moved down the steps.

She crouched when she reached the bottom, laying her fingers against the P.I.'s neck. And knew the explanations she'd posed for the lies they were.

Any doubt she might have had about what had happened to him disappeared as she leaned forward, trying to see his face in the spill of moonlight. The dark, precisely placed hole in the middle of his forehead eliminated all possibility of a heart attack or an accident.

Douglas Reemer had been shot. And whoever had killed him was still somewhere out there, waiting in the darkness.

CHAPTER EIGHTEEN

AFTER SHE'D CLOSED the back door, throwing the dead bolt that had been installed above the regular lock, Cait leaned against it, trying to deal with what she'd just discovered. The man who was supposed to protect her had been murdered and she was alone in the wilderness with his killers.

In her shock, she hadn't even thought about turning the body over to search for his weapon. Stupid. So frigging *stupid,* she berated herself.

She could always open the door and go out there again. No one had shot at her. No one had attacked her. Not this time.

Maybe that was because she'd caught them by surprise. They had probably figured she wouldn't come to look for Reemer. Not this soon.

Did that mean that they were even now making their way to the front of the house? Trying to find an easier means of access than the solid wood door she was leaning against.

She didn't even know if the windows were locked. She assumed someone, either Will or the P.I., had at some time checked them, but she certainly hadn't.

Although she thought about doing that now, she decided it would be smarter to pick an area in the interior to retreat to, some place she had a reasonable chance of being able to defend herself, and check only the windows there.

She had to assume they knew she was here alone. And she should also assume that they would get into the house. They could break a window or, if they were determined enough, knock down the door. Unless...

Paul or Will would have given Reemer the key before they'd left. It had probably been in his pocket when he'd gone out to investigate.

Her throat ached with the enormity of the admissions she'd just made. She was alone. Whoever had murdered Douglas Reemer had come here to kill her. And more than likely they had the key to the front door.

Expect the unexpected and then deal with it. That was the essence of what she'd been trained to do.

She had already wasted too much time by letting her fear control her. She pushed away from the door, bringing her weapon back into firing position.

Ideally she needed a room with one entrance. Make them come through it in order to get to her. The only place she could think of that fit that criteria—

She'd already started moving toward the windowless bathroom when she heard some sound from the front of the house. This time she didn't stop to try to figure out what it was.

She ran back along the route she'd taken minutes before. Through the kitchen and into the den, dimly lit by the dying fire. Then a turn and back down the hall toward the light she'd left on in the bath.

She eased the door closed and turned its lock, the kind that could be opened with a credit card, before she reached out to flick off the light. As darkness surrounded her, the fear she'd fought in the kitchen returned with a vengeance.

She wanted to put her forehead against the door and give in to it. She backed away instead, bringing the SIG-Sauer up, left hand automatically slipping under the trembling right.

Just as the weight of the weapon had comforted her, the effect of bringing it into position provided some semblance of resolve. She could do this. All the hours she'd spent at the range during the last few weeks were proof that, despite her injuries, she was still capable of defending herself.

That was all she had wanted when she'd begun going there. Now she had a chance to prove that she'd been successful.

A chance...

One clip. Fifteen rounds.

The sounds that had come from the front of the house had stopped, which wasn't comforting. They were probably already inside. And since she could think of only one thing they wanted here...

She concentrated on not allowing the fear that had paralyzed her to build again, knowing panic would

make her forget the practiced sequence. Just like shooting at a paper target, she told herself, keeping the familiar outline of the human shape firmly in her mind's eye.
Aim for the widest part to give yourself the best chance
of putting your shots into the kill zone.

She could hear them in the hallway now. There was
no one sound that was distinguishable. The noises
were more like the rustle of rats in a wall. Subtle and
terrifying.

She resisted the urge to take another breath. As flooded
with adrenaline as her system was, too much oxygen
would make her light-headed. What she needed now—

Someone pushed against the door, causing it to tremble in the frame. The impact of a shoulder against its
solid wood.

Her eyes strained to see through the darkness, expecting it to burst open at any second. If they were smart
enough to flip the switch out there at the same time,
she'd be blinded by the influx of light.

Instead of trying to force the door, however, they did
the unexpected. It seemed that she felt the rush of the
first bullet, which struck the wallboard behind her, at the
same time she heard the sound of the shot.

She ducked reflexively and then squeezed as much
of her body as she could into the space between the wall
and the toilet. Once there, she turned so that she was
again facing the door.

The sound of gunfire echoed and re-echoed in the enclosed room. The hint of soap that had been left in the

air from her shower was replaced by the unmistakable smell of cordite wafting in from the hallway.

She resisted the urge to put her hands over her ears and close her eyes. She held her weapon aimed at the door instead, her forearms resting on the closed seat of the john, her cheek against the cold porcelain of its tank.

Her eyes had adjusted to the darkness enough that she thought she could distinguish the outline of the white door. Something of the right size and shape interrupted the continuity of the line of dark blue trim, which topped the ceramic tiles running halfway up the wall. All she had to do was to focus on that and at the first sign of movement, squeeze the trigger.

As she mentally reiterated the sequence, the hail of bullets stopped. The silence was eerie after the barrage, more terrifying than the noise.

She imagined them standing outside, one with his ear pressed against the door. Expecting moans? A surrender?

If so, you're in for a disappointment.

More scurrying. She held her breath, listening intently.

When the attack came, however, she was shocked, both by its speed and suddenness. One of them kicked the door, hitting it hard enough to jar the flimsy lock out of the latch. It crashed open, striking the wall.

Two or three bodies filled the opening. With the lack of light it was impossible to be sure.

Instead of the neat outline she'd targeted at the range, a mass surged into the room. Without her conscious volition, her finger closed over the trigger. Somehow she managed to squeeze off the first shot without allowing the weapon to jerk out of alignment.

The second was easier, reflex taking over as she continued to shoot round after round. Although the entire sequence could have occupied no more than seconds, time stood still.

She was conscious of each separate movement of her finger. Of each inch of forward motion by her assailants. Of the upward track her weapon made as they drew closer and closer to where she cowered.

The tank beside her head shattered, struck by return fire, which she'd been oblivious to. Water, smelling faintly of antifreeze, gushed outward from the crack in the porcelain, drenching her left shoulder and breast. Ignoring the icy shock of it, she continued to fire at the shadowy forms rushing in slow motion across the room.

At some point she knew only one attacker remained. Then, almost before she could digest that information, he was on her. Her last shot was fired with her weapon pointed almost straight up as he lunged at her over the seat of the commode.

He landed on top of it and of her, seeming to shut off all the light and air from the room. Although he was draped over the SIG-Sauer, she pulled the trigger one more time. Given their positions, she couldn't miss.

As the sound of that shot died away, the same unnerving silence that had fallen just before they'd broken down the door filled the room. All she knew for sure was that, against all odds, she was alive.

She held her breath, listening for someone else's breathing. There was nothing.

Something wet and warm fell on her cheek. She tried to pull her head back to escape whatever it was, but she was trapped in the cramped space where she'd taken refuge by the body of the man lying above her.

She began to believe, as impossible as it seemed, that she must be the only one who'd survived. The thought of surviving, only to be unable to get out from under the corpse of the man she'd killed, panicked her.

She wanted out of here. If there was *someone* else in the hall, she'd deal with them. Right now—

She tried to push up, using her left forearm, which was resting on top of the closed seat of the toilet, for leverage. Although she also bent her head, putting it under what she believed to be the man's shoulder, she couldn't budge the dead weight.

Her breath sobbed in and out as she struggled. She had never before understood the horror of claustrophobia. After this, she would never disparage anyone for their fears. Not now that she knew…

She tried to bring her knees up so she could get her feet under her to bring the muscles of her lower body into play. The space she was caught in was too confining to allow her to do that.

Again, panic ballooned in her chest. She wanted out. No matter what else might happen, she couldn't stand another second of—

As before, everything seemed to happen at once. There was a flicker from the overhead light. She looked up and glimpsed the face of the dead man.

Glimpsed because almost as soon as the fluorescent buzzed on, his body was dragged away. As it slid off the toilet and onto the floor, she brought her weapon up, her finger already closing over the trigger as she squinted into the flood of light. It formed a halo around the still-dark figure looming above her.

"It's me, Cait."

Although she still couldn't see Will's features, she recognized his voice. Her hands, however, couldn't seem to release their grip on the semiautomatic.

He reached out and put his hand over the barrel, pushing the weapon to the side. "It's over."

"They're dead? Are you sure they're dead?"

She could make out his features now, although the overhead still created an aureole around his head. She couldn't identify the emotion in his eyes. It was nothing she'd ever seen there before, not even on the morning he'd shown up at her back door.

Whatever was in them frightened her, and she couldn't imagine why. They were both alive.

"What's wrong?"

Again she tried to rise, using leverage from her left arm to push herself to her knees. At the same time Will stooped, so that they were at eye level.

"Don't try to move."

"What is it?"

Instead of answering, he began to push aside the neck of the sweatshirt she'd pulled on over her still-damp body. Although she didn't understand why, she didn't question what he was doing.

It was as if she no longer had the will or the strength to resist. Weakness washed over her. It was over. And they were both safe, she told herself again.

At least she had believed they were. If she could only figure out why Will was acting so strangely...

"What's wrong?" she asked again.

She released the gun, letting it fall from her hand onto the closed lid. She caught his fingers, which were still pulling the neck of her shirt down.

"What are you doing? You're scaring me, Will."

"I'm trying to find out where you're hurt."

...where you're hurt...

She wasn't hurt. She would have known if she'd taken a bullet. Even as badly injured as she'd been that day two years ago, she'd known she had been shot.

She'd been aware of the rush of cold water when the tank had broken. She had felt the blood that had dripped down on her from the man she'd killed—

She looked down to where Will's hands were still working. The front of her sweatshirt was covered with blood.

"It's not mine."

His fingers continued their task, pushing aside the fabric in an effort to find the wound and staunch the flow of blood. She put her hand over his, holding it.

"It's not mine, Will. It's his. I wasn't hit."

His eyes came up, searching hers to verify what she'd said.

"I'm okay. I swear. Just— Just get me out of here."

She saw the realization that she was telling the truth form in his eyes. Then, before she could protest, he reached down and gripped her right arm above the elbow, using it to pull her to her feet.

Damaged nerves and muscles screamed. Her vocalization of that agony was more subdued, but apparently it was enough to make Will aware of what he was doing. He completed the process he'd begun by taking her left arm.

As soon as she was standing, he retrieved the SIG-Sauer from the seat of the toilet. Despite her trust in his skills, she felt a little bereft without the weapon. After all, she'd acquitted herself well enough.

Damn straight.

For the first time, she looked across the commode and at the man that had fallen over it. And then at the second body sprawled on the white tile floor, a pool of blood seeping from under his out-flung arm.

There had only been two of them and not the half dozen it had seemed. Still, given the hail of bullets...

She shivered, aware again of how remarkable it was that she was the one standing. The one unscathed.

"Come on."

She looked up, finding an answering incredulity in Will's face. They had both survived. Against all odds.

"Where?"

"I don't know yet. All I know is that this place is no longer safe."

Because whoever was after him had made the connection. The process had probably started as soon as he and Paul had shown up at the police station. Or maybe, given the leak to the media, even before. Once they'd had Paul's name—

"Reemer said Paul was coming back here."

"I think Reemer's dead, Cait."

"I know. I saw him. That's how I knew they were here."

His free hand against the small of her back, Will directed her past the second body and through the open doorway into the hall. "You need shoes and something besides that." He nodded toward the bloody sweatshirt.

He waited in the doorway of the darkened bedroom while she slipped on her shoes. She dragged the wet shirt over her head, wiping at the moisture it had left on her skin with a shirt she took from her suitcase. Dropping that on the bed, she slipped into the cardigan Will had packed, buttoning it as she walked toward the door.

"How'd you get here?" she asked as Will moved to allow her to step into the hall.

"I stole a car. By now it's been reported. And so has yours, by the way."

"Reemer has a car." *Had* a car, she corrected mentally. "The keys may still be in his pocket, but—"

"What?"

"I think they searched him. Paul gave him the key to the front. I think that's how they got in."

"They'd have no reason to take the car keys."

They had reached the den, and Will headed toward the front of the house. As she hesitated, resisting the urging of his hand, he glanced back at her.

"He's out back. They got him when he went out to investigate. The door closed behind him."

Without answering, Will changed directions, heading toward the kitchen. It was the same journey she'd made only minutes before, but despite the fact that neither of them could be certain the danger was over, there was none of that sense of threat she'd felt before.

She had no idea where Will intended to take her, but she trusted him to make that decision. The ones he'd made for himself had so far been infinitely superior to those that had been made for him.

CHAPTER NINETEEN

"REEMER'S DEAD, and they almost got to Cait. You can forget any idea you might have of giving them another chance."

Will had again stopped to call Paul from a roadside booth. This time he'd chosen one where he could stay in the car and talk.

He had pulled the investigator's SUV into a position that would allow him to watch the cars that passed on the narrow two-lane. Traffic had been almost nonexistent, as it had been since they'd left the summerhouse, attributable to both the rural location and the fact that it was night.

"I found your guy," Paul said.

His mind on the carnage they'd left behind, it took a second for that to sink in. "The guy from the restaurant?"

Although he'd pointed the man out to Paul, he'd never expected Paul would be able to track him down in that crowd. Especially with the chaos when the sniper had opened fire.

"Except he has nothing to do with the restaurant."

He could hear the undercurrent of excitement in

Paul's voice. It was a tone from their childhood, when his friend had information he intended to make Will work for, but he was too tired for that kind of guessing game tonight.

"What the hell does that mean?"

"That he used to work for Vincent."

"For Greg?"

Given the guy's appearance, Will had a hard time fitting him into the narrow framework of the millionaire's world. Not unless he'd worked for Greg in some menial role.

"Actually, for his brother," Paul said.

For Ron Vincent? That seemed stranger still. "As what?"

"As a pharmaceutical researcher."

Paul's voice again indicated that the information was key. For the life of him, Will couldn't figure out why. "So?"

"So Ron Vincent fired him."

Will still wasn't making whatever connection Paul intended him to make. If the guy was a disgruntled employee who'd been let go by Ron, what connection did he have with Greg's murder?

"Does this have something to do with the patent challenge?"

"Only if you consider what the simultaneous loss of two of its top three profit-producing drugs would do to Vincent's stocks."

The loss of two of the top three... The HIV drug

would certainly be one of those. That's why Greg had fought against the patent challenge, despite the cost in legal fees and the hit the company's reputation had taken. Even with that battle, given just the threat of a cheaper replacement for it, Vincent's stock had taken a nosedive. If there was another, similar disaster on the horizon...

"Are you saying Vincent was facing another patent fight?"

"Something worse. At least according to our new mutual friend. Something that had the potential to take the company under."

"And that second threat has something to do with Greg's murder?"

"According to our source, it was the cause of it."

"Where is he?"

If the man from the flashback could provide an explanation for the murder, Will's life depended as much on his staying alive as it did on Cait's survival. And the people behind all this would be just as determined to take him out as they had been to get rid of her.

"He's here with me. And don't worry. Nobody knows I've found him."

The same reassurance Paul had made about leaving Cait at the summerhouse. Will had reluctantly gone along with it then because he trusted his friend. He wasn't buying it this time.

"Where are you?" he asked.

"Headed your way."

"Then we need a change of plan."

"Your call."

There was no other convenient "safe" house. Not that Will could think of. Maybe that was just as well, considering his track record with them since this had begun.

In spite of that, he was hesitant to name a specific location. His pursuers had so far been too good, or too lucky, in figuring out where he would go next. His paranoia now extended to the possibility that Paul's cell might be bugged. Far-fetched in normal circumstances, but these were anything but.

"You remember Darryl Craven?"

"Yeah. What about him?" Skepticism had replaced the excitement in Paul's voice.

"You remember where he was from?"

The small Virginia town of McGoo had evoked its share of laughter, especially at the upscale prep school they'd all attended. He was betting Paul would remember some of those sophomoric jokes they'd made.

"You want me to—"

"You remember Darryl's favorite pastime while he was there?" Will had deliberately broken in before Paul could complete the question.

There were a few seconds of silence. Will held his breath, hoping he wouldn't have to be more specific.

"How long before you'll arrive?" the lawyer asked.

"Less than an hour."

"Find something to do for an additional thirty minutes or so. I'll see you then."

The connection was broken before Will had time to agree. Apparently Paul's memory was as good as it had ever been. All that remained now was to meet with the witness his friend had found to determine if Paul was still as smart.

DELAYED REACTION had set in. Cait couldn't stop shivering as she huddled in the passenger seat of the P.I.'s car. That had a lot to do with the cold outside, but at least a part of what caused the periodic tremors had to do with the night-mare images of what had happened back at the summer-house. She couldn't seem to get them out of her head.

Will's preoccupied silence after he'd talked to Paul hadn't helped her to put the memory of the men she'd shot behind her. She wasn't sure what she had expected him to say that would do that. She wasn't sure there was anything he *could* say that would put those deaths into a different perspective.

And that was not his job, she reminded herself. Just as if she had been forced to shoot someone during the course of a security detail, she had fired her weapon in self-defense. This time the life she'd been defending had been her own, but that didn't change the morality of it.

She couldn't rationalize her need for Will to help her deal with the trauma. She just wanted him to. Just as he'd helped others get through the difficult times that were sometimes necessitated by their job.

He hadn't done that tonight. Other than what he'd said in the immediate aftermath of the attack, he'd hardly spoken two words since he'd guided her out of that gory bathroom.

"Are you sure Paul understood where you wanted to meet?"

Her question was more an attempt to destroy the oppressive silence than to solicit information. Will had told her that Paul had located the man from his flashback, but she'd been too caught up in what had happened at the summerhouse to contemplate something that seemed tangential to what was going on.

"He knows."

She could have pressed the point. Instead, with a mental acknowledgment of the terseness of Will's reply, she wrapped her arms around her body, trying to draw some warmth from its heat.

"I'm sorry."

She looked up to find Will had turned from his contemplation of the front windshield to face her. The light from the streetlamp outside the entrance to the high-school football stadium where they were waiting illuminated his features. The natural leanness of his cheeks had deepened in the last three days, making them almost gaunt. It was as if he'd aged years in that very short period of time.

"For what?" Maybe he'd finally realized how much she needed some reassurance that she'd done the right thing.

"I should never have gotten you involved in this."

She acknowledged the truth of that, especially after what she'd gone through tonight. Despite those horrific events, however, she knew that if she had been given a choice between having to endure them and not having Will back in her life, she would have chosen the former.

"We were partners," she said.

And we were lovers. They were again. Both of those.

"That didn't give me the right—"

He stopped, straightening in the seat. His gaze was no longer focused on her, Cait realized. He was looking out into the darkness through the window behind her.

She turned, watching the headlights grow larger and larger as the vehicle he'd spotted approached. When she looked back at him, Will was removing the SIG-Sauer from where he'd placed it on the console between them.

Weapon in hand, he waited, intent on the car that was now pulling into the parking lot. It crossed the asphalt toward them and was guided into a position parallel to theirs. Only when it stopped beside them was Cait able to identify the vehicle as the black Lexus in which Paul and Will had driven off this morning.

After a moment, the driver's side door opened. The interior light revealed two occupants—Paul and someone who matched the description of the man in Will's flashback.

In response to their arrival, Will opened his door. As he stepped out of the car, he bent and directed a command at her, "Stay here."

Unwilling to be left alone, and even more unwilling to be out of the loop on whatever Paul had discovered, Cait ignored him. As soon as she'd closed her door behind her, the cold struck her like a knife, cutting through her sweater and jeans.

Despite Will's order, neither he nor Paul seemed surprised to find her standing beside them. The lawyer's passenger had not yet exited the car.

"There might be a problem," Paul said, his voice low. *So that the man sitting in the Lexus couldn't hear?*

"What kind of problem?" Will's question expressed the same sudden trepidation she felt.

If the man Paul had brought with him wasn't what they'd all hoped, then Will's options were the same as they'd been this morning. He could again attempt to turn himself in, if not to the Metropolitan police, perhaps to the locals. Or he could do what she had urged him to before. He could run.

"The reason he was in the alley that night," Paul said. "The same reason that kept him from being able to get an appointment with Greg Vincent to tell him what he knew before it was too late."

Before it was too late for the millionaire? Cait held her breath, waiting for Will to ask the questions that would clarify for them both what that reason might be.

"You said he'd worked for the company. So why wouldn't he have been able to get in to see Greg?"

"I told you he'd been dismissed."

"You told me Ron Vincent had fired him."

"Yeah, well, not without reason, apparently."

"What kind of reason?"

"Stewart Espy had a psychotic break two months ago."

"A psychotic break? What the hell does that mean?"

"It means he was hospitalized."

"Hospitalized?"

"He was committed to a psychiatric ward because, according to his doctors, he'd lost touch with reality."

"THE INITIAL TRIALS indicated there were problems, but Vincent knew there were competitive products on the horizon. The key was getting Romoxidin on the market first, accompanied by an aggressive advertising campaign, of course. That was something he excelled at."

Driven inside by the cold and the need to evaluate Espy's story where they could see him as he told it, they had taken a chance on the twenty-four-hour coffee shop in the town square. Will had chosen a booth that looked out on the parking lot, but so far there had been no traffic.

Only a couple of the other tables were occupied. And none of the customers seated at them seemed to be paying any attention to the group. Cait had quickly decided that even if they did, the trade-off for light and heat was worth enduring their curiosity.

"You're talking about Ron?" Will asked, attempting to clarify which Vincent their "witness" was describing.

"Yeah," Dr. Stewart Espy agreed, taking a sip of his coffee. He held the white ceramic cup cradled between his palms. The liquid it contained occasionally sloshed over the sides as his hands trembled.

"So…you're saying they put the drug on the market *knowing* there were problems with it?" Cait asked.

The dark eyes above those sunken, bewhiskered cheeks focused on her face. "You think that's unusual?"

"Isn't it?"

"There are always side effects. That's why those miles of fine print appear on the label."

"But the problems with this drug were beyond the norm?" Paul prodded.

"People were dying."

"The drug *killed* people?" Will asked. "And Vincent *knew* it?"

"He knew because I told him. We all told him. The dangers were apparent almost from the beginning."

"Then he had to know they would eventually come out," Cait said.

"He thought it was worth the risk. After all, it might be years before anyone figured out what was going on." Espy's bitterness was apparent.

"How could it take years? If the drug was having adverse side effects—"

"The people Romoxidin was developed to treat were very ill to begin with. Vincent knew their deaths would be blamed on other factors. At least in the beginning."

Espy set the cup down on the table with the same careful attention he'd devoted to holding it steady. He put his hand over the breast pocket of his shirt as if he were searching it for cigarettes.

"What kinds of things?"

Espy had been feeling the outside pocket of the battered knapsack he had insisted on bringing into the restaurant from the car. Cait suspected that if, as it appeared, he'd been living on the streets, the bag might contain everything he now owned.

His dark, bloodshot eyes had come up at Will's question. "Depression."

"Depression?"

"That's what Romoxidin was prescribed for, so it was easy enough to hide those deaths."

"I don't understand." She didn't. What did any of this have to do with Greg Vincent's murder? "You said the people who took this drug were already seriously ill. Depression doesn't kill people."

"If they commit suicide it does."

"Depressed people sometimes commit suicide," Will said carefully.

"Not in the numbers they did when they were taking Romoxidin," Espy said.

None of them commented for a moment, trying to figure out the logic behind what they'd just been told. Finally Will leaned forward, his forearms resting on the table as he bent to peer into Espy's eyes.

"But if they were, as you said, already 'very ill,' then doesn't it seem likely that some of them *would* commit suicide?"

"That's the argument they used. That the suicides were the result of the depression."

"You believe they weren't?" Will asked.

"Not in that number. The double-blind trials demonstrated the effect quite clearly. We did several of them, actually, because we couldn't believe what we were seeing. Romoxidin was supposed to be some kind of miracle. Most patients reported an almost immediate response to it, especially in contrast to SSRIs, which can take up to several weeks to make a difference in mood and outlook."

"If there was such a positive response, then how did the suicides come into play?"

"We didn't know. And we couldn't figure it out. I worked on that drug. Believe me, I wanted it to do what it had promised in the lab. For a while it would. They got better, a lot better and rather quickly, and then..." Espy hesitated, his eyes lifting to look through the plate-glass window and onto the empty parking lot. "And then they killed themselves. In far greater numbers than the subjects who were taking any other SNRIs, which is the class of antidepressant Romoxidin is."

Cait had known what SSRIs were. She had taken an antidepressant in that class for a time after the extent of her injury and the accompanying disabilities had finally hit her. The drug had helped her to put things into perspective, such as how grateful she was to still be alive, but she knew from the things she'd read that wasn't always the case.

"Severely depressed people kill themselves," Cait said softly. "It happens all the time. Maybe—"

"They argued that the drug relieved the inertia, the inability to act, that's a common symptom of deep depression. They said it allowed the patients to develop the strength of will to carry out their *original* intent, which was to end their lives. Something they hadn't been able to achieve while they were so sick."

"But you don't believe that's what happened?" Will's question had been as soft as hers.

"I wish I could. Romoxidin was my polio vaccine, Mr. Shannon. My triumph. I wish I could believe that what caused those people to do what they did had anything at all to do with an improvement in their depression. It didn't. And that was evident from the trials. Mr. Vincent, however, preferred the other explanation. And there was a great deal in the literature that seemed to back up that hypothesis."

"You yourself believed that those suicides were caused by some other effect of the drug?"

Espy turned to look at her, his cup halfway on that perilous journey to his lips. "A few months after that aggressive advertising campaign kicked into high gear, the anecdotal evidence started to come in. It backed up what we'd seen in the double blinds."

"And yet the company still denied what was happening?"

"Vincent filed the letters away, just as they had the questions and concerns we'd expressed from early on in the trials."

"If this is all true, then surely *someone* put it together."

Paul obviously meant someone other than the man sitting before them. If this witness represented their best hope of getting Will off the hook for those murders, then that hope appeared to be as fragile as the man himself.

"No one *could* put it together. Not unless they'd seen the documentation, both from the trials *and* the letters. There were dozens of those. From doctors. Psychiatrists. Counselors. Even bereaved family members."

"And they all blamed Romoxidin."

"They all made the same connection. There had been little threat of suicide until the victims reached a certain point in their treatment. And it was always the *same* point. That isn't the kind of thing that happens by chance."

"You're saying that when they got enough of the drug into their systems," Will attempted to clarify, "it triggered something that made them want to kill themselves."

"I'm saying that when the drug reached a certain pharmacological level, something went wrong. People suffering from depression attempt suicide, but not in the numbers we saw in the patients who had taken Romoxidin for a period of at least six months."

"And you're also saying that the company knew about this phenomenon and kept it to themselves."

"If they'd admitted it, they would have had to pull Romoxidin from the market. That was something they couldn't afford to do. Not while they were fighting the patent challenge. It would have been the death knell for the stock. And for the company, of course."

"So they just put all the documentation of all you're saying went on into a file and ignored it?" Cait asked, finally realizing the magnitude of what Vincent had done.

"Oh, they did more than that, Ms. Malone," Espy

said, his voice for almost the first time filled with emotion. "They silenced those of us who knew and attempted to tell the truth."

There was an evangelical fervor about the statement, both in the wording and in the tone. Cait looked up and saw the same unease she'd felt on hearing it reflected in Will's eyes.

According to Paul, Espy had been hospitalized because he'd had a psychotic episode. Was it possible the conspiracy he believed he had discovered to keep a questionable drug on the market was simply the figment of a disordered mind?

"How?"

Will's demand brought Espy's attention back to him. He held Will's gaze a moment, before he lowered his head, taking another sip of coffee.

"Dr. Espy? I asked you a question."

"How did they silence us? Is that what you want to know?"

"If I'm right, then the people who murdered Greg Vincent have killed at least four people. I'm asking why they didn't kill you."

"They've tried. Not at first, of course. At first they simply ignored us. And without access to the necessary documentation…" Espy shrugged.

"What do you mean 'without access'? I thought you'd seen the letters you mentioned?"

"I have. At first, they treated them just as they would have treated those kinds of letters at any other time.

Then, when they realized how many there were, and when those of us who had worked on the trials directed their attention to the commonality…"

"What did they do?" Paul asked when the scientist seemed to have run down.

"They took the files away. They never intended for anyone else to see them."

"But if the fact that they existed was common knowledge—"

"It wasn't. Only to those of us who had helped develop the drug. And we were employees. We were told to forget what we'd read. We were told that Romoxidin was no different in this respect from any of the other dozen or so antidepressants. That the effects it had were exactly the same for all of them."

"But you knew from the trials and the letters that they weren't," Paul reiterated.

"As did they."

"So…what happened?" Will's question seemed almost cautious.

"Dr. Russell had a cerebral hemorrhage. Chad Lowell, his assistant, died in an accident on his motorcycle. Dr. Gail Abernathy…" Espy laughed, the sound without amusement. "She committed suicide. Ironic, isn't it?"

"And you? They didn't try to get rid of you?"

"Unfortunately—or fortunately I suppose, since it kept me alive—they had the perfect excuse to discredit anything I might say about Romoxidin."

"You were hospitalized," Cait said.

Of all those seated at the table, she was probably the one who would have the most understanding of mental illness. She had fought her own emotional demons.

"I was confined to the psychiatric ward."

There was a small silence. It was again obvious no one wanted to ask the hard questions that confession called for. They didn't have the luxury, however, of respecting Stewart Espy's privacy. Or his pain.

He was Will's witness. His get-out-of-jail card. If the researcher didn't come through for them...

"Can you talk to us about why that happened?"

No one could doubt the compassion in Will's soft question. And after all, he, too, had confessed to struggling to make sense of what had happened to them on the day of the assassination attempt.

"Ron Vincent isn't a doctor, but he knows enough about the drugs Vincent Pharmaceutical manufactures to be dangerous."

"Are you saying...Ron Vincent *drugged* you?"

"I believe he read the protocols until he found something we produced in-house that would do what he wanted."

"A drug that caused psychotic symptoms?"

"At a high enough dosage. Actually, we produce quite a few of those."

"And you think he gave you one."

After the ruthlessness these people displayed, Cait wasn't sure why she would be shocked. For some reason she was. She knew they'd given Will something, but the idea of simply pumping someone full of a drug without knowing or caring what effect it would have made her flesh crawl.

"It's the only explanation I have for what happened. I tried to get the documentation about what was going on into his brother's hands, and the next thing I know, I'm confined to a padded room."

"Documentation?" Paul interrupted. "I thought you said they'd gotten rid of that."

"I said they'd moved the files. Some of us had had the foresight to make copies of what they contained before that happened."

"And you still have those copies?"

For the first time in days, Will's voice was filled with hope. As he had asked the question, he'd glanced toward her, briefly meeting her eyes before he'd looked back at the scientist.

"That's what I tried to give the other Mr. Vincent that night. Either they didn't reach him or they were taken away."

"That night. At the restaurant? That's why you were there? To try to give that information to Greg?"

"The waiter came outside the kitchen to smoke. I gave him the information for Mr. Vincent. I had hoped that if he knew…" Again Espy's eyes contemplated the outside darkness. "I got him killed instead."

"You aren't to blame for what happened to Greg," Will said. "If his own brother was willing to murder to prevent him from seeing those files—"

"I have no doubt that's what happened. The waiter promised me he would hand the disk to Mr. Vincent personally. *And* unobtrusively. I stressed to him how important that was. Apparently he succeeded in the first, but not the second."

The waiter. Emilio Garza. Who was also dead. Not because he'd put something in Will's drink as they'd thought, but because he'd handled the information that had gotten Greg Vincent killed.

"You're assuming that because Greg was murdered?"

Espy didn't look at her, despite her question. Instead his eyes remained focused on Will, a small smile playing about his lips.

"And because he sent you out into the alley to find me. I knew then that I'd failed."

"I came out to look for you?"

"And I ran. I didn't know who you were. You don't remember?"

"Another of Ron's experiments I think. I remember very little about that night."

"But…you recognized me at the police station."

"A long story," Will said. "About the information…"

"I put it into the waiter's hands. It was on a disk. I'd inserted it into a small kraft envelope."

Will shook his head. "I don't remember an envelope from the restaurant. Or at the house."

"Maybe that's what they were looking for at Emilio's," Cait suggested.

"Obviously he handed it over to Greg. Why else

would he have sent me out to find Dr. Espy? If that disk isn't back in Ron's hands, then it would be at Greg's. And I doubt anyone is going to let us search for it there."

The hope she'd seen in Will's face had dissipated with his realization that, despite knowing what had happened, they were no closer to proving it than they'd been before. Espy wasn't anyone's idea of a credible witness. Without documentation that results from the drug trials had been suppressed...

"Then we should go to the source," Espy said.

"The source?"

She tried to control the skepticism in her tone, but the story he'd told had taken them from despair to hope and back again. She didn't want him dangling something in front of Will that would prove to be another cruel mirage.

"The laboratory."

"You're saying..." Paul hesitated, obviously unsure of exactly what Espy *was* saying.

"I'm saying that I don't believe they could have erased all evidence of the trials or of those letters. My colleagues all had their own computers and their own record-keeping secrets. They knew what was going on as well as I did. They paid the ultimate price for that knowledge. If I could get into the facility, I'm convinced I could find the information we need."

His eagerness to do that was a little frightening, especially combined with his evangelical zeal and the look in his eyes. Maybe Ron Vincent had had nothing to do with this man's hospitalization. Maybe he was simply as crazy as any good prosecutor would be able to make him out to be.

Yet, what other choice did they have? Which was apparently the conclusion Will reached as well.

"You think if you get inside the lab, you can find the information."

"I'm sure of it. I just need someone to help me. I thought it might be to our advantage to help one another, Mr. Shannon. Are you game?"

CHAPTER TWENTY

"THIS IS INSANE."

"Probably," Will acknowledged without turning to look at her. "Insane or not, I don't have any other choice."

They were back in the cars, Espy and Paul in the Lexus ahead of them, he and Cait in Reemer's SUV. They were headed back to the Beltway, although no specific destination there had been determined. Not even Vincent Pharmaceutical. Not yet.

"Espy can testify to what he knows," Cait argued. "All those people he mentioned. Surely there's evidence somewhere that their deaths weren't what they appeared to be."

Will wished he could believe that. Actually, he did believe there would be evidence of what the researcher had suggested. He just didn't believe that anyone was going to look for it.

That would require exhuming bodies, which would mean getting permission from family members. Even if they gave it, an autopsy might not provide the proof they'd need in the case of the assistant killed in the motorcycle accident. And maybe not for the woman who'd supposedly committed suicide. There were too many ways to arrange either scenario without leaving evidence behind.

"If Espy and I are caught breaking into the lab, you can suggest to the cops they look for it."

He didn't mean his answer to sound as sarcastic as it did, but he'd long ago lost faith in the system. No matter how much Cait wanted to believe that his innocence was a shield against being convicted for murder, he couldn't. And judging by what had happened when he'd tried to turn himself in, he might not live long enough to make it into a courtroom.

"I can't believe you're really thinking about breaking into that lab."

Cait was smart enough to know that he had no other option. That was her heart speaking, not her intellect.

"You have another suggestion?"

"We can still leave," she said softly.

"No, *we* can't. That, too, is reality, whether you want to accept it or not."

"You don't want me to go with you?"

"You know better than that."

"Then stop saying it isn't possible."

"Our pictures and our prints are in the system, Cait. Even if we managed to get good identification, they'd track us down."

"How?"

"The same way they find other fugitives. The need

to communicate with family and friends. To know what's going on back here. The need to hold on to some particle of the life you once had."

"Since we know the dangers, we can avoid them."

"And you never talk to your mother again." He waited through the resulting silence, giving her time to think about all fleeing would entail.

"And if you go by yourself?" she asked finally. "Does that mean you won't give in to that temptation?"

Cait was his temptation. The siren call he'd hear in his dreams. Maybe if he had left before they'd made love again...

"It's a choice I won't have to make."

"Because you aren't going." Her intonation was flat.

"I'm going to break into Vincent's main lab with Dr. Espy and locate the documentation he says is there."

"And if he's wrong?"

"It won't be the first mistake I've made since all this started."

Going to her house. Trying to talk to the waiter. Trusting the cops. Believing, against his instincts, that Paul's private investigator would protect Cait.

He couldn't think of any decision that hadn't turned into a nightmare. His reactions to the situations those choices had created had been a reflection of his training. He couldn't fault them. It was the initial decision in each case that had gotten him into trouble.

Like this one? He ignored the niggling doubt, speaking more forcefully, perhaps to convince himself as well.

"This is for all the marbles. If I can find proof they concealed knowledge of deadly side effects for one of their premier drugs, then the cops will be forced to listen. Especially given the list of the deaths of researchers involved with Romoxidin."

"If they catch you, you and Espy will become additions to that list."

"Probably. Since that was their mistake the first time."

"Their mistake?"

"Not killing either of us when they had the chance."

"Somehow I don't find it comforting to think that they've probably figured that out by now."

IN THE END THEY HAD RENTED a motel room on the outskirts of Chevy Chase. Although there were two queen-size beds, despite the sleep they'd all missed, no one had opted to take advantage of them.

Cait had stood behind Stewart Espy's chair, avoiding the dirty knapsack he'd hung over its back, while he had sketched the layout of the lab. His drawings were incredibly detailed, despite the continual trembling of the hand that held Paul's Montblanc.

They'd gone through the drive-in of one of the all-night burger places near the motel, but most of what they'd bought lay uneaten in the center of the table they were gathered around.

Exhaustion had taken its toll on all of them. Espy, who had seemed fragile in the coffee shop, appeared on the verge of collapse. Only Will seemed to be operating with any degree of alertness. Cait knew him well enough to know that he was running on adrenaline and hope.

"And this is the room where they keep the actual paperwork on the drugs?" he asked, pointing to one of the small rectangles on Dr. Espy's diagram.

"You aren't expecting to find the letters, are you?" The pen Espy was using stilled as he looked up.

"You said they'd moved them. Any idea where?"

"Probably to the shredder. Why would they keep them?"

"Then…exactly what do you expect to find in lab?"

"A lot of the data is stored in the system."

"The computers," Paul interpreted.

"Someone had to compile it. We might not be able to find the actual reports, but believe me, they've all been correlated and studied. That's when the questions began."

"What about the results of those original double-blind trials?"

"Those would have been saved as well."

"How can you possibly know all that information will still be there?" Cait asked, her voice expressing her frustration with this plan. She had called it insane before. Now that she'd listened to Espy's explanations, it seemed even more so. "If Ron Vincent isn't a complete idiot, that material has long since been cleared from the hard drives."

"I'm afraid you don't understand how this all works, Ms. Malone."

Espy's eyes, as he focused them on her, were even more bloodshot. The tremors now seemed to be affecting more than his fingers, although he'd laid down the pen and was sitting with his hands clasped tightly together, possibly to control them.

"What I *don't* understand is someone holding on to data that could send them to prison. Ron Vincent isn't that stupid or he wouldn't be in the position he's in today."

"He's in that position because his father owned the company. And because his brother put up with mistakes and failures that no other CEO would have tolerated. It's called nepotism, I believe."

"Not any longer," she said, angered by his condescension. "Right now it's called being the guy in charge."

"Or fratricide," Will reminded her. "Ron didn't really achieve anything on his own except *not* getting charged in his brother's death."

"Or in Emilio's. Or those of the researchers Dr. Espy mentioned. None of that seems characteristic of someone too stupid to hide stuff that could condemn him."

"Not too stupid," Espy corrected. "Too arrogant. And that will be his downfall."

Again that flash of evangelical fervor appeared in his eyes. Cait didn't know if Paul had even had an opportunity to check on the researcher's credentials or his medical history. Apparently, from what he'd said before, that was the kind of thing his firm had used Doug

Reemer for. Obviously that wasn't going to happen in this case.

"Even if what you say is true," she conceded, "how can the two of you get into the lab without alerting security?"

If she couldn't stop Will with logic, perhaps she could bring a halt to this by pointing out the impossibilities of the clandestine raid they were planning. Every mom-and-pop drugstore had a security system these days. One of the most successful pharmaceutical manufacturers in the country would employ one that was state-of-the-art.

"I still have a key to the back delivery door. Vincent uses card scans for access to the lab area. I also still have my card."

She almost laughed. She controlled the instinct, shaking her head instead. "Unless they've changed the locks and denied your access."

"Believe me, Ms. Malone, they aren't that efficient. Or that worried about me."

"Ron Vincent was worried enough that he had his brother and a waiter murdered because of material you tried to pass on to them. If he wasn't alerted then to the danger you represent, Dr. Espy, he certainly is now."

"Even if my card is denied, I can still get into the lab. I know that building intimately. I spent almost fifteen years of my life there."

"And if you're really foolish enough to try this, you may spend the very short time that remains of it there as well."

"Security guards are seldom given permission to shoot people, Cait."

She turned at Paul's comment, looking him straight in the eye. "And drug companies are seldom involved in wholesale murder. Obviously we aren't dealing with the norm here. Something all of you seem to have forgotten."

"If anything goes wrong, they'll call the cops and have us arrested," Will said.

She could tell from his expression that he didn't believe that anymore than she did. Security had probably been alerted to watch for something just like this ill-conceived raid since Espy had surfaced with his package in the back alley of the restaurant that night.

"You don't believe that."

"I believe that if we're going to try to implicate Ron Vincent in his brother's death, we're going to have to have proof of his motive. Apparently that proof can be found within Vincent Pharmaceutical. Dr. Espy is willing to help me find it. It's a chance I have to take."

It was the same argument he had made in the car. And she knew that no matter what she felt, Will believed this was his only chance to get his life back. And he was willing to risk everything for it.

"Then take me with you."

Will's eyes widened slightly, one of those physiological reactions no one can guard against. And then his lips began to tilt, slowly slanting into a smile.

"Why not?" she demanded, seeing it. "You said we were partners. You said that's why you came to my house."

"I *said* a lot of things. But you *know* why I came to you that night."

Because they had been much more than partners. They still were.

"That doesn't negate the rest. We worked together. I have the training Dr. Espy lacks. If you really believe this is your only chance...you have to know it's mine, too."

"I don't need to have to worry about you getting hurt."

"If security is only going to arrest you, how could I get hurt?"

He obviously had no answer for that. It served him right for trying to pass off that lie.

"It isn't an option."

"Because two years ago I was slow to react? Is that why you don't trust me to be on this team?"

"There is no team. This is my fight, Cait. Mine alone."

"You're taking him."

She glanced down at Stewart Espy, who was sitting with his forehead propped on his hands. His posture was hardly conducive to having confidence that, if placed under stress, he would be able to perform.

"Dr. Espy is familiar with the lab."

Because of that I have to take him. Will didn't say it aloud, of course, but it was obvious what he meant. And just as obvious that if he could think of any way of carrying this off without involving the scientist, he would leave him here.

"While all I'm familiar with is watching for the unexpected. You don't think that would be a valuable skill in a situation like this?"

"We can argue this all day, Cait. It won't change anything. There are a dozen valid reasons for not taking you into that lab—"

"No. No matter what you say, Will, there's really only one reason. You don't think I'm capable of doing what I was trained to do. Of doing what you, yourself, trained me to do."

"This isn't about you."

"Of course it is. I let you down two years ago. You don't want to take a chance that I might do it again."

"That's ridiculous. You know it, and I know it. This ploy isn't going to work."

"Why is it ridiculous? If I'd reacted sooner, there would have been no investigation. You wouldn't have lost your position with the Service. You'd never have been Greg Vincent's bodyguard. And if you hadn't been, then you wouldn't be in this situation."

"If you want to start assigning blame, start with having your supervisor take advantage of you."

She laughed. She couldn't help it.

"Nobody ever took advantage of me sexually. Especially not you."

Will stood so suddenly that Espy started. "I'm going outside to get some air. I'm sure Paul and Dr. Espy aren't thrilled at being made privy to this conversation."

"Actually, I'm finding it very informative," Paul said. "I've never pictured you as a debaucher of young women."

"Because he isn't," Cait said. "He's just stubborn and opinionated and convinced of the rightness of any position he takes."

"I'm convinced of this one." Will had already started toward the door when Paul's question stopped him.

"Are you sure you want to go outside? Unless I'm mistaken about what that is," he said, nodding toward the narrow streak between the edges of the blackout drapes, "it's daylight."

Will hesitated, his eyes tracking in the direction Paul had indicated. "Maybe a shower will serve the same purpose. It's been a couple of days since I've managed one."

In her bathroom. In her bedroom. Then into her bed.

The progression of images his words had produced wouldn't be denied. Nor would the feelings that went with them, intensified after yesterday morning's tryst in the boathouse.

"It probably will," she said, "if the purpose is not to listen to what I'm saying."

"I couldn't have said it better myself."

He turned, striding across the room toward the bath. He closed the door sharply, without quite slamming it.

"Damn you," she said under her breath.

"He's right," Paul said. "He doesn't need to have to worry about you on this one."

"I know what I'm doing. He knows that. He saw—"

She had almost said that he'd seen the men she'd killed at the summerhouse. As if that were some kind of badge of honor.

Maybe in this case it was. Their enemy was ruthless and would obviously stop at nothing—not even killing innocent people—to accomplish their goal. On the other hand, the men she'd killed were hardly innocent. So why should she feel guilty about what she'd done?

"You can argue. You might even win," Paul said. "But if you do, then ultimately you also lose."

"Is there supposed to be some logical thought behind that mumbo jumbo?"

"Will's life depends on what we're going to do tonight. Dr. Espy's, too." The lawyer looked pointedly at the man whose bowed head once more rested in his hands. "Will doesn't want you there because he knows that having you in danger would make him less effective. It would interfere with his concentration. If you can't accept the reality of that…" He shrugged.

She wanted to say he was wrong. That they both were. She wanted to say a lot of things, but none of them would rebound to her credit because she knew Paul was right.

No matter how sure she was of her abilities, her presence would be one more thing Will would have to worry about. Given the risks involved in this, he didn't need anything to distract him.

Paul must have seen acceptance in her face. Either that or he was concerned that just the argument would prove to be a distraction.

"Why don't you get some sleep?" he suggested. "Dr. Espy, you should probably try to rest as well. If you're determined to do this tonight—"

The scientist lifted his head, looking from one to the other. "I thought you understood. Like Mr. Shannon, I don't have a choice. I, too, would like my life back. And proving what a murderous bastard Ron Vincent is seems to be the only way to accomplish that."

CHAPTER TWENTY-ONE

ONLY DESPERATE MEN would believe they could break into a secure location and remove data. And, Will acknowledged as he followed Stewart Espy along the tree-shadowed walk at the back of Vincent Pharmaceutical, that's exactly who they were and what they were about to try to do.

In the darkness, he almost bumped into the researcher who had come to an abrupt halt in front of him. Espy turned, whispering over his shoulder.

"The door I told you about is just ahead."

Espy claimed he still had the key for the back entrance where deliveries of routine supplies for his section of the lab had been accepted. Whether or not the lock had been changed since he'd worked here was another question.

Although the scientist was convinced it would not have been, Will had spent the afternoon going over Espy's drawings, trying to formulate a contingency plan. One he hoped he wouldn't have to use.

"Let's try it."

As Will put his hand on his companion's shoulder to

urge him forward, it brushed against the filthy backpack Espy had again insisted on bringing with him. He had become almost hysterical when Will had attempted to talk him out of carrying the thing inside.

It was ironic that Cait thought he wouldn't allow her to come because he doubted her competency. Instead of a partner he knew he could rely on, he was stuck with a guy who seemed primed to fall apart at the first sign of trouble. Even now he could feel under his palm the vibration of the researcher's body, which trembled like a tuning fork.

Espy nodded, but he didn't move. Not until Will literally grasped him by the elbow and encouraged him.

Suddenly the back wall of the building, to which they'd been walking parallel, was broken by a bay, large enough to accommodate a good-sized delivery truck. In its center was a single door with five or six steps leading up to it from the asphalt. Above the entrance, a security light was shielded from vandals by a metal cage. Beside it was a loading dock, perhaps four feet above the ground, which was topped by a roll-up door.

Espy hadn't mentioned the light, but perhaps he'd assumed Will would expect one. It made him wonder, however, what else the researcher had forgotten to tell him.

Will debated trying to break the bulb somehow, but finally decided that the risk involved in doing that was as great as simply walking up to the door and trying the key. Still holding Espy's elbow, Will made him wait while he took another survey of their surroundings.

Only when he had, did he release his arm with the whispered instruction, "Go."

The scientist hurried toward the steps, holding on to the metal handrail as he climbed. Will followed more slowly, his gaze moving between his companion and the deserted service road behind the building. So far, so good.

He reached the steps, but stopped at their foot to continue his reconnaissance while he waited for Espy to open the door. After perhaps thirty seconds without any sign that the task had been accomplished, Will turned, looking up the stairs.

The researcher appeared to be struggling to make the key work. It should have become obvious to him that if it hadn't by now, it probably wasn't going to.

Just as he decided that, Will remembered those trembling hands. Maybe the reason Espy couldn't get the door open had nothing to do with the lock.

He took the steps two at a time, coming up onto the landing behind the scientist. Espy turned at his approach, the key still in his fingers.

"They've never changed the locks. Not in all the time I was here."

"A few murders will make a difference in how things have always been done."

Will's mind was already considering alternative ways to get into the lab. Despite Espy's confidence, he'd known this wasn't going to be easy.

"What about the door on the loading dock?" Will

held out his hand for the key, but his mental focus had already shifted to the metal roll-up above the platform.

"I never had a key to that."

"I meant how does it work?"

"I don't know. There's a pulley system, I think. Chains. I'm not sure about the lock."

If it didn't involve something within his domain, obviously Espy hadn't been interested. He had known about this door because the researchers had used it if they'd ever had to come back to the lab when the main reception area was closed.

Inside was a utility corridor that eventually led to the lab where Espy had worked. It was the entrance to that section that required the card scan for admittance.

The scientist placed the key on his palm. Will almost slipped it into his pocket, but something, perhaps his compulsion for control, made him step over to the door to try it for himself.

The key slipped into the lock, but he couldn't get it to turn. Without his conscious volition, his left hand, which had been fastened around the knob, exerted an upward pressure. It was an unthinking act based on his own sometimes recalcitrant apartment door. The lock had to be pulled into better alignment with the latch before the key would work.

Despite all expectations, as soon as he lifted the door that fraction of an inch, the key turned, unlocking the mechanism. Under his hand, the door swung open on to a darkened corridor.

Shocked by his success, Will froze, expecting an alarm. When that didn't happen, he glanced at his companion, who seemed as dumbfounded as he had been.

"You were right," Will said. "They *don't* change the locks."

"Hubris," Espy said as he stepped past him, entering the utility hallway as if his confidence had been restored.

He quickly punched a series of numbers into the box beside the door. Together they watched as the small red light that had been blinking steadied. The alarm the broken circuit would have triggered had been stilled with the correct code.

"Or the codes," the researcher said with a note of triumph. "You arrogant bastard."

He meant Ron Vincent. Arrogant *and* stupid, Will thought, but tonight that combination had been to their advantage. And according to Espy, there was only one more barrier to their reaching the records they needed.

The researcher reached back and pulled the metal door closed. Shut off from the security light, the corridor was plunged into darkness.

It took Will's eyes a moment to adjust, but Espy had already started walking toward the dim green light at the other end of the hall. That glow was generated by an emergency light, the kind that would continue to function in case of a power outage. Apparently, this hallway was not normally illuminated. Of course, since it was only used during the daytime that made sense.

Espy was having no trouble navigating in the semi-darkness. Forced to follow the sound of his footsteps until his pupils had adjusted, Will had slipped his weapon from its holster.

Both the dimness and the realization that he would have no idea whether anyone they encountered was an innocent bystander or one of the people who had plotted to kill and frame him for murder increased his tension. He might have only a split second to make a decision about using the semiautomatic.

"This way."

In his excitement, Espy had no longer bothered to keep his voice down. Will started to remind him, but as they rounded the corner, that caution went out of his head.

Before them lay the double-glass doors he knew from the drawings would lead into the main part of the laboratory. The final barrier. And the final test. If they hadn't changed the lock or the code—

"You stand in front of the door," Espy instructed, his voice filled with renewed enthusiasm. "When the scan's complete, the latch will release with an audible click. Step forward as soon as you hear it because the doors will begin to open immediately."

The plan was that they would go through together. Espy had assured him there was nothing about the system that would allow it to recognize that two people were entering although only one card had been scanned. He had said it with such assurance during the discussions in the motel room that Will hadn't questioned the assertion.

Now doubt began to surface. Given the stakes involved in their business, surely a major drug manufacturer would have a fail-safe system to guard against the very thing they were about to attempt.

"Have you ever done this before?" he asked.

"There was never any need."

"Then how do you know it will work?"

"Because I've read the specifications of the system."

"Are you sure you understood them?"

"I read English, Mr. Shannon," Espy said, his tone as condescending as it had been to Cait. "It's my native tongue."

"Then I hope you got it right."

At this point, Will had nothing to lose. Either they got lucky and found what they needed during this suicidal excursion or they got caught.

He positioned himself in front of the place where the glass doors met. He turned and nodded to Espy, who mirrored the gesture. Then the scientist stepped forward, running a card through the scanner.

For a heartbeat nothing happened. Long enough that the anxiety sitting like a cold weight in the bottom of Will's stomach expanded in a wave of disappointment. Just as he was about to turn his head to ask Espy what they did next, he heard the click he'd been warned to expect.

He stepped forward, as close to the doors as he could get. As they began to slide apart, the researcher jumped to the side so that he was directly behind him. Will took

a step forward, aware that the man following him mim-
icked his movements.

They cleared the doors, which closed with a soft
pneumatic wheeze behind them. They both stopped,
waiting for lights to blink or alarms to sound. Neither
happened.

Gradually the pump of adrenaline into his blood-
stream slowed. Will drew a shuddering breath before he
turned to face his companion. "Now what?"

"Now we go hunting."

CAIT LIFTED HER WRIST, trying to read her watch by the
light of the halogen lamp in the parking lot across the
street. Although the front of Vincent Pharmaceutical
was well lit, Paul had deliberately pulled the Lexus
into the deep shadows cast by the trees that lined the
service drive.

Unable to believe what the hands of her Timex were
telling her, she raised her arm higher, trying to direct
more of the light onto its face. It had been less than
twenty-five minutes since Will and Dr. Espy had disappeared around the back of the building. She felt as if
they'd been gone for hours.

She glanced across the front seat at Paul. He was
leaning forward, wrists crossed on the top of the steer-
ing wheel. His gaze was focused intently in the direction of where the two of them had disappeared.

"What do you think?"

The lawyer turned, his face a spectral white in the

dimness. "I think they must have gotten in. What else could they be doing for this long?"

If the key Espy had claimed would open the delivery door hadn't worked, they might well be trying to find another means of access. She knew Will wouldn't give up without a fight. Too much was riding on it for him.

And for her.

"Yeah, I think they're in," she agreed. "I'm not sure that makes me feel any better. Do you believe Espy?"

The pause before Paul answered confirmed her own doubts.

"What he says makes sense of Greg's murder. The company couldn't take two hits that severe on major products and survive. As for the rest..." The lawyer shrugged.

"There's something about his eyes when he talks about Ron Vincent that gives me the creeps. It's like he's on a mission to get him. Like it's become the reason for his existence."

"Revenge is a normal human emotion. If what he says is true, then Vincent destroyed his life."

"And killed his co-workers. So why hasn't he just run away? Why keep poking at the wasp's nest?"

"I don't understand."

"He shows up at the restaurant where Greg is meeting with his brother to give him documentation that will prove Ron is a murderer. Why not mail the disk? Why not do something—anything—other than what he did?"

"You think he really *is* insane?"

She shook her head, still trying to put her impressions of Espy into some kind of perspective. "I don't know what I think. He just…" She shook her head, remembering the wildness in the researcher's eyes.

"Creeps you out." Paul's repetition of the word she'd used sounded slightly amused.

"And to know that Will's depending on him… That creeps me out even more."

"Will can take care of himself."

Paul was right. If there was anyone capable of dealing with the unexpected, it was Will. Why then was her sense of foreboding so strong?

"Why didn't he come here by himself?"

The thought had begun as a slightly troubling, unanswered question. Now, as her anxiety built, it loomed in her mind as more and more important.

"Will?"

"Dr. Espy. If Ron Vincent took the disk he tried to give Greg that night, and he knew he could recreate it by retrieving the records he claims are here, then why didn't he just do that? Why show up at the police station? Why convince Will to come with him?"

"Because he's a basket case. You saw him. Hell, he isn't capable of changing his clothes. What makes you think he could carry off something like this on his own?"

Paul was right. The scientist had seemed to be hovering on the verge of another breakdown since he'd been with them. That was what she should be worried about. Espy having some kind of "psychotic break," whatever that meant, while he and Will were in the lab.

Knowing Will as she did, she knew that if that happened, he would feel responsible for the man. He wouldn't leave him behind no matter what.

"I don't know. Just...nerves I guess. I was never good at waiting."

"You were in the wrong profession for this kind of stuff," Paul said, turning his eyes back to the building. "You should have chosen the law. Waiting is all lawyers ever do."

Her gaze followed his. The building was deceptively peaceful in the moonlight. There was nothing to indicate, not from here at least, that a life-and-death search was going on inside.

And no way to know until the two men emerged, if they did, whether or not it had been successful.

"I THOUGHT YOU SAID that everything would be on the computers."

Will was frighteningly conscious of the passage of time. Something that didn't seem to bother the scientist at all.

"It is," Espy assured him without looking up from the file folder he was going through.

They hadn't turned on the lights in the narrow room where the physical files were kept, so he was using the light from the computer room to read by.

"Then why are we looking there?"

"I'd rather have the original data if we can locate it. Especially that from the double blinds where the problems with Romoxidin first showed up."

"We need to grab whatever we can get our hands on and get out of here."

"*You're* the one who needs this information the most, Mr. Shannon. I'm just trying to help you retrieve that which will be most useful."

"If we get caught in here, none of this will do either of us any good."

"There are only a few more cabinets for clinical trials. It has to be here."

Unless they'd already trashed it. Which is what anyone with half a brain would have done when the first questions surfaced. Why murder people to prevent that kind of information from becoming public and then keep it in your company's files?

"Leave those," Will ordered. "See what you can find in the system."

At his tone Espy looked up, his finger marking his place in the drawer. In the dimness his eyes appeared cold, almost feral.

"But I'm sure it's here."

"Maybe. But we don't have time to go through all of this."

Will gestured to the row of filing cabinets that faded away into the dimness at the end of the narrow room. Although organized by date, from what the researcher had told him the data on the drug had been compiled over a lengthy period of time. It didn't make sense to do a physical search when the computers would find what they were looking for in a matter of seconds.

"If the alarms had gone off, someone would have been here by now. Relax."

The researcher returned to his search, thumbing through the next folder. Obviously Will had not effectively communicated his sense of urgency.

"Why don't you try the computers?" he suggested. "I'll look through these."

"You wouldn't know it if you found it," Espy said, moving on to the next folder.

"They're labeled, aren't they?"

"With both the names of the drugs and the methodology. Only someone who is very familiar with the protocols would be able to determine which trials are relevant, however."

"Look, I appreciate what you're trying to do. I never would have known about any of this if it weren't for you, but if they find us in here—"

"No one comes to this lab at night. Not anymore."

Will wasn't sure what that meant. Maybe that the scientists Espy had worked with were all dead.

The tone of the comment bothered him. As did the man's painstakingly slow examination of each file. Nothing Will had said to him about the need to get this done and get out had gotten through.

"Then tell *me* how to get into the computers. This will go faster if both of us are working at it."

He was surprised when Espy immediately acquiesced.

"The system should be up. Use Espy as your log-on. My password was brigadoon. Lowercase, of course."

Almost as bizarre as Espy himself, but Will didn't argue the point. He walked out of the files section, which was separated from the computers by a wall that was glass on top, and into the main room.

He sat down at one of the monitors, moving the mouse to wake it up. When the log-on screen came up, he typed in the information he'd been given and was surprised when he was granted access.

"How do you spell it?"

He could see the researcher in the file room from the desk where he sat. He was still on his knees, his ever-present backpack at his feet.

"Brigadoon?" Espy asked without looking up.

"Romoxidin."

"That's the marketing name. You'll need the name under which the trials were run. Try RX157."

Will typed it in and then, again holding his breath, hit Search. The screen filled with a listing that went on for what would be several pages.

He scrolled down, his eyes scanning the items. Just as Espy had warned him, none of them meant anything to him. If he opened each and printed them out, they would be here all night. Despite Espy's assurances, that wasn't something he was comfortable with.

The easiest way would be to transfer everything to a disk, which was probably what Espy had done before.

It would take a while, especially since this was a system he wasn't familiar with, but it would be far less time-consuming than printing the stuff. Unless Espy could point him in another direction...

He glanced over to the row of filing cabinets where the researcher had been working. The drawer he'd been going through was still open, but Espy wasn't there.

He turned his head, looking at the other side of the lab. Only dimly lit by the row of lights they'd turned on in this section, it appeared to be deserted, too.

What the hell...

"Dr. Espy?"

There was no response.

"Dr. Espy, are you here?"

Will pushed back his chair and stood, hoping that he'd be able to see to the end of the line of filing cabinets through the glass top of the wall that separated the two rooms. Although he could see most of it, the room appeared to be empty.

He walked toward it, his footsteps loud in the silence. Although he had been uneasy before, the researcher's sudden disappearance had pushed that tension into overdrive. Once more, he began to ease his weapon from its holster.

He reached the doorway that separated the rooms, the SIG-Sauer gripped in both hands. Holding his weapon out before him, he stepped around the corner, bringing the entire area into view. There was no one there. And no door at the end, as he had expected.

His gaze and the muzzle of his weapon tracked back along the line of file cabinets. Only then did he notice what he'd missed before.

The battered knapsack Stewart Espy had insisted on taking everywhere with him lay on the floor near the open drawer, but there was something different about its configuration. It had been unzipped, the top half had been thrown back, revealing that, whatever the contents had been, they, too, like the scientist, had disappeared.

CHAPTER TWENTY-TWO

"WHAT THE HELL?"

Cait glanced over at the lawyer, but he was peering through the windshield toward the front of the building. She turned to see what had prompted his comment.

Two cars were pulling up along the curb. They must have entered the service road from the other direction, since they hadn't passed by the Lexus.

As they watched, five men piled out, making no attempt at stealth. The slamming doors were audible even at this distance.

A couple of them visually checked out the area around the building. She held her breath, expecting one of them to point toward Paul's car, but they didn't. Apparently the spot he'd chosen in the shadows under the trees had served its purpose.

"Not the cops," he whispered.

"Would you recognize Ron Vincent?" She thought Paul had mentioned seeing Greg's brother on television.

"Not at this distance."

And not in this light. Even as she thought that, the men who'd been doing the visual scan turned, obviously in response to instructions from whoever was in charge, and started toward the service entrance.

"Call Will."

"Espy," Paul said, flipping open the case of his cell and beginning to dial.

"What?"

"I gave Espy your phone. He's the one with the bag."

Although her instinct was to question the wisdom of that decision, it was too late for anything she might say to make a difference. And what could that matter? Anyone could answer a phone.

Her eyes on Paul, she waited, imagining the rings he was obviously listening to, at the same time wondering if the men from the cars had already entered the building. If so, would they be able to hear the phone?

She stifled the urge to warn Paul that he might be giving away Will and Dr. Espy's location. He would be as aware of that danger as she was. The greater danger lay in *not* warning them that they were about to have company.

"No answer."

Paul had turned so that his eyes met hers. The panic that was building in her chest was reflected in them, despite his attempt to appear calm.

"Hang up," she ordered.

"What? We have to warn them."

"Something's obviously gone wrong. All you're doing by letting it ring is telling those men where they are." She reached out, her fingers closing around the door handle.

"What are you doing?"

She looked back at Paul's question, discovering that he'd at least listened to her advice. As she watched, he closed his phone, turning in the seat to face her.

"Call the cops," she said. "The locals. The sheriff's department. Whoever. Get them out here as fast as you can."

"If I do, it's all over, Cait. You understand that?"

"If you *don't* do it," she warned, "it's over. *Really* over. If those men work for Vincent, then they aren't going to make the same mistake they made before." She opened her door to get out of the car, throwing the last over her shoulder as she began to run. "This time they aren't going to leave either of them alive."

A DOZEN EXPLANATIONS for Espy's disappearance ran through Will's head as he crossed over to examine the empty bag. He touched it with his foot, pushing back the top half to verify that his impression had been correct. It was indeed empty.

So what had the researcher brought into the lab in the knapsack? And an even more important question, where had he gone with the contents?

Will had already taken a step back toward the room with the computers when his gaze swept over the still-open file drawer. Then, his mind belatedly registering what he'd just seen, his eyes returned to it.

Two folders had been placed flat on the tops of the others. The ones Espy had been looking into when he'd decided to leave? Or something he had wanted to draw Will's attention to?

Hardly daring to hope it might be the latter, Will stooped beside the drawer. The files appeared to have been taken from the cabinet. The material they were made of seemed the same.

He leaned forward, trying to read the tab on the first without touching it, but he couldn't see the lettering from this angle. With his left hand he reached out to lift the cover.

The original name of Romoxidin, which Espy had called out to him as he'd typed, leaped up at him from the first page. Below it were a series of dates. The trials the scientist had told him about?

Still operating one-handed, his gun in the other, he inserted his thumb into the middle of the thick stack of papers the folder contained, lifting them before letting them fall back onto the bottom half. Although he couldn't be sure, the material appeared to be exactly what they'd come here to retrieve—the compiled data on the double blinds that had alerted the researchers to the problems with the drug that would eventually be marketed as Romoxidin.

He set the top folder down on the floor and opened the one that lay beneath it. When he fanned its pages, both their format and the handwritten signatures at the bottom indicated these were the letters that had finally convinced someone other than the researchers that the company had a problem. Together the two files constituted the proof Espy had promised.

Proof that Ron Vincent had had a very good reason
to murder his brother. He'd had to do that in order to
keep this information from coming out and destroying
the company they had inherited from their father.

It was obvious Espy had left these for Will to find.
This was exactly what the researcher had offered when
he'd convinced him to make this raid. The fact that he'd
come through with the information didn't begin to explain his disappearance.

Stewart Espy wasn't his responsibility, Will reminded
himself. He had what he had come for. All he had to do
was carry the folders out of the lab and get them into
the hands of someone qualified to interpret the data they
contained, something Paul would help him accomplish.

He picked up the second folder, stacking it on top of
the one he'd laid on the floor. Then, still working only
with his left hand, he attempted to pick both up.

Too thick to be grasped one-handed, the top file
slipped to the side as he tried to lift it, pages sliding out
onto the tile. Using the hand in which he held his
weapon, he hurriedly caught them and shoved them
back inside.

As he did, his eyes found the open knapsack. He
couldn't leave it here since its presence would give away
the fact that someone had been inside the lab. Putting
the folders inside and then carrying the bag with him
would ensure that none of the documents were lost.

He reached out and pulled the knapsack toward him.
He inserted the thicker folder first and then pushed the

file with the letters inside on top of it. They slipped into place with an ease that made him wonder if the two might have come out of the knapsack rather than from the drawer.

Even as the thought crossed his mind, he admitted it made no sense. If Espy had had these all along, why not simply hand them over? Why go through the charade of having to break into the lab to retrieve this data? And more importantly, why disappear?

Unless, just as the doctors who had committed him two months ago had believed, Stewart Espy had indeed lost touch with reality.

Will zipped the knapsack and then slung it over his left shoulder. As he did, he could smell the miasma of unwashed body that had also surrounded Espy.

He stood, pushing the file drawer back into the cabinet with his foot. Then he took a last look down the length of the narrow storage room. There was nothing that would indicate to the employees reporting for work in the morning that anyone had been here.

Will pivoted, turning to make that same survey of the larger room behind him. The chair where he'd sat to log in to the computer was pulled out.

Since he now had the two file folders, he needed to decide if there was any reason to copy the information that had come up on the screen onto a disk. That would be a time-consuming process since he believed that each entry would have to be transferred separately, and there were a large number of them.

Whether copying them would be worthwhile or a duplication of what he already had was a question only Espy could answer. And Espy wasn't around to do that.

Son of a bitch. It wasn't enough that the guy might have hoodwinked him. Now, at a crucial time in the operation, he was playing hide-and-seek, and Will didn't have time to find him.

He walked over to the computer he'd awakened. Without sitting down, he clicked on the first item on the list that had come up in response to his query. While the information loaded, he laid his weapon on the desk and pulled the knapsack off his shoulder. He removed the thicker of the two folders, spreading it out open on the desk beside the monitor.

The report that appeared on the screen was dated. As were those in the file, he discovered. If he could match the one that had come up to a duplicate in the folder, then he would assume they were all there and get the hell out of here. If he couldn't...

He began to thumb through the contents of the file, turning the ones he'd checked facedown onto the inside cover of the folder. His fingers shook slightly in his haste, reminding him of the researcher's trembling hands.

The seconds ticked away as he examined the documents, looking for the one currently displayed on the monitor. He was no longer sure this process was quicker than copying the files would have been. All he knew for certain was that he'd been here too long.

He looked at his watch, surprised to find that they'd

been inside the lab for almost forty minutes. *Too long.*
Too long.

Despite his sense of urgency, he turned another page,
his eyes running over the heading in an attempt to locate
the date. Just as he reached out to lay it aside, there was
a metallic noise from somewhere beyond the double-
glass doors he and Espy had walked through together.

He stopped in midmotion, cocking his head to listen
for a repetition. There was none, but whatever he'd heard
was enough to cement the decision his instincts had been
screaming at him to make for the last ten minutes.

Still standing, he quickly completed the log-out sequence. When he finished, he punched off the monitor
in order to darken the screen. If anyone noticed that tomorrow, it probably wouldn't trigger any alarms. None
that were as loud as the one sounding inside his head.

He closed the folder, at the same time throwing open
the unzipped bag to slide it back inside. This time the
odor that floated upward from its fabric wasn't reminis-
cent of body odor.

It *was,* however, something he'd smelled before. In
the stress of the moment he couldn't quite identify it. He
spent a second or two trying, even bringing the knapsack
closer to his nose, but the identification eluded him.

Knowing he had no more time to devote to the mystery,
he zipped the bag, throwing it over his shoulder again.
Only then did he pick up the gun he'd laid on the desk.

He crossed to the wall switch with a couple of long
strides and clicked off the lights that Espy had turned

on when they'd entered the records section. Standing in the sudden darkness, he listened again.

This time there could be no doubt about the sounds or where they were coming from. Someone was walking down the hallway toward this room.

His exit cut off by their approach, Will retreated to the only place he could—the narrow room lined with the filing cabinets. If he crouched down beside the last one…

The door to the outer hallway opened, throwing light into the room containing the computers. Will ducked, scrambling soundlessly across the carpet to reach the end of the row of file cabinets. Just as he'd hoped, there was a small space, perhaps two feet wide, between the last of the them and the wall. He slipped into it, working to control his breathing.

The knapsack was behind him, pressed against the wall. He clutched his weapon in both hands, pointing it out and slightly upward.

Whoever had entered the outer room was making no noise now. Through the glass top of the wall, he could still see light spilling in from the hall. Other than that, and the initial sound of the door opening, there was no evidence that anyone was there.

Still, at any moment he expected the overhead light to come on in the file room. Anticipating that, he eased back as far as he could so that his feet wouldn't be exposed. And then he waited.

As his eyes adjusted to the darkness of the corner where he'd hidden, he realized there was a faint light coming from behind the cabinet he was hiding beside. He turned his head, putting his cheek against the coolness of the wall.

There was a gap of perhaps three inches between the back of the file drawers and the wall behind them. Except there was no wall. Not in that particular spot. Instead there was a door, almost completely hidden by the tall cabinet.

Maybe hidden was the wrong word, he realized. Maybe it was just a matter of making use of every available inch of storage space. Maybe if no one used that door any longer—

No one except Espy?

Had Espy pulled the cabinet out to gain access to the door and then pulled it back into place when he'd gone through into the other room? If so, he'd made no noise doing it. Not enough to alert Will to what was going on.

Another sound came from the main room. Someone was moving around in there. If they were searching for whoever had set off an alarm he'd never even been aware of, then they would surely come in here, too.

A security guard with a flashlight? If so, everything was over.

He turned his head, rolling the back of it against the wall. The thread of light under the hidden door was still visible. It was so faint it obviously wasn't coming from the room just beyond. Perhaps it filtered into that area from an interior hallway or from the halogen lamps in the parking lot outside.

He closed his eyes, trying to decide what to do. If whoever was out there had come far enough into the main room to reach the area where the top half of the wall became glass, then they would notice an increase of light if Will opened the door. Or he could do nothing, hoping whoever was out there wouldn't search this far back.

If they were responding to an alarm, however, there was no doubt they'd look in this area. If they did, they'd find him.

More importantly, they would find the files he carried. As company property, they would be confiscated before the cops ever got here. His only chance to get proof of Ron Vincent's guilt out of this building and into public scrutiny was to get out of here now.

He switched the SIG-Sauer to his left hand. Then he inched upward, his back still against the wall.

A buckle on the knapsack made a scraping noise as he moved into a semi-upright position. He stopped immediately, waiting for some reaction from the adjacent room.

When there wasn't one, he reached into the space between the back of the cabinets and the wall, trying to locate the doorknob. He grasped it, turning until he felt the door begin to move.

Not locked.

He took a breath in relief and then left the door ajar, knowing that the next part of what he had to do to get out would be the most dangerous. He used his palm and the inside of his forearm against the back of the cabinet, determined to push it forward. Instead of the resistance he'd expected, it moved away from the wall with almost no effort on his part and, incredibly, without making any noise.

The damn thing was on wheels or casters. That's how Espy had gotten out without making any sound.

Will took a step to the side, easing the cabinet out far enough to move behind it. At the same time he felt for the knob again.

Once he had it in his hand, he took the final step that would put his body in front of the hidden door. Without giving himself time to think about what he was doing, he pushed it open and stepped backward into the room.

He fought the urge to step around the door and close it, using it as a barrier between himself and whoever was searching in the data-storage area. Instead, he made himself reach out and pull the file cabinet back into place. Only then did he step aside and shut the door.

He turned and realized he'd entered some kind of janitorial supply closet. He could make out the labels on the bottles and jars on shelves lining either side. Directly across from him was another door, under which the thread of light he'd noticed before seeped into the darkness.

Only this time, it was unfiltered. The room that lay beyond that door was lit.

Again the choice was clear. He could wait here, hoping to escape detection. Hoping whoever was searching the storage area didn't know or wouldn't discover the entrance to this closet.

Or he could take his chances by opening the door before him and attempting to get the hell out of here. And getting the information he carried out, too.

There was a faint noise from somewhere behind him. It might have been a rat he'd frightened. It might even have been the folders settling in the knapsack. It was enough to make the decision for him.

He opened the closet door and was immediately confronted with proof that his speculation that this had been Espy's escape route had been correct. The researcher was bending over a desk, one of several in the room.

He had looked up as soon as door opened. The expression on his face was not surprise. More like regret, perhaps.

He straightened, his thin torso almost overbalanced by what was strapped to it. A harness, obviously homemade, came from around his back to fasten in the front with a set of buckles. Just above them, approximately over his heart, was a rectangular shape, perhaps eight by ten inches, wrapped in olive-drab cellophane. Wires protruded from it, and attached to those was what appeared to be a small alarm clock.

Will's recognition that Espy was wearing a bomb was almost instantaneous. And with it came an identification of the elusive odor that had permeated the knapsack the scientist had kept with him at all times.

Something Will had smelled before and never wanted to smell again.

The Army, which had once used it extensively, called it C-4. The rest of the world simply called it plastique.

CHAPTER TWENTY-THREE

CAIT WASN'T SURE, even when she got out of the car, what she could do. She had no gun. No key. No way to communicate with Will. And no plan, she added as she ran.

It was the kind of stupidity Will would be the first to condemn. That didn't slow her. Paul was calling the cops, so there was nothing else she could do out here.

If there was a chance that she could find Will before the men in the cars did, she had to take it. She had studied Espy's diagrams, too. She knew where the two of them had been going.

And Ron Vincent wouldn't?

She had no proof Vincent had been with those men. Based on what he'd done in the past, he seemed to be a firm believer in having hired help do his dirty work.

She slowed as she approached the corner of the building. Her back to the wall, she peeked around it. The delivery bay and its entrance were exactly as the researcher had described them. Except he had a key and she didn't.

The effects of the adrenaline that had surged through her body when she'd seen the men arrive were now mitigated by reality. She wasn't going to be able to get in and warn Will. All she was going to do was get herself killed.

A sound behind her caused her to turn in time to see Paul slip into place at her back. She could hear his ragged breathing in the stillness.

"You get the cops?" she whispered.

Still winded from the run he'd made, he nodded. "What are you going to do?"

As if she knew. She wished to God she did.

"That's the service door," she said, leaning back so he could look across her and into the delivery bay. "It's probably locked, but there's only one way to know that for sure. If it's not, I'll go in. When the cops arrive, just get them inside the building as fast as you can."

Paul nodded, seeming to hang on her every word, just as she had once hung on Will's. "Maybe…"

"What?"

"Maybe I should be the one to go. I don't think Will would want you—"

"Stick to what you know, Paul. And let me do what I know."

He nodded, seeming relieved at her show of confidence. "I thought you might want this."

She turned to find that he was holding a snub-nosed .38 on his palm. She looked up into his eyes, hers questioning.

"I keep it in the car. Don't worry. It's licensed."

Of all the things she *wasn't* worried about, that would top the list. Instead of telling him that, she said, "Thanks."

When she took the gun from his hand, it didn't have the comforting heft of the SIG-Sauer, but at least she had a weapon. As for the rest…she'd figure it out as she went along.

She took a breath and then blew it out hard between pursed lips before she sprinted for the door. Hand on the metal railing, she took the concrete steps two at a time.

She hesitated before allowing her fingers to close around the knob. When she turned it to the right, the door moved.

Unlocked. The damn thing was unlocked.

Maybe Will had left it that way in case they needed to get out in a hurry. Or maybe neither he nor Espy had thought to throw the bolt. In any case…

Trying not to think about what might lie ahead, she pushed open the door and stepped inside.

"I'M TRULY SORRY, Mr. Shannon," Espy said. "I thought you'd be out of the building before they arrived."

He should have been. The researcher had given him everything he'd needed. All he'd had to do was to pick up those folders and get the hell out of here. Instead, he'd tried to get it all. Every bit of evidence he might need to get his life back. *His life…*

"What are you doing, Dr. Espy?"

The question was rhetorical. The knowledge of what the man intended had already turned Will's guts to water. There was enough plastic explosive strapped to Espy's body to blow them, along with anyone else unfortunate enough to be in this wing of the building, to kingdom come.

"I'm going to wipe a foul evil off the face of the earth."

It was a bad movie line, the kind of thing no one should be able to say with a straight face. Espy just had. And the look in his eyes when he'd said it was the same one that had made Will uneasy last night at the motel.

"I understand your anger, Dr. Espy, but believe me, this isn't the way to—"

"You think the police are going to do something about what's going on here? The FDA? Believe me, I've tried to convince both of them to act. Look where it got me."

In a psych ward. Will couldn't blame the man for having lost faith in the system. Especially not if what Espy had told them about being drugged was true.

Considering that he was wearing several pounds of plastic explosive, that might *not* be true. Maybe Espy had been crazy all along. And if he was, what were the implications for the "proof" Will carried in the knapsack?

"With the documents you've given me, we can put a stop to what they're doing," Will said, working to make his voice reassuring. "We just need to get the information out of here."

Only when the word *we* came out of his mouth did he realize that wasn't what he'd wanted to say. With the cargo the scientist was carrying, he didn't want to take

Espy with him. He just wanted to get out himself. For the first time since he'd found Greg's body, he felt as if he had a chance to clear his name. To get his life back. And not only that…

The image of Cait's face looking up at him that morning in the boathouse was far more motivation than that which had driven him on the desperate run through Rock Creek Park that night. He had more to live for now than he'd had at any time since his dismissal. If he could just get out of here alive—

"I appreciate your concern, Mr. Shannon, but I'm afraid it's too late for me. I have nothing to go back to, even if we were able to prove what happened. No one will hire me now. Ron Vincent saw to that. And without my work, I have no life."

"So…you planned this all along." Will nodded toward the bomb.

"Once Mr. Vincent was dead, there was no other option. His father, whom I admired greatly, spoke highly of his elder son. I knew he couldn't be aware of what his brother was doing. Keeping silent and letting people die. I thought if I could show him the documentation, he'd put a stop to it. That's all I wanted. Instead…I got him killed."

"You weren't to blame for Greg's death, Dr. Espy. And we can still make sure the authorities know the truth."

"That was your role, Mr. Shannon. Mine was to see that no one else died."

The fact that Espy had spoken in the past tense made Will wonder what time he'd set that clock for. Minutes from now? Or seconds?

"It's not too late," he urged, hoping that was true. "We can go back out through the lab—"

"You're certainly free to try. Believe me, I shall hope for your success, but…you really should have left when I gave you the chance."

"You *knew* they were coming? You were expecting them?" That explained both the folder he'd been given and the bomb.

"Let's say I had hoped they would. The system records which access card has been used to open the doors. I'm sure there's been an alert on mine since I walked out of the hospital. Certainly since the night I came to the restaurant. They'd been looking for me before then, but I'd managed to avoid them. Once they found the information I'd given to Mr. Vincent, they knew I would try to come back here. It was the only place where there were copies of the material."

Which meant Espy hadn't brought those folders in with him. They had been hidden in the file drawers, just as he'd claimed.

"You think security was just waiting for you to show up."

"*Not* security, Mr. Shannon. Ron Vincent doesn't want to arrest me. He wants to kill me. But this time I'm prepared for him." Espy touched the explosive, his fingers gliding over the slick cellophane in a caress.

Will wondered if Vincent really was one of the searchers. Of course, Espy was right. Vincent would undoubtedly want to take care of the problem the researcher represented himself.

"If you do this," Will said, "a lot *more* people will die."

"Only those who deserve to."

"Even if you manage to kill Vincent, the company will go on. At least for a while. Romoxidin will still be on the market. Someone *might* discover what you know, the information that's in these papers..." Will touched the knapsack on his shoulder. "But that could take months, even years. There's a better way if you really want to stop those suicides."

Something in what he was saying had had an effect. He could see it in Espy's eyes.

"Take that off," Will urged, "and let's get out of here."

"It's too late," Espy said, shaking his head.

Because the device had some kind of fail-safe to make sure he didn't back out?

"What does that mean, Dr. Espy? Why is it too late?"

"There are only a few outside exits. Part of building security. I'm sure they'll have them covered by now."

Actually there were six, Will remembered from the diagram. And unless Vincent had sent an army...

"I'm willing to take that chance. If they're guarded, we fight our way out." Will gestured with the semiautomatic. "Don't let any more people die from a drug *you* developed, Dr. Espy. Not when you have the opportunity to put a stop to it. I'll get you out of here.

And I'll help you get the evidence to the right people. This time we'll force them to act."

Will waited, watching the thoughts moving behind those strange, dark eyes. Espy's hands started toward his chest, and Will's heart stopped. Then he lowered them, shaking his head.

"Your job, Mr. Shannon. That's why I brought you here. You take the data from those trials out. Show them to the world. And then, even if you don't succeed—" He opened his hands, holding them palm out on either side of the plastique.

"Without your testimony, no one will ever know the truth about Dr. Russell's death. Or Dr. Abernathy's. Don't you owe it to them to let the world know why they died?"

"Gail was my friend. I had been foolish enough to hope that some day…" The words faded as the thin hands again made that upward journey.

If Espy didn't defuse the explosives this time, Will would have to leave without him. Whether he could get out of the building before the bomb exploded, he had no way of knowing. All he knew was that there were too many possibilities waiting beyond those doors not to take that chance.

As the seconds he'd allotted for the other man's decision ticked down to zero, Espy reached down and pulled the wires out of the detonator he'd planted inside the square of plastique, breaking the circuit. Then his hands closed around the buckle, pressing the catch that would release the lock. He shrugged out of the harness and opened the bottom drawer of what Will assumed had been his desk. He carefully laid the explosives inside, still connected to the vest he'd worn, before he closed it.

"The main reception area, I think," the researcher said, looking up at Will. "They won't expect us to be that bold."

"Lead the way."

Wherever they went, Will knew they'd have to fight their way out, something he was more than willing to do. *This* time someone worth fighting for was waiting for him.

THEY HAD GONE BACK through the closet and file room. Whoever had been in the main computer area had apparently finished their search and moved on.

"This way," Espy said, confidently leading Will through the maze of lab equipment despite the lack of light.

They were approaching another set of glass doors, exactly like the ones they'd come through on their way in from the utility hallway. Instead of scanning his card, Espy pushed a red button on the right-hand side and they slid open.

Apparently only the entrance to the lab was secure. The quick exit was probably a mandated safety feature in case of an emergency. Tonight it had worked to their advantage.

"Which way?" Will whispered once they were through.

He was bothered by the fact that they'd seen no one. Someone had been searching the records area. Although not eager for a confrontation, he preferred to know the whereabouts of whoever was inside the building. And he wasn't as convinced as Espy that it was anyone but security.

"The hall around that corner leads straight to reception." Espy had leaned close to his ear to whisper the instructions, putting his hand over his mouth like a child.

Will nodded. Using the same technique as before, he edged along the wall before he leaned forward to check out the corridor Espy had pointed out. It stretched before him, wide and empty, polished tile gleaming softly in the reflected glow of the halogen lamps from the parking lot out front.

It couldn't be this simple, Will thought. But then nothing else about the last three days had been easy. Maybe he was due.

He looked back over his shoulder. Espy was watching him, eyes wide in the darkness. Will gestured for him to follow and then slipped around the corner.

On either side of the hallway were a half-dozen offices, their doors open. He could check out each as he approached them, a time-consuming process. Or they could simply make a break for it and take their chances.

He glanced back to communicate that decision to Espy and realized the researcher wasn't behind him. Either he hadn't yet rounded the corner or—

Will turned, starting to bring his weapon up. Before he could, the lights in the corridor came on. A man stepped forward from around the corner, propelling Dr. Espy in front of him with the arm he held twisted behind his back. The muzzle of his gun was pressed against the researcher's temple.

Just as it had that morning in Cait's bathroom, a memory exploded in Will's brain, destroying the present by giving him a glimpse of the past. This man had held a gun to *his* head. He and another man had forced Will to lie still while someone—

The image was gone as suddenly as it had appeared. In spite of that, he now knew what they'd done. He could feel the sting of the needle they'd inserted between his fingers. And while whatever they'd injected had burned its way into his veins, he had been looking up at that green-shaded lamp on Greg Vincent's desk.

"Drop the gun, Will. Or, as my father would say, this is going to be like shooting fish in a barrel. You *are* familiar with that expression, aren't you?"

Stunned by the suddenness of the flashback, Will had let his guard down. He whirled in the direction from which that mocking statement had come. Ron Vincent stood at the other end of the corridor, a man on either side of him, their weapons pointed at Will.

"From what I've heard about your father—" Will began. He held his arms away from his body as he stooped to lay the SIG-Sauer at his feet.

"From my sainted brother no doubt. They were two of a kind. Far too noble for their own good."

"At least too noble for yours."

"What Greg wanted to do would have destroyed the company. There's no way we were going to win the patent fight. If he withdrew Romoxidin from the market, too, it was over."

"You killed those people," Espy said from behind him, "as surely as if you'd put a gun to their heads."

"They killed *themselves*, Dr. Espy. I tried to explain that to all of you."

"You lying piece of filth."

"You've already caused far more trouble than you're worth, Espy. Say something like that again, and I'll tell Alton to pull the trigger."

Vincent sounded as if he were enjoying this. Why wouldn't he be? As reckless as he'd been, everything he'd done had worked. And the last two people who stood between him and complete success were, as he had taunted, fish in a barrel.

"Tell him," Will said, glancing over his shoulder.

"Tell me what?" Vincent's tone was still cocky, but he had taken the bait.

"About the bomb," Will said. "Tell him, Dr. Espy, or we'll all die."

"Do you really think I'm stupid enough to fall for that?" Ron's laugh was almost convincing.

Behind him, Will heard a movement. Espy struggling to get free or his captor getting nervous?

"Dr. Espy says you've destroyed his life. Nobody will listen to him about Romoxidin, so he's…taken matters into his own hands. Whatever you gave him seems to have worked a little too well."

Before the flashback, Will had had doubts about Espy's story that he'd been drugged. He no longer did.

"You insane bastard. If you *did* bring a bomb in here…" Vincent started down the corridor toward them, his face flushed with anger.

His henchmen, caught off guard, hurried to catch up. When he had closed half the distance between them, Ron reached over and took the semiautomatic out of the hands of the man on his right. As he advanced, he held the gun out in front of him, one-handed, the muzzle pointed at the researcher.

"Kill him," Will warned, "and you'll never find it in time."

"Then you tell me," Vincent said, swinging the gun toward Will as he continued to advance.

"His desk," Will said. "Bottom drawer. Right side. I don't know how long before it goes off."

Vincent gestured angrily with the weapon, as if he intended to fire. Despite his attempt at intimidation, it was becoming increasingly obvious that he didn't have a lot of experience with guns.

"Go see if he's telling the truth." Vincent took his eyes off Will to bark the order to the man beside him.

Exaltation surged through Will's chest. He'd hoped that if he mentioned the bomb, they would take the two of them out of the building, which might give them a chance to get away. To have Vincent split his force was a far better outcome than Will had anticipated.

The man didn't move. Neither did the one to Vincent's left. Across his body, their eyes met briefly, but Vincent seemed oblivious to that exchange.

"I don't know where his desk is," the first one said.

"Take him with you. Show them the way, Dr. Espy. If he doesn't, persuade him."

Obviously still reluctant, the man whose gun Vincent had taken walked past Will. "Bring him," he said to the man holding Espy.

"Persuade him like they did Emilio?"

"Emilio?" Vincent seemed genuinely puzzled.

"Emilio Garza. The waiter. You had him beaten to death."

"That was you, Will. Don't you read the papers?"

"I didn't kill Emilio."

"Yeah, well, the ironic thing is I didn't either. The cops said he was dealing. Somebody must not have liked his product."

"Are you saying…you *didn't* have him killed?"

"Why would I? I didn't want anything to tie me to Greg that night. If you hadn't gone looking for the waiter, nobody would have made the connection. Not to the restaurant. Not to me."

That might even be true. From what Paul had told him, Vincent hadn't gone public about dinner with his brother until *after* the busboy had called the police. It made sense he wouldn't want to be one of the last people to see his brother alive.

Considering the environment in which Emilio had lived, his death could have happened exactly as Vincent suggested. That would explain why the apartment had been searched.

"So…if not from Emilio, how did you find out about the disk Espy gave Greg?"

Vincent laughed. "My brother called me. He wanted to talk about the information he'd been handed. What could I do? I came right over to his house. Just like he asked me to."

"And you murdered him."

"You were the one hired to protect him. Not a great recommendation of your skills, Will."

"I shouldn't have had to protect him from his own family."

"Most victims have a close relationship with their murderer. I'm surprised someone with your experience didn't know that."

If Ron had shown up at the house that night, even with his entourage in tow, Will wouldn't have been suspicious. He'd been given no reason to doubt Greg's brother at that point.

"You drugged me, and then you put my gun and Greg's body in his bed. Clever for the spur of the moment."

"You were always my contingency plan, Will. That's why I hired you. I knew Greg would eventually run the company into the ground. If he'd ever found out about

Romoxidin, he would have pulled it off the shelves, no matter the cost. He actually wanted to go to production with a couple of Espy's 'wonder drugs,' even if there was no market for them."

"And no possibility of profit. Just saving a few lives."

Vincent had relaxed his hold on the weapon, his anger evaporating as he clearly enjoyed telling Will what he'd done.

"When someone had to take the fall for Greg's death, you came with certain…built-in credentials. I just had to improvise a little that night because of Espy."

Ron had wanted Will on the job because if anything happened to his brother, with his background Will would be a believable scapegoat. As Cait had said, it was diabolical.

"And it all would have worked, except I regained consciousness before the cops got there."

"You must have the constitution of a horse. With what I saw you drink at the restaurant, you should have been out for at least a couple more hours."

Ron hadn't realized that what Will had been drinking was club soda. If they'd injected him with something like GHB or ketamine, Vincent had expected the effects to last much longer.

"You're the one who called the cops that night."

"I wasn't taking any chances. Then, when they called me as Greg's next of kin, I found out you hadn't been there when they arrived. Since the drug didn't work like it was supposed to, I couldn't be sure what you might remember. Or how much you might figure out."

"So you had to find me before I could find someone who might listen."

"Not as hard as it sounds. I had lots of personal information about you, some from your former employers. It's amazing what people will tell you when they find out you're hiring someone to protect your beloved brother."

There were no more questions to ask. He had drawn this out as long as he could, hoping Vincent would give him an opening. He hadn't, and if Will didn't act soon, the men who had taken Espy would return, doubling the odds.

"Now what?" he asked.

He lowered his shoulder, allowing the strap of the knapsack to slide down his arm. With his right hand, he reached over as if to pull it up. There was no reaction from Vincent.

The man to Vincent's left would be the real danger. If he could get Ron between them to use as a shield, it might be possible he could bargain his way out of the building.

Once outside and in the darkness, he'd take his chances. Besides, Paul and Cait were out there. Maybe if they'd seen Vincent and his entourage arrive, they'd notified the locals.

As if in response to the thought, there was the distant wail of a siren. Will's eyes focused beyond the two men before him, looking out through the expanse of glass in the reception area. Light bars, strobes flashing, could be seen approaching the front of the laboratory.

"What the hell?" Vincent said, turning to look behind him. As he did, the man to his left shifted, too, his head swiveling toward the front doors.

It was the chance Will had been waiting for. He grabbed the strap of the knapsack, ripping it off his shoulder and swinging the bag at Vincent. It caught the gun he'd had been holding so casually and sent it skittering across the tile.

The other man turned at the sound, trying to bring his weapon back into firing position. The knapsack completed its arc, striking him on the arm. Although he held on to the gun, it was pointed toward the wall when he fired.

By the time that bullet struck, Will was on him. They fell together, fighting for control of the semiautomatic. As he clawed at the man's arm, trying to wrench the weapon away, Will was also conscious of what Vincent was doing. He might not know much about guns, but he knew enough to pick one up and fire it. At this range, it would be hard to miss.

As he gripped the wrist of the man under him, trying to keep him from bringing the weapon into play, Will glanced to the side. Vincent was scurrying toward the gun that had been knocked out of his hand.

The roundhouse punch his opponent landed on his temple brought Will's attention back to the battle he was waging. When he got another chance to look at him,

Vincent was turning, the gun extended in front on him, this time secured with both hands.

Will realized there was not much he could do about that now. He tried to roll and take his opponent with him, but he couldn't get leverage to complete the move.

He heard the gun's report, but unbelievably, given the distance, Vincent must have missed. Will managed another glance to his right as a second shot rang out.

With the sound, Vincent's knees bent, the gun he held slowly lowering until it pointed straight down at the floor. He pulled the trigger as he toppled forward, his head landing at Will's elbow.

He had no idea who'd fired the shot that had taken Vincent down, but the odds were now even. Encouraged, Will released the wrist he'd been holding. Ignoring the gun, he drove his elbow downward into the center of the man's face, once and then again.

As the man stilled, Will pushed himself to his knees, looking for any sign his opponent might have more fight left in him. When it became apparent he didn't, Will finally looked behind him.

Cait stood in the center of the corridor, her feet slightly apart, knees bent, and her weapon extended. There was no one behind her.

At least not yet.

"Come on," he said, scrambling to his feet.

He grabbed the knapsack from the floor, slinging it over his shoulder. By then, Cait was beside him. Together they ran for the front of the building, where it seemed every police cruiser in the county might be gathered.

"Drop the gun and put your hands up," he ordered, watching the officers, weapons drawn, converging on the glass doors.

He glanced at Cait to make sure she understood what he wanted her to do. Her eyes met his as she tossed the weapon she'd used to kill Vincent to the side and raised her hands.

There would be a time for everything he needed to say. Paul and the documents he carried would ensure that. Right now—

"Let them in," he said.

Her eyes held his for what seemed an eternity before she walked forward to unlock doors. Will waited until the first officer came through them before he spoke, his hands high in the air, the knapsack and its precious contents over his shoulder.

"My name is Will Shannon. The Metropolitan police have an APB out on me. I'm surrendering into your custody. The bag I'm carrying has evidence relating to the Gregory Vincent murder. Please take very good care of it."

He was relieved to see Paul making his way toward the door. He knew he could count on him to see that those papers were taken care of. And that Cait was taken care of as well.

"Dr. Espy, who used to work here, is back in the lab," he said to the cop who had taken his right hand, pulling it behind his back. "He's being held at gunpoint. There are also a few pounds of plastic explosive in a desk drawer there. You might want to call in the bomb squad as soon as you've rescued Espy."

As they cuffed him, Will resisted the urge to say something else to Cait. To tell her he loved her. To make promises he couldn't know right now whether or not he would ever be able to keep.

It would be far better to say nothing than to say too much. Until this was all straightened out, he would have to trust that she knew how he felt.

And trust she would also know that, if he could, he would come find her. If he couldn't—

He destroyed that thought, looking back at her as they shoved him through the doors. He didn't take his eyes off her until the deputy put his hand on Will's head and helped him into the back of the cruiser.

EPILOGUE

ARMS FULLY EXTENDED, Cait held her weapon, the left hand supporting the right. She deliberately cleared her mind of outside distractions, focusing on the white torso at the end of the lane. Without pausing, she fired six shots, placing each within the black outline of the heart that centered the target.

Still holding her position, she allowed herself a moment to relish the accomplishment. Then she laid down the SIG-Sauer and took off the headset she'd worn to protect her ears. Unable to resist, she took one last look at the circle of holes before she turned to let the next person waiting for the lane take her place.

"Nice," Will said.

He was leaning against the wall behind her. It was obvious he had been there awhile, but, conscious of nothing but her goal, she'd been completely unaware of him.

With the Metro police dragging their heels, in spite of the growing evidence against Ron Vincent, it had been nearly three weeks since she'd seen him. Despite the fact that Will had been incarcerated most of that period, he looked better than he had at any time during the three days they'd been on the run for their lives.

He was clean-shaven, dressed in khaki slacks and a navy wool blazer, which he wore over a white dress shirt. There was no evidence of injury or fatigue, both of which had marked his features during the few days they'd spent together.

Instead, he looked like the man she'd fallen in love with. And very much "the senior agent in charge."

"Thank you."

She had known he would seek her out as soon as he was free of the legal entanglements from Greg Vincent's murder and its aftermath. Based on what Paul had told her last week, however, she hadn't been expecting that to happen so soon. In spite of the hours she'd spent thinking about this moment, now that it was here, she was unprepared.

"That's a qualifying round," Will said, nodding toward the target.

Although some part of her had wanted to prove she was still capable of doing the job she'd once held, she had no plans to rejoin the Secret Service. She'd had enough adrenaline rushes to last a lifetime.

"I guess so," she said, glancing back down the lane, "but that isn't why I'm here."

"Why *are* you here?"

"To prove something to myself, I suppose."

"I can't imagine there's anything left you need to prove to anyone."

She examined the words, finally deciding that they were indeed the compliment they'd seemed. "You'd be surprised."

"I am. Constantly. That's why *I'm* here."

Despite their long association, despite his claim that he never had to explain things to her, that comment was harder to interpret. Maybe because she was afraid the words didn't mean what she wanted them to. What she *needed* them to mean.

"I *was* wondering," she said.

"You were? Now *that* surprises me."

She had moved away from the lane, realizing that the next shooter was growing impatient. As she stopped in front of Will, she could again smell the faint, pleasantly masculine scent of his aftershave. Just as it had that morning in her kitchen, it triggered memories of other times and places. Other intimacies.

"Why would that surprise you?" she asked.

"Because I assumed you'd know that I would come as soon as I could."

There was no answer she could make to that. Not unless she wanted to bring up things that, as yet, remained unspoken between them. They'd made no plans for the future during those frantic days on the run. The subject of what might come next in their relationship hadn't even come up.

At the time, there had been no guarantee either of them would have a future. Much less one they might spend together. Now, however...

"Then...it's over? The police are satisfied?"

"Thanks in a large part to Paul. And to Dr. Espy, of course. To the documents he provided. They're even talking about opening investigations into the deaths of his colleagues. I think their families might eventually agree to all that entails, simply to get closure. Especially the Abernathys."

Gail Abernathy was the researcher who had supposedly committed suicide. Cait could understand why her relatives would want to know if that was what had really happened. The knowledge that she had been murdered might even be easier for them to deal with.

"So what happens next?"

"Paul's firm has an opening. He's asked me to think about it."

Douglas Reemer's job, she realized. Working as a private investigator. She could see Will in the role, although given what had happened to Paul's previous employee—

"I wanted to know what you thought about that."

"What *I* thought?" Her response was more of a delaying tactic than anything else.

First, because she hadn't had time to decide how she felt about Will in that role. Granted, the situation that had cost Reemer his life had probably been as far from the norm for him as for the two of them. That didn't change the fact that he was dead.

And secondly, she didn't know how to answer because she wasn't sure what the implications of the fact that he was asking were. As things stood now, she had no right to comment on whatever Will wanted to do with his life.

As things stood now...

"It will help me decide," he said.

"What I think will help you decide?"

"Surely you aren't surprised by that."

She shook her head, still unsure how personal the conversation they were having really was. Maybe he was asking her to comment as a friend. Or as someone who knew his professional strengths and weaknesses as well as anyone could. She would certainly qualify on both counts.

If he were asking her on another, more intimate level, that seemed to indicate some degree of commitment between them that hadn't been articulated. And before she started offering opinions about what Will should do with the rest of his life, she thought it needed to be.

"I guess I *am* surprised. I don't have any right to tell you what you should do, Will. Just as you'd have no right to tell me that I'd be a fool to try to qualify."

"I would never tell you that."

"And I wouldn't listen if you did. Not unless..."

She stopped, knowing she'd gone too far. This might be at the heart of what she needed to hear him say, but he hadn't said it yet. She had to remember that.

"Unless what?"

"Unless I felt that whatever decisions I made would also impact your life in some way."

"You don't feel that way?"

"I'm not the one who asked for an opinion."

They were silent for a few minutes as she retrieved her coat. He helped her into it and then held the outer door for her to walk through.

It had begun snowing again while she'd been inside. Although the city had gotten a sprinkling last night, several inches were predicted for later this afternoon.

That was the reason she'd taken the opportunity to come to the shooting range this morning. The weight of the weapon in her hand and the satisfaction of being able to place multiple shots in the kill zone helped to keep the nightmares at bay.

"How about if I buy you lunch?" Will asked as they walked toward her car.

"Actually, I'm meeting my mom."

That was true, unfortunately. The timing couldn't be worse, but given the animosity between her mother and Will, she wasn't sure she wanted to invite him to join them.

If things went as she hoped, that was something that would have to happen eventually, but not today. And not without giving her mother warning.

"She said to tell you that she'd give you a call later on so you two could set up another day."

Cait had been rummaging through her purse for her car keys when the sense of that registered. She lifted her eyes from the disorder inside her bag to search Will's face.

"You talked to my mother?"

"I thought it was about time. Especially since you'd already gone public with our relationship."

That was the most important thing she'd done with her second fifteen minutes of fame. As soon as she'd straightened out the media's nonsense about Will kidnapping her, she had told them where he'd spent the night before the assassination attempt.

Telling the truth about that had felt as if a weight had been taken off her shoulders. One she'd carried for the last two years. The hardest part was not revealing the other guilt she'd carried so long.

Will had sworn to her that she hadn't hesitated that day. At the time, she hadn't believed him. Perhaps because she thought she'd acquitted herself fairly well both at the summerhouse and the lab, she had managed to keep those doubts to herself in the interviews she'd done.

She wasn't sure how grateful the Secret Service would be for that, since she *had* revealed that she and Will had been involved, but that was another thing she'd decided not to worry about. She wasn't planning on going back to them, hat in hand, so what did it matter?

"Yeah, well, my mom wasn't too happy about that."

"About you and me?"

"About me telling the world. I think she enjoyed the 'my daughter, the hero' bit. More than I did, that's for sure. She was less thrilled at the thought of my sexual exploits making headlines instead."

"Is that what it was? A sexual exploit?"

"To everyone else."

She used the excuse of her still-undiscovered keys to look down again. This time she searched until she found them, only then raising her eyes to his.

"Maybe we should do something about that," Will said.

"About my mom?"

"About me making an honest woman of you."

The words created a hollow sensation in the bottom of her stomach and her heart began to beat too rapidly. Still, this wasn't exactly how she'd been envisioning the moment.

"I finally did that in the interviews."

There was an awkward silence. If she had expected him to explain what he'd meant by the phrase he'd just used, she was disappointed.

"Can I at least say I'm grateful?"

"You can do anything you want, Will. Thanks to Paul, you're a free man. Enjoy."

Feeling an unexpected sting of tears, she turned, punching the remote to open the door of the Altima. Will reached over and put his hand around the fingers in which she held the keys.

"What are you doing?"

"You said I could do anything I wanted."

He used the hand he'd taken to turn her. He slipped his left arm inside her coat and, applying pressure against her back, pulled her body against his.

As his head began to lower, hers automatically tilted to meet his kiss. Although the sexual hunger that flared between them was undeniable, she sensed something that hadn't been there before. Will had always been both protective and proprietary, but there was something different about the way he held her. And about the way he kissed her.

After only seconds he lifted his head, breaking the contact between their lips. Surprised, she opened her eyes to find he was looking down at her.

"I told your mother I was going to ask you to marry me. I don't think she was enamored of the idea, but she didn't threaten to have me arrested this time."

"You asked my mother's permission to marry me?"

"No, and if I had, I'm not sure she would have given it. I just thought she should be informed. She loves you and wants to take care of you. And while I might not like it if the taking care of you part means she wants to keep you away from me, I can certainly empathize."

With wanting to take care of her? If so...

"I spent two years fighting to reach the point where I can take care of myself. I don't need anybody else to do that. Not my mom. Not even you, Will."

"Fair enough. What about the other? Surely you're not opposed to that."

She loves you and wants to take care of you...

"To being loved?"

"That's what I had in mind. I know... I know there's a certain notoriety that's always going to surround me. I can see the questions in people's eyes when we're introduced. They wonder if I'm guilty of any of the things

I've been accused of. I've developed a pretty thick skin since the inquiry, but I thought I should warn you. Some of those same questions will be in their eyes when they look at you."

"If there's anyone in this world who knows the truth about you—"

"It's not a matter of knowing the truth," he interrupted. "It's about always having to face the doubts. And the doubters."

"Is that supposed to warn me off?"

"It's an effort to be fair."

"Fair to who?"

"To you. I don't want you to decide one day that you can't deal with that anymore. That's the one thing I couldn't take, Cait."

"You think I'm going to run because someone looks at me funny? I'm made of sterner stuff, Shannon. I would think you'd know that by now."

"I know I love you. I know that I don't ever want you to be where I can't reach out my hand and touch you at night. I know that I want to have children with you. A houseful of scruffy, risk-taking, freckled-face boys and a couple of tall, elegant, red-haired girls."

"I don't have freckles," she said, leaning forward.

"One or two," he said softly, his lips touching the tip of her nose. "In places only I have ever seen."

"I don't believe you."

She stood on tiptoe, putting her arms around his neck. The words had been said. All the ones she had needed to hear and some she'd not even dreamed about. And all of them had been right.

"I've never lied to you. And I never will."

"Swear," she whispered, her mouth just below his.

Snowflakes were caught in his eyelashes and in the midnight hair, but the brown eyes were warm and open. And they, too, said everything she had needed to know.

"On every memory we've ever shared," he said, repeating the vow he'd made at the summerhouse. "And especially on all those yet to come."

* * * * *

Turn the page for
an exciting preview
of
multi-RITA® award winner
Gayle Wilson's
new novel of
romantic suspense
THE INQUISITOR
coming
July 2006
From MIRA

THE SOUND OF HER OFFICE DOOR being flung open brought Jenna's eyes up. The secretary she shared with three other therapists was well aware that she used the last ten minutes of the hour to make notes on the session that had just ended. Why Sheila would come in now…

Except it wasn't Sheila. Not *just* Sheila, anyway. Her secretary was looking at her over the broad shoulders of the man who seemed to fill the doorway.

"I'm sorry, Dr. Kincaid," she said. "I tried to tell him—"

"We need to talk."

The intruder was clearly not offering an apology for the interruption. The curt sentence had been more of a command than a request. Whatever his problem—and Jenna wasn't using that term in the sense of something needing treatment—she didn't have either the time or the inclination to deal with it today.

"I'm afraid you'll have to make an appointment—"

"How much?"

"I beg your pardon?"

"How much is it going to cost to talk to you? What I have to say won't take a full hour, but I'm willing to pay for one if that's what it takes to get you to listen."

As if to prove his point, he took his wallet out of the back pocket of the jeans he wore. Behind him, Sheila pantomimed dialing a phone and then bringing it to her ear, her brows raised in inquiry.

Jenna shook her head, the movement slight enough that she hoped it wouldn't be noticed by the man now in the process of opening his billfold. She was unwilling to call the cops until she knew more about what was going on.

The guy didn't look deranged. Actually... Actually he looked pretty normal, she admitted.

If you think normal is six-foot-something of solid muscle enclosed in black chamois and denim.

He carried nothing in his hands and the well-worn jeans hugged his hips too tightly to conceal a weapon. He was also clean-shaven, although there was a hint of a five o'clock shadow on the lean cheeks.

His coal-black hair was so closely cropped it couldn't possibly be disarranged, which might have given her some indication of his mental state. The fact that it had so recently been trimmed seemed a point in his favor. People who had really "lost it" usually weren't concerned about personal grooming.

His eyes, however, were the most compelling argument that there was nothing seriously out of whack with his psyche. They were a clear, piercing blue, the color almost startling against the darkly tanned skin and ebony hair.

And right now they were focused on her, she realized belatedly. They seemed perfectly calm as he waited for her answer, billfold open, long, dark fingers poised to pluck from it whatever amount she named.

Still evaluating him, as she would any patient, Jenna noticed that his nails were neatly trimmed. The hands themselves were completely masculine, the fingers square despite their length.

"Hundred and fifty?" he asked as she continued not to respond to his initial question. "That do it?"

She blinked, breaking the spell he'd cast. She realized she had simply been staring at him rather than trying to formulate an answer.

"I'm sorry. I'm completely booked this afternoon, as I'm sure my secretary told you. If this is an emergency, I can try to work you in early tomorrow—"

"Lady, I'm here in an attempt, obviously misguided, to save your life. I'm even willing to pay for the opportunity. All you have to do is say how much."

He strode across the room, stopping when he reached her desk. Her gaze followed, her chin automatically lifting as he approached until she was looking up into those ice-blue eyes. Above the right, a dark brow was raised in inquiry.

"One seventy-five? Two hundred? I'm not up on the going rate for therapy. Just name your price."

Jenna realized that her lips were still parted from her

uncompleted sentence. She closed them, glancing back at Sheila to indicate with a nod that she would see him.

The secretary's mouth opened, obviously to protest that decision, but then she snapped it shut. She reached out for the knob of the door, pulling it closed behind her as she returned to the outer office.

Jenna wasn't completely sure that Sheila wouldn't place that call to the cops, even though it had been vetoed. And she wasn't totally sure she wouldn't be relieved if her secretary did.

She looked back at the man who had invaded her office and now seemed to fill it. He, too, had watched the secretary's departure.

He turned back just as Jenna's gaze refocused on his face. There was something in his eyes now that looked like approval.

Because she'd been crazy enough to let him stay?

Maybe he was pleased at the ease with which he'd gotten his way. Something he seemed accustomed to doing.

"How much?" he asked again.

"You can put your money away, Mr...."

"Murphy. Sean Murphy."

Although she waited, he didn't offer to elaborate on that information, so she went back to the most salient part of what he'd said. Salient to her, at least.

"You said you're here in an attempt to 'save my live.' I'm not sure what that means, but given how serious it sounds, I'm willing to listen. You have—" she glanced at her watch to make her point "—exactly ten minutes before my next appointment."

Actually, he had said he was here in a *misguided attempt* to save her life. That ambiguity made her more uncomfortable than the implied threat in the other.

He held her eyes a moment, perhaps assessing how serious she was about the time frame she'd just given. After a few seconds, he closed his wallet with a snap. He struggled briefly to push it into his back pocket, verifying her initial assessment about the tightness of his jeans.

Now if only she'd been equally correct in gauging his mental state.

"I saw your interview yesterday."

Something shifted in the bottom of Jenna's stomach, cold and hard and frightening. She swallowed, determined not to display any outward sign of her fear.

"The one on holiday stress?"

"I must have missed that part. What I saw was you giving your professional opinion about the man who killed the three women here."

Her heart began to race, although she told herself the murderer who had carried out those crimes, was, according to every indication, far too organized to pull anything like this. Whatever this man was here for, it wasn't to kill her. Especially considering the way those poor women had been brutalized.

This wasn't his methodology. And this wasn't the setting he would choose to carry out those unspeakable acts.

"I tried to make it clear to the reporter that serial killers don't exactly fall within my area of expertise—" she began, choosing her words carefully.

"What you made clear, Dr. Kincaid, was that you thought that poor, mistreated bastard just couldn't help himself."

The anxiety Jenna had felt at the beginning of his tirade was suddenly replaced by anger, most of it self-directed. She had known she should have cut the reporter off when he'd started that line of questioning. Instead, she'd been too conscious of the public-relations aspect of the interview. If she had seemed uncooperative, that might well have been the only part of the segment to be aired.

And what if it were?

Of course, it was easy to sit here now, without the red light of the camera focused on her face, and know exactly what she should have done. She'd made a mistake, but she didn't deserve to be chastised for it by someone who clearly had his own agenda. Just as the reporter yesterday had.

"I never said that."

She hadn't. And she didn't have to sit in her own office and listen to someone's misinterpretation of what she *had* said.

"Close enough. As a psychologist, you had to know he'd feed off your comments."

She had thought something similar yesterday. Not that the killer would "feed off" her remark about sociopaths being the products of abuse, but that he would delight in hearing anyone talk about the murders on the air. Just as she had known he would relish the increased terror that kind of interview would bring to the community.

"He's *already* feeding off the media frenzy," she said, refusing to allow this jackass to intimidate her, despite his size and his surety. "I doubt anything I said yesterday is going to add appreciably to his enjoyment."

Since the police had announced the connection between the three homicides, not only had the local media been all over the story, the twenty-four-hour cable news stations were carrying it as well. It seemed now that the killer had been linked to several murders in other parts of the country.

She hadn't had time to do much more than look at the lead story in the morning paper. That had been enough to let her know this was going to remain at the top of the front page until the killer was caught. Or until things got so hot for him here that he moved on to another location.

Which was essentially all she'd said yesterday, she reiterated mentally. Actually, there was *nothing* she'd said that wasn't completely accurate.

She had talked to Paul Carlisle, the founder of the practice, when she'd come in this morning. That's when she'd discovered that the station had replayed her comments about the murders on both the late-night news and again this morning, although they hadn't bothered to repeat the rest of the interview.

Maybe Sean Murphy had heard one of those broadcasts. In any case, there was nothing she needed to apologize for, she decided. No matter what he thought.

"You really don't have a clue, do you?"

"I'm *sorry?*" Her voice rose on the last word. The initial spurt of anger his attitude had evoked came roaring back in force.

"You tell someone who likes torturing women that he's just some poor abused kid who can't help himself—"

"Wait just a minute. I never said that. I never said anything *like* that."

"Yeah? Well, you can bet that's what he heard."

"And who made you the expert on what he heard?"

"A long and very intimate acquaintance."

That stopped her. Her analytical mind took over, replaying the words in her head.

"Are you saying…you *know* him? You know who he is?"

"I know *what* he is. And I know what he does. A whole hell of a lot better method of 'knowing' him than whatever crap you were spouting."

"I think we're through here."

Jenna stood so quickly that her desk chair rolled back to hit the wall behind her. She reached across the desk to punch the button on the intercom. If he didn't leave immediately, she would tell Sheila to do what she had wanted to when he'd first barged in.

"You're his type, you know."

Startled by the change in tone, Jenna looked up, her finger hovering just above the phone. There was no longer any trace of approval in his eyes. They were cold now. And angry.

"What the hell does *that* mean?"

"You can look it up when the cops here finally get their act together. Dark hair. Dark eyes. Tall. Slender. And not a prostitute or a waitress among them."

The same anxiety she'd felt when he said he'd come to save her life fluttered again in her stomach. The story on today's front page had featured pictures and profile of the three local victims. And the description he'd just given fit all of them.

"I don't know that he's ever done a psychologist before," Sean Murphy went on, seeming to relish the impact his warning was having, "but I've got a feeling he'd be very interested."